JO TO THE RESCUE

ELINOR M BRENT-DYER

Girls Gone By Publishers

COMPLETE AND UNABRIDGED

Published by

Girls Gone By Publishers
4 Rock Terrace
Coleford
Bath
Somerset
BA3 5NF

First published by W & R Chambers Ltd 1945
This edition published 2006

Typeset in England by AJF
Printed in England by Antony Rowe Limited

ISBN 1-84745-003-2
978-1-84745-003-6

'It was a huge lump of raw meat!'—PAGE 134

CONTENTS

INTRODUCTION

In 1925 W & R Chambers Ltd published *The School at the Chalet*, the first title in Elinor Brent-Dyer's Chalet School series. Forty-five years later, in 1970, the same company published the final title in the series, *Prefects of the Chalet School*. It was published posthumously, EBD (as she is known to her fans) having signed the contract three days before she died. During those 45 years Elinor wrote around 60 Chalet School titles, the School moved from the Austrian Tirol to Guernsey, England, Wales and finally Switzerland, a fan club flourished, and the books began to appear in an abridged paperback format.

How Many Chalet School Titles Are There?

Numbering the Chalet School titles is not as easy as it might appear. The back of the Chambers dustwrapper of *Prefects of the Chalet School* offers a simple list of titles, numbered 1–58. However, no 31, *Tom Tackles the Chalet School*, was published out of sequence (see below), and there were five 'extra' titles, of which one, *The Chalet School and Rosalie*, follows just after *Tom* in the series chronology. In addition, there was a long 'short' story, *The Mystery at the Chalet School*, which comes just before *Tom*. Helen McClelland, EBD's biographer, helpfully devised the system of re-numbering these titles 19a, 19b and 19c (see list on pages 16–18).

Further complications apply when looking at the paperbacks. In a number of cases, Armada split the original hardbacks into two when publishing them in paperback, and this meant that the paperbacks are numbered 1–62. In addition, *The Mystery at the Chalet School* was only ever published in paperback with *The Chalet School and Rosalie* but should be numbered 21a in this sequence (see list on pages 19–21).

Girls Gone By are following the numbering system of the original hardbacks. All titles will eventually be republished, but not all will be in print at the same time.

Apart from *The Chalet School and Rosalie*, Chambers published four other 'extra' titles: *The Chalet Book for Girls*, *The Second Chalet Book for Girls*, *The Third Chalet Book for Girls* and *The Chalet Girls' Cookbook*. *The Chalet Book for Girls* included *The Mystery at the Chalet School* as well as three other Chalet School short stories, one non-Chalet story by EBD, and four articles. *The Second Chalet Book for Girls* included the first half of *Tom Tackles the Chalet School*, together with two Chalet School short stories, one other story by EBD, seven articles (including the start of what was to become *The Chalet Girls' Cookbook*) and a rather didactic photographic article called *Beth's Diary*, which featured Beth Chester going to Devon and Cornwall. *The Third Chalet Book for Girls* included the second half of *Tom Tackles the Chalet School* (called *Tom Plays the Game*) as well as two Chalet School short stories, three other stories by EBD and three articles. (Clearly the dustwrapper was printed before the book, since the back flap lists three stories and two articles which are not in the book.) It is likely that *The Chalet School and Rosalie* was intended to be the long story for a fourth *Book for Girls*, but since no more were published this title eventually appeared in 1951 in paperback (very unusual for the time). The back cover of *The Second Chalet Book for Girls* lists *The First Junior Chalet Book* as hopefully being published 'next year'; this never materialised. *The Chalet Girls' Cookbook* is not merely a collection of recipes but also contains a very loose story about Joey, Simone, Marie and Frieda just after they have left the School. While not all of these Chalet stories add crucial information to the series, many of them do, and they are certainly worth collecting. All the *Books for Girls* are difficult to obtain on the secondhand market, but most of the stories were reprinted in two books compiled by Helen McClelland, *Elinor M. Brent-Dyer's Chalet School* and *The Chalet School Companion*, both now out of print but not too difficult to obtain secondhand. Girls Gone By have now published all EBD's known short stories, from these and other sources, in a single volume.

The Locations of the Chalet School Books

The Chalet School started its life in Briesau am Tiernsee in the Austrian Tyrol (Pertisau am Achensee in real life). After Germany signed the Anschluss with Austria in 1938, it would have been impossible to keep even a fictional school in Austria. As a result, EBD wrote *The Chalet School in Exile*, during which, following an encounter with some Nazis, several of the girls, including Joey Bettany, were forced to flee Austria, and the School was also forced to leave. Unfortunately, Elinor chose to move the School to Guernsey—the book was published just as Germany invaded the Channel Islands. The next book, *The Chalet School Goes to It*, saw the School moving again, this time to a village near Armiford—Hereford in real life. Here the School remained for the duration of the war, and indeed when the next move came, in *The Chalet School and the Island*, it was for reasons of plot. The island concerned was off the south-west coast of Wales, and is fictional, although generally agreed by Chalet School fans to be a combination of various islands including Caldey Island, St Margaret's Isle, Skokholm, Ramsey Island and Grassholm, with Caldey Island being the most likely contender if a single island has to be picked. Elinor had long wanted to move the School back to Austria, but the political situation there in the 1950s forbade such a move, so she did the next best thing and moved it to Switzerland, firstly by establishing a finishing branch in *The Chalet School and the Oberland*, and secondly by relocating the School itself in *The Chalet School and Barbara*. The exact location is subject to much debate, but it seems likely that it is somewhere near Wengen in the Bernese Oberland. Here the School was to remain for the rest of its fictional life, and here it still is today for its many aficionados.

The Chalet Club 1959–69

In 1959 Chambers and Elinor Brent-Dyer started a club for lovers of the Chalet books, beginning with 33 members. When the club closed in 1969, after Elinor's death, there were around 4,000 members worldwide. Twice-yearly News Letters were produced, written by Elinor herself, and the information in these adds fascinating, if sometimes conflicting, detail to the series. In 1997 Friends of the Chalet School, one of the two fan clubs existing today, republished the News Letters in facsimile book format. A new edition is now available from Girls Gone By Publishers.

The Publication of the Chalet School Series in Armada Paperback

On 1 May 1967, Armada, the children's paperback division of what was then William Collins, Sons & Co Ltd, published the first four Chalet School paperbacks. This momentous news was covered in issue Number Sixteen of the Chalet Club News Letter, which also appeared in May 1967. In her editorial, Elinor Brent-Dyer said: 'Prepare for a BIG piece of news. The Chalet Books, slightly abridged, are being reissued in the Armada series. The first four come out in May, and two of them are *The School at the Chalet* and *Jo of the Chalet School*. So watch the windows of the booksellers if you want to add them to your collection. They will be issued at the usual Armada price, which should bring them within the reach of all of you. I hope you like the new jackets. Myself, I think them charming, especially *The School at the Chalet*.' On the back page of the News Letter there was an advertisement for the books, which reproduced the covers of the first four titles.

The words 'slightly abridged' were a huge understatement, and over the years Chalet fans have made frequent complaints about the fact that the paperbacks are abridged, about some of the covers, and about the fact that the books were published in a most extraordinary order, with the whole series never available in paperback at any one time. It has to be said, however, that were it not for the paperbacks interest in the Chalet series would, in the main, be confined to those who had bought or borrowed the hardbacks prior to their demise in the early 1970s, and Chalet fans would mostly be at least 40 and over in age. The paperbacks have sold hundreds of thousands of copies over the years, and those that are not in print (the vast majority) are still to be found on the secondhand market (through charity shops and jumble sales as well as dealers). They may be cut (and sometimes disgracefully so), but enough of the story is there to fascinate new readers, and we should be grateful that they were published at all. Had they not been, it is most unlikely that two Chalet clubs would now be flourishing and that Girls Gone By Publishers would be able to republish the series in this new, unabridged, format.

Clarissa Cridland
2002

ELINOR M BRENT-DYER: A BRIEF BIOGRAPHY

EBD was born Gladys Eleanor May Dyer in South Shields on 6 April 1894, the only daughter of Eleanor (Nelly) Watson Rutherford and Charles Morris Brent Dyer. Her father had been married before and had a son, Charles Arnold, who was never to live with his father and stepmother. This caused some friction between Elinor's parents, and her father left home when she was three and her younger brother, Henzell, was two. Her father eventually went to live with another woman by whom he had a third son, Morris. Elinor's parents lived in a respectable lower-middle-class area, and the family covered up the departure of her father by saying that her mother had 'lost' her husband.

In 1912 Henzell died of cerebro-spinal fever, another event which was covered up. Friends of Elinor's who knew her after his death were unaware that she had had a brother. Death from illness was, of course, common at this time, and Elinor's familiarity with this is reflected in her books, which abound with motherless heroines.

Elinor was educated privately in South Shields, and returned there to teach after she had been to the City of Leeds Training College. In the early 1920s she adopted the name Elinor Mary Brent-Dyer. She was interested in the theatre, and her first book, *Gerry Goes to School*, published in 1922, was written for the child actress Hazel Bainbridge—mother of the actress Kate O'Mara. In the mid 1920s she also taught at St Helen's, Northwood, Middlesex, at Moreton House School, Dunstable, Bedfordshire, and in Fareham near Portsmouth. She was a keen musician and a practising Christian, converting to Roman Catholicism in 1930, a major step in those days.

In the early 1920s Elinor spent a holiday in the Austrian Tyrol at Pertisau am Achensee, which she was to use so successfully as the first location in the Chalet School series. (Many of the locations in her books were real places.) In 1933 she moved with her mother and stepfather to Hereford, travelling daily to Peterchurch as a governess. After her stepfather died in November 1937 she started her own school in Hereford, The Margaret Roper, which ran from 1938 until 1948. Unlike the Chalet School it was not a huge success and probably would not have survived had it not been for the Second World War. From 1948 Elinor devoted all her time to writing. Her mother died in 1957, and in 1964 Elinor moved to Redhill, Surrey, where she died on 20 September 1969.

Clarissa Cridland
2002

PUBLISHING HISTORY

Jo to the Rescue was first published in 1945 by Chambers and was produced in a wartime economy format—see illustration below left—which was a requirement of all published books at this time. It was thus thinner than usual, and also smaller in size, being 4¼ x 6¾ inches (approx 11 x 17 cms). When I left Macmillan

Miss Oxenham,
with love from
Elinor
March 1946.

Publishers in 1994, I was lucky enough to be given, as a leaving present, a first edition (without a dustwrapper) of *Jo to the Rescue* which is inscribed by Elinor Brent-Dyer to Elsie Jeanette Oxenham (see above right). It is interesting that EBD signs 'Elinor', whereas the inscription is to 'Miss Oxenham'! The dustwrapper illustration and the black-and-white line frontispiece were by Nina K Brisley. We have used the front of the dustwrapper as our front cover, and the spine is shown on the back, with the text of the original blurb; we have also reproduced the frontispiece. The 1945 edition was reprinted in 1946 in the same size, with the frontispiece.

The book was reprinted in 1951 in the by then normal hardback format of 5 x 7½ inches (approx 12½ x 18½ cms). For this edition, the front of the dustwrapper had to have a white border round it in order to make it fit (see illustration opposite, top left). There was no illustration on the spine, which was a standard 'blue spine' of the period—ie the spine was blue, with white lettering. This edition had no frontispiece.

The second hardback edition was issued in 1955, with a new dustwrapper (above right) by an unknown artist, but no frontispiece. This edition was reprinted in 1960.

Armada did not publish *Jo to the Rescue* in paperback until 1994, because it was previously considered by the company that the 'family' stories would not sell as well. The cover was by Gwyneth Jones (see right). This edition was reprinted the same year.

To the best of my knowledge there have been no other printings until this GGBP edition.

Text

For this edition we have used the text of the original hardback edition; the only change we have made to the layout is to begin each chapter on a new page. The resolution of errors in the first edition is explained in the Appendix.

Clarissa Cridland
2006

COMPLETE NUMERICAL LIST OF TITLES IN THE CHALET SCHOOL SERIES

(Chambers and Girls Gone By)

Dates in parentheses refer to the original publication dates

1. *The School at the Chalet* (1925)
2. *Jo of the Chalet School* (1926)
3. *The Princess of the Chalet School* (1927)
4. *The Head Girl of the Chalet School* (1928)
5. *The Rivals of the Chalet School* (1929)
6. *Eustacia Goes to the Chalet School* (1930)
7. *The Chalet School and Jo* (1931)
8. *The Chalet Girls in Camp* (1932)
9. *The Exploits of the Chalet Girls* (1933)
10. *The Chalet School and the Lintons* (1934) (published in Armada paperback in two volumes—*The Chalet School and the Lintons* and *A Rebel at the Chalet School*)
11. *The New House at the Chalet School* (1935)
12. *Jo Returns to the Chalet School* (1936)
13. *The New Chalet School* (1938) (published in Armada paperback in two volumes—*The New Chalet School* and *A United Chalet School*)
14. *The Chalet School in Exile* (1940)
15. *The Chalet School Goes to It* (1941) (published in Armada paperback as *The Chalet School at War*)
16. *The Highland Twins at the Chalet School* (1942)
17. *Lavender Laughs in the Chalet School* (1943) (published in Armada paperback as *Lavender Leigh at the Chalet School*)
18. *Gay From China at the Chalet School* (1944) (published in Armada paperback as *Gay Lambert at the Chalet School*)

19. *Jo to the Rescue* (1945)
19a. *The Mystery at the Chalet School* (1947) (published in *The Chalet Book for Girls*)
19b. *Tom Tackles the Chalet School* (published in *The Second Chalet Book for Girls*, 1948, and *The Third Chalet Book for Girls*, 1949, and then as a single volume in 1955)
19c. *The Chalet School and Rosalie* (1951) (published as a paperback)
20. *Three Go to the Chalet School* (1949)
21. *The Chalet School and the Island* (1950)
22. *Peggy of the Chalet School* (1950)
23. *Carola Storms the Chalet School* (1951)
24. *The Wrong Chalet School* (1952)
25. *Shocks for the Chalet School* (1952)
26. *The Chalet School in the Oberland* (1952)
27. *Bride Leads the Chalet School* (1953)
28. *Changes for the Chalet School* (1953)
29. *Joey Goes to the Oberland* (1954)
30. *The Chalet School and Barbara* (1954)
31. (see 19b)
32. *The Chalet School Does It Again* (1955)
33. *A Chalet Girl from Kenya* (1955)
34. *Mary-Lou of the Chalet School* (1956)
35. *A Genius at the Chalet School* (1956) (published in Armada paperback in two volumes—*A Genius at the Chalet School* and *Chalet School Fête*)
36. *A Problem for the Chalet School* (1956)
37. *The New Mistress at the Chalet School* (1957)
38. *Excitements at the Chalet School* (1957)
39. *The Coming of Age of the Chalet School* (1958)
40. *The Chalet School and Richenda* (1958)
41. *Trials for the Chalet School* (1958)
42. *Theodora and the Chalet School* (1959)

43. *Joey and Co in Tirol* (1960)
44. *Ruey Richardson—Chaletian* (1960) (published in Armada paperback as *Ruey Richardson at the Chalet School*)
45. *A Leader in the Chalet School* (1961)
46. *The Chalet School Wins the Trick* (1961)
47. *A Future Chalet School Girl* (1962)
48. *The Feud in the Chalet School* (1962)
49. *The Chalet School Triplets* (1963)
50. *The Chalet School Reunion* (1963)
51. *Jane and the Chalet School* (1964)
52. *Redheads at the Chalet School* (1964)
53. *Adrienne and the Chalet School* (1965)
54. *Summer Term at the Chalet School* (1965)
55. *Challenge for the Chalet School* (1966)
56. *Two Sams at the Chalet School* (1967)
57. *Althea Joins the Chalet School* (1969)
58. *Prefects of the Chalet School* (1970)

Extras

The Chalet Book for Girls (1947)
The Second Chalet Book for Girls (1948)
The Third Chalet Book for Girls (1949)
The Chalet Girls' Cookbook (1953)

COMPLETE NUMERICAL LIST OF TITLES IN THE CHALET SCHOOL SERIES

(Armada/Collins)

1. *The School at the Chalet*
2. *Jo of the Chalet School*
3. *The Princess of the Chalet School*
4. *The Head Girl of the Chalet School*
5. *(The) Rivals of the Chalet School*
6. *Eustacia Goes to the Chalet School*
7. *The Chalet School and Jo*
8. *The Chalet Girls in Camp*
9. *The Exploits of the Chalet Girls*
10. *The Chalet School and the Lintons*
11. *A Rebel at the Chalet School*
12. *The New House at the Chalet School*
13. *Jo Returns to the Chalet School*
14. *The New Chalet School*
15. *A United Chalet School*
16. *The Chalet School in Exile*
17. *The Chalet School at War*
18. *The Highland Twins at the Chalet School*
19. *Lavender Leigh at the Chalet School*
20. *Gay Lambert at the Chalet School*
21. *Jo to the Rescue*

21a. *The Mystery at the Chalet School* (published only in the same volume as 23)

22. *Tom Tackles the Chalet School*
23. *The Chalet School and Rosalie*
24. *Three Go to the Chalet School*
25. *The Chalet School and the Island*
26. *Peggy of the Chalet School*

27. *Carola Storms the Chalet School*
28. *The Wrong Chalet School*
29. *Shocks for the Chalet School*
30. *The Chalet School in the Oberland*
31. *Bride Leads the Chalet School*
32. *Changes for the Chalet School*
33. *Joey Goes to the Oberland*
34. *The Chalet School and Barbara*
35. *The Chalet School Does It Again*
36. *A Chalet Girl from Kenya*
37. *Mary-Lou of the Chalet School*
38. *A Genius at the Chalet School*
39. *Chalet School Fête*
40. *A Problem for the Chalet School*
41. *The New Mistress at the Chalet School*
42. *Excitements at the Chalet School*
43. *The Coming of Age of the Chalet School*
44. *The Chalet School and Richenda*
45. *Trials for the Chalet School*
46. *Theodora and the Chalet School*
47. *Joey and Co in Tirol*
48. *Ruey Richardson at the Chalet School*
49. *A Leader in the Chalet School*
50. *The Chalet School Wins the Trick*
51. *A Future Chalet School Girl*
52. *The Feud in the Chalet School*
53. *The Chalet School Triplets*
54. *The Chalet School Reunion*
55. *Jane and the Chalet School*
56. *Redheads at the Chalet School*
57. *Adrienne and the Chalet School*
58. *Summer Term at the Chalet School*
59. *Challenge for the Chalet School*

60. *Two Sams at the Chalet School*
61. *Althea Joins the Chalet School*
62. *Prefects of the Chalet School*

NEW CHALET SCHOOL TITLES

In the last few years several authors have written books which either fill in terms in the Chalet School canon about which Elinor did not write or carry on the story. These are as follows:

Juliet of the Chalet School by Caroline German—set in the gap between *Jo of the Chalet School* and *The Princess of the Chalet School*; it tells of Juliet's debut as Head Girl. (Girls Gone By Publishers 2006)

Visitors for the Chalet School by Helen McClelland—set between *The Princess of the Chalet School* and *The Head Girl of the Chalet School* (Bettany Press 1995; Collins edition 2000)

Gillian of the Chalet School by Carol Allan—set between *The New Chalet School* and *The Chalet School in Exile* (Girls Gone By Publishers 2001; reprinted 2006; out of print)

The Chalet School and Robin by Caroline German—set after *The Chalet School Goes to It* (Girls Gone By Publishers 2003; out of print)

A Chalet School Headmistress by Helen Barber—set during the same term as *The Mystery at the Chalet School* (Girls Gone By Publishers 2004; out of print)

Peace Comes to the Chalet School by Katherine Bruce—set in the gap between *The Chalet School and Rosalie* and *Three Go to the Chalet School*; the action takes place during the summer term of 1945 (Girls Gone By Publishers 2005)

New Beginnings at the Chalet School by Heather Paisley—set three years after *Prefects at the Chalet School* (Friends of the Chalet School 1999; Girls Gone By Publishers 2002; out of print)

FURTHER READING

Behind the Chalet School by Helen McClelland (essential)*

Elinor M. Brent-Dyer's Chalet School by Helen McClelland. Out of print.

The Chalet School Companion by Helen McClelland. Out of print.

A World of Girls by Rosemary Auchmuty. Out of print.

A World of Women by Rosemary Auchmuty*

*Available from Bettany Press, 14 Warrener Close, Swindon, Wiltshire, SN25 4AH, UK
(http://users.netmatters.co.uk/ju90/ordering.htm)

JO TO THE RESCUE

BY

ELINOR M. BRENT-DYER

AUTHOR OF THE CHALET SCHOOL SERIES, 'JANIE OF LA ROCHELLE,' 'HEATHER LEAVES SCHOOL,' 'GERRY GOES TO SCHOOL,' 'THE LITLE MISSUS,' ETC.

CONTENTS

For

The Prefects of the Margaret Roper School

Joan, Mary, Doreen, Judith, Monica,

Vera, Phyllis

With love from their Head Mistress

Chapter I

Phoebe

The lattice window, already ajar, was pushed wide open, and a shock head was thrust through.

'They're coming, Miss Phoebe!' proclaimed a shrill voice. 'They've got a huge waggon. There's four of them, and a whole squad of kids.'

Phoebe looked up eagerly from her knitting. 'Coming, Reg? You've seen them, then? Where are they? Oh, if only I could get out to see them!' She finished with a sigh and an impatient glance round.

'I'll come in and wheel you, Miss Phoebe, if that's all,' said Reg promptly. 'Where's Debby gone, any-road?'

'She had to go into Garnley to the bank. She locked the door and took the key with her. You'd need to get the chair round by the back. Do you think you could manage?' Phoebe sounded doubtful.

'Manage right enough. There's no step, and the chair runs easy. I know. I helped Debby oil her last night.' Reg looked about. 'No flowers nor anything I'd upset, is there? Then I'll get through.' And he swung a sturdy leg over the window-sill and dropped down into the room easily. 'There y'are, Miss Phoebe! Got a shawl or summat to put over you?'

'It's over there on the end of the sofa. Give it to me, Reg, and go and unbolt the back door while I put the shawl on. Hurry, do! They'll be at The Witchens and into the house before you get me round if you don't.'

'Not them! They wasn't only halfway up the bank, and you

know what sort of a pull Tedder's Bank is. Besides, they were mostly out of the waggon, and the kids was gathering flowers. Little kids they are, all on 'em.' Reg called this back from the passage, where he had gone to open the back door after he had given Phoebe the great grey shawl from the end of the sofa. 'There's plenty o' time.'

He came back a minute or two later to find Phoebe muffled in her shawl, a flush of excitement on her thin cheeks. He paused only to tuck in the ends of her wrap from the wheels, and then, seizing the handle of the invalid chair in which she sat, he wheeled it deftly out of the room, down the passage, and through the back door into the little cobbled courtyard which divided the house from the long vegetable garden. Phoebe lay back with a sigh of relief as the soft summer breeze touched her face and ruffled the smooth hair across her brow. She had so longed to go out, but Debby, the loving tyrant who had ruled her life ever since rheumatic fever had left Phoebe an invalid at the age of twelve, had refused to permit it, since Debby herself must go to Garnley, the near-by market town, to cash a cheque at the bank, and get one or two needful things which were unobtainable at Garnham, the village up on the moors where they lived, and it might rain while she was gone.

Phoebe had said no more. How could she? If Debby ever left her, there was no one else to look after her, for she was singularly destitute of relations. The long years of invalidism had left her timid and uncertain; and the death of her father, eighteen months before this, had taught her to cling desperately to her one prop.

Reg pushed the chair carefully round the house to the front garden, and installed it at the bottom, where a break in the hedge enabled Phoebe to see without being seen. He himself squatted on the grass at her feet, and applied his eye to another break lower down.

'There's the waggon coming, Miss Phoebe,' he said, a few

minutes after they had established themselves, as a big waggonette, pulled by a pair of fine bay cart-horses, topped the rise. 'There's one lady in it, see. She's got a baby on her knee. Here comes the rest, running after them.' And a bevy of small children came racing along, followed by a very tall lady, carrying another baby over her shoulder, and chattering eagerly to another lady not quite so tall; while a third, very small and dark, with a tiny girl on her back, acted as whipper-in to the rest of the crowd.

'Four of them! And all quite young! I don't believe any of them can be much older than I am,' half-whispered Phoebe. 'Oh, I wonder how long they are going to stay at The Witchens?'

'It's taken till the end of September, any-road,' said Reg, who had his own methods of getting to know news. 'That's two months, Miss Phoebe. Likely you'll get to know 'em all. They look friendly enough. I'll bet they'll be running over for a crack with you in a day or two.'

'They may not,' sighed Phoebe. 'There's four of them. They probably won't want anyone else. And then they've got all the children. If they're going to look after them and do the work as well, they won't have much time for making new friends.'

'Mrs Purvis is going three mornings a week to redd up for them,' replied Reg. 'She was over at our place last night, and told Auntie so. And Lily Purvis—her that's a bit daft—is to go every day to clean the steps and peel potatoes and such-like. Lily's rare and set up about it, I can tell you.' Then, as the party came nearer: 'Gee! What a lot o' kids! Three—five—and the three they're carrying—that makes eight. And here comes another—older'n the rest,' as a girl of about ten, with a mop of chestnut curls that gleamed in the summer sunlight, came racing over the rise, her hands full of wild-flowers, and caught up with them. 'How are they goin' to fit all that crowd into The Witchens? It's nobbut more'n a big cottage.'

'They'll manage, I expect,' said Phoebe. She looked at the

happy, chattering crowd with wistful eyes as they crossed the wide white road and made for the grey-stone house opposite. 'There's four good bedrooms and two wee attics. The Witchens isn't all that crowded, Reg. Debby told me—for she went over it before we came here. It was too big for us; but I expect they can fit in somehow.'

The waggonette had stopped, and the lady with the baby handed over her burden to the red-curled girl with a merry 'Here you are, Sybs! Got him safely? Do not let him drop, whatever you do!'

The tall lady laughed, a golden ripple of laughter, and her voice as she spoke matched it. 'You needn't be afraid, Frieda. Sybs is quite safe.'

'What a lovely voice!' whispered Phoebe, afraid of being heard.

Reg gave her a quick, inquisitive glance. 'Aye; it is that!' he agreed.

'She *must* sing with that voice. I wonder if she's been trained—if she knows anything about instruments—'cellos, I mean?'

'Mebbe she does. You can ask her when you get to know her,' he said.

'If I ever do—I'd love to, she looks so kind. See how she's helping those little girls. She might be able to advise me. I wish she would. I do so need advice, and Debby is no good there.'

'That chap been bothering you again about the 'cello, Miss Phoebe?'

'Yes; he says his girl has set her heart on having Father's 'cello. I don't want to sell it—it's the thing he loved best on earth, and it seems to bring him nearer to me when I can touch it. But I'll never be able to use it myself, and Mr Burthill seemed to think it would be selfish of me to keep it when I can't and she can—this daughter of his.'

'I don't see it,' said Reg bluntly. 'Keep it if you want to, Miss

Phoebe. It's yours. Why should you sell it if you want it?'

'But I'm so afraid of being selfish,' sighed Phoebe. 'It's awfully easy to be selfish when you're a cripple, Reg. Ever since I was at that hydro and saw that poor Miss Emery, I've tried so hard not to get like her. She didn't mean it; but she was horribly selfish. She wanted everything she could have for herself, and she never thought of anyone else. I should hate to get like that. And Father would have hated it for me.'

By this time the newcomers had crowded into the house, but the door had been left open, and someone was running from room to room, pushing open all the windows, so that the sound of the merry voices and laughter came across the road to the pair in the garden.

Phoebe listened eagerly. It was two years since her father, a 'cellist who had just begun to make his name after years of hard struggling, had brought her to this quiet place where he hoped the fresh moorland breezes and pure air and water would do something for her. Six months later he had died, and in the first freshness of her grief Phoebe had shut herself away from the few old friends who had known that Nicholas Wychcote was a widower and the father of a daughter. She had never known her mother, who had died when she was only six months old; and Debby, who had been her grandmother's old cook, and had come to keep house for Mr Wychcote when he was left alone with a baby-girl to look after, had known very little of her either, since both he and she had married against the wishes of their families. Her father's agent had been very urgent that she should apply to her mother's people when he had died, since old Mr and Mrs Wychcote had gone some years before. But Phoebe's shyness and timidity, together with her pride, had forbidden it. Nicholas Wychcote had left his daughter the house in which she now lived, together with its contents, the contents of his rooms in town, and a tiny income. She and Debby were just able to live in modest comfort, and that was all.

Among his other possessions had been his 'cello, a valuable Lott, which had come to him from his godfather. Phoebe loved it because from it her father had drawn the beautiful music which was making his name when he died. But three months ago a letter had come for her from her father's agent, enclosing another from a wealthy man who informed her that his only child had been devoted to the 'cello, and had greatly admired the playing of Nicholas Wychcote. She was not making the progress she had hoped, and she had been seized with the idea that if she could only have his 'cello, she would be able to become a great player, which was her pet ambition. It was only recently that Mr Burthill had heard that Wychcote's possessions had come to a daughter. Now he wrote, wishing to buy the instrument, and offering the sum of £100 for it. £100 seemed a lot to honest Debby. Spread out, it would mean an additional ten shillings a week for the best part of the next four years, and that was a great matter when their income was so small. She completely failed to realise what the instrument meant to her young mistress as a memorial of her father; and, more than that, as Phoebe herself knew dimly, if anyone could make such an offer, it meant that the 'cello was probably worth considerably more. From Debby's point of view, this was foolishness. It *might* be worth more; but Miss Phoebe was not sure. £100 was £100, and the gentleman was willing to pay it on the nail. Why not clinch the bargain? If she wanted a 'cello—though that again was foolishness since she could do nothing with it nowadays—she could perhaps get a cheap one to take its place.

For once Phoebe felt that Debby had failed her. But to whom could she turn for advice? The doctor, a busy country practitioner, knew less than nothing about music, and would probably agree with her faithful old nurse. The Vicar was even more out of the question. He was a man who was ruled by his wife, who was a big, bustling lady with a loud voice and very decided views on every subject. Very early in their life at Garnham she had called. Nicholas Wychcote had been at home at the time, and he had taken an instant dislike to her. She had alluded to Phoebe, in the latter's hearing, as 'that poor, afflicted child of yours.' She had broadly hinted that all musicians were a lackadaisical, lazy, good-for-nothing lot; but since he was there, it was his bounden duty to put his talents at the service of the parish and play at the village concerts. One was coming off on Friday fortnight, and he should be put down for two solos.

Mr Wychcote had declined. In the first place, he did not wish to play at the village concert under the patronage of this insufferable woman. In the second place—which he made his excuse—he had an engagement to play at the Free Trade Hall at one of the big concerts there.

Mrs Hart was not to be put off. Well, then, would he play at the next one? She would take no excuse—play he must.

Mr Wychcote told her that he was sorry, but he could make no engagement without consulting his agent. He was under bond to him to accept none of anyone else's making. Seeing that nothing else would put an end to Mrs Hart's importunities, he gravely gave her the agent's name and address, advising her to write to *him*.

Unfortunately, the lady did so, and the agent calmly sent her the usual notice of fees. Mrs Hart nearly had an apoplectic fit at the Vicarage breakfast-table, where she read it. Unhappily, the Vicar was away for the week-end—though it is doubtful if he could have restrained his wife, even had he been at home. She marched over to Many Bushes, where Mr Wychcote was just going off to London to play in a big broadcast concert, and accused him of gross insult.

Like all creative artists, he was nervy, especially just before a performance, and he was irritated by her manner. He answered her with a bland, 'But, dear lady, you would not expect a bus-driver to use his bus for the purpose of bringing people to your entertainment free of charge. Why should you expect me to play free of charge? I am not an amateur: I am a professional. Naturally, I charge professional fees. Does your husband marry or bury his friends without *his* professional fees?'

After that there was no hope of friendship with the Vicarage folk; nor any hope of help from them. The Vicar had called twice to see Phoebe after her father's death. But on both occasions Debby refused to admit him to see her mistress, who was too ill to see anyone. And when Mrs Hart called, there was a real passage-of-arms between her and the faithful handmaid, greatly to the joy of one or two people who overheard most of what passed, and who had endured much at the hands of the Vicaress.

As for the village folk, they knew nothing of the matter and could not be looked to for help, though many of them were friendly enough, and many a cake or bag of buns from the weekly baking appeared at the cottage door, as well as offers to 'do a bit of shopping in Garnley as we're going to-day, if so be as you wants owt.'

The Witchens had been empty ever since the Wychcotes had come to Garnham, and when Phoebe heard through her usual medium, Reg Entwistle, that it had been let for the summer, she had hoped wistfully that there would be someone there who would be friendly with her; Debby was a dear, but she was limited. So long as her mistress was fairly well—for her—and the cottage was in its usual speckless condition, all should be well. Phoebe, missing more than she had realised the companionship of a cultured mind that had been hers for twenty-one years, in spite of her father's busy life, was moping inwardly. Now she felt excited. She would surely get to know these people. Perhaps they could help her. The one with the lovely voice might know something about 'cellos, and be able to advise her. But whether she did or not, it meant that at least there was a chance of companionship of the kind she had not known since her father left her.

She was roused from her happy day-dream by Reg's fidgeting, and, glancing at her wrist-watch, she gave a cry: 'Reg! It's half-past four! You must be dying for your tea! Wheel me back to the parlour, please, and then you must go. It was so kind of you to bring me out, and I have so enjoyed it.'

Reg jumped up. 'Right y'are, Miss Phoebe. Coom along! Over she goes!' He pushed the chair back to the parlour, bolted the back door again, and then wheeled up the tea-trolley, which had tea ready laid on it, with a little electric ring and kettle of water on the under shelf. The ring was plugged in, and Phoebe could make tea for herself easily. After asking if there was anything more he could do for her, and accepting one of Debby's cinnamon buns, he vaulted through the window. Phoebe, her mind in a happy turmoil, had her tea, and then picked up her knitting, and went on with it till six o'clock brought the bus from Garnley, and Debby herself hurrying up the narrow front path, anxious about her charge.

'I'm sorry to be so late, Miss Phoebe,' she said as she bustled into the room, her basket piled high with parcels. 'I missed the three bus, and had to wait for the five-fifteen. You've had your tea?'

'Yes, thank you, Debby. Did you do all you wanted?'

'Aye; I even matched up that silk you wanted at Burnside's, so you can get on with your cushion-cover.'

'Oh, Debby! How nice! I'm getting so sick of knitting. I've done nothing else for the last three days. But it was no use beginning something else until I'd finished the cushion.'

Since Phoebe had been so tied to her chair, it had been necessary for her to find something to occupy her time. She could scarcely read all day, and there were few games she could play alone. She had turned to needlework as soon as she could manage it. Her father, glad to indulge her, had seen to it that she had the best lessons available, and her plain sewing and embroidery were both exquisite now. For years Mr Wychcote had been in the habit of bringing her skeins of silks of every shade and colour and texture whenever he went to a fresh town to play, so that she had drawers full of them. He had also bought her lengths of material for embroidery—linens, crash, satin, muslin. When she was able to think about such things again after his death, Phoebe had decided to try to add to their slender income by selling her work, and she was beginning to work up a small connection. The great drawback lay in the fact that she could never rely on being able to ply her needle at any time. When the cruel rheumatic pains attacked her fingers and wrists, as they sometimes did, she was helpless—unable, even, to feed herself. So she always had to warn her customers that she could never promise work for a certain date, though she always tried to get it done in the right time, often working when it was torture to hold her needle and the material. There was real heroism in the way she tried to overcome her disabilities, and Debby, watching over her with a gruff tenderness, could often have wept to see her struggles. Of late, the pains had been less frequent, and less severe when they did come. She was able to move about a little on crutches on her best days, which was something no one had hoped for during the first years. When she could not do that, Debby, a brawny countrywoman, would pick the girl up in her arms and carry her about as if she had been a little child. Phoebe was small and thin, and very light, and Debby made nothing of her weight.

'Debby, I've news for you,' said her young mistress presently.

'Aye, Miss Phoebe? What's that, now?' asked Debby, who had doffed her hat and coat, and tied a large white apron over her dress.

'Reg Entwistle came this afternoon to tell me that the people for The Witchens were coming. I got him to take me out through the back door to see them. Oh, Debby! They do look so nice—four ladies, all of them about my own age, or not much older, anyhow; and a lot of children.'

'I heard there was a bonny parcel o' bairns,' replied Debby, laying hands on the tea-trolley and wheeling it towards the door. 'Mind you don't go tiring yourself with them, Miss Phoebe—that is, if you get to know 'em. That Sodger at the Vicarage'll do her best to stop it if she can; but mebbe we'll meet 'em first.'

There came a knock at the door, and Debby, pushing the trolley back into a corner, made haste to answer it. From where she was sitting, Phoebe could not see who was there, but a thrill ran through her as she heard the golden voice she had admired so short a time before ask anxiously, 'I say, could you tell me where we can get some milk? I'm so sorry to trouble you, but we can't find any, though the agent from whom we took the house said he'd see there was some, as well as bread, waiting for us when we got here. We've found the bread, but we can't run the milk to earth, and I'm afraid he's forgotten it. We've a whole pack of babes who are yelling for supper; but unless we can get that milk, supper won't be forthcoming.'

She heard Debby—blessed Debby!—say, 'Come in, Ma'am, and I'll put off my apron and come and show you where it likely is.'

Then the door was pushed wider, and through it came the tall, slender being she had seen that afternoon. Debby's voice said, 'This is my mistress, Miss Wychcote. She'll spare me a minute or two, I'll be bound.'

The next moment her hands were taken in a warm, gentle grasp, and the lovely voice cried, 'Wychcote? Did you say *Wychcote*? But of course, I can see the likeness for myself! You couldn't be anyone but Nicholas Wychcote's daughter! I'm Joey Maynard!'

Chapter II

JOEY

TAKEN completely aback by these whirlwind tactics, Phoebe first stared and then demanded, 'But how do you know?'

'By the likeness, of course. I said so. You're the image of him.' And Joey Maynard stood back and surveyed the broad brow from which the thick brown hair with its golden lights sprang back to give a square effect; the pointed chin with its deep cleft; the wide-set, large eyes, and the long, sensitive mouth. 'I saw—and heard—him five times in all; and the last time, I met him. A friend of mine was solo soprano, and I went round after the concert and she introduced me to everyone. Vanna di Ricci told me after that he had a daughter who was about our age, she thought; but I never thought I'd have the luck to meet you!'

The luck! Phoebe's lips suddenly quivered. She had hoped to be on terms of friendship with the newcomers; but she had never even dreamed of being so rapturously greeted. Jo saw it, and her eyes softened as she dropped into a near-by chair and bent forward.

'Don't you call it luck for me? I admired his playing so much. I've always loved the 'cello, and his was such wonderful music. I met him, and liked him personally. And now I've found his daughter. Vanna couldn't tell me much about you, and she didn't know where you were, or anything about you, after he left you. I'd have written to you then if I could. Besides, I was rather in the thick of things myself at that time. But I'll tell you later, for I see your maid is ready, and we can't keep the babes waiting any longer than we can help. They've been very good, dear lambs; but they are tired and hungry, and the sooner they're in bed the better. I'll run over tomorrow if I may.'

'Oh, do!' implored Phoebe. 'Father told me about Vanna di Ricci, and said she had a lovely voice. She was to have come and have tea with us, only I got ill again, and after that he brought me here, and then—well, then things happened so fast, and so she never came. I'd have loved to meet her, for he said she was a charming girl, and I have so few friends.'

'So she is. Vanna's a dear,' declared Joey Maynard as she got up to follow Debby. 'When I write, I'll tell her about you, and see if she can come to us for a few days. Then you *will* meet her. Now I must go. Thank you so much for sparing your maid to us for a few minutes.'

'Debby will be glad to help you,' replied Phoebe, smiling. 'Ask her if there's anything else you want, won't you?'

'If she can guide us to the milk, that's all we're likely to need tonight, anyhow. Goodbye for now, Miss Wychcote. I'll see you in the morning. And you shall meet the rest—by instalments, I think. You might be rather overwhelmed if we all surged in on you at once!' And with this Jo departed, leaving a happy Phoebe behind her.

As they crossed the road, Jo said to Debby, 'Debby—I may call you that, may I?—will it be possible for Miss Wychcote to come over to us sometimes, do you think? We'd love to have her if she could.'

'Debby's my name,' said that person drily. 'Yes, Ma'am, Miss Phoebe can come. Her chair's on wheels, and I could bring her. Or on her well days she can walk with crutches.'

'Oh, I'm glad! What was it—an accident?'

'No, Ma'am. When she was twelve, she had rheumatic fever very bad, and it left her like you see her. Sometimes the pain is very bad, and then she can't do nothing for herself. But just now she's a bit better, and I'm hoping when Dr Mitchell comes again he'll see an improvement.'

'Dr Mitchell?' began Jo with a startled look. Then she closed her lips.

Debby had noticed nothing. 'Yes, Ma'am. That's the specialist that's had charge of her for the last three years. He comes to see her once in six months unless we have to send for him. Now, Ma'am,' as they reached The Witchens, 'if we go round the house to the shed, I'll show you where the stone trough is; for that's where the milk'll be. It's been a hot day, and whoever brought it would put it there to keep it fresh.'

Joey led the way round the house to the big, airy shed at the back. Arrived there, Debby opened a door inside and showed a stone-paved, stone-lined place, with a deep stone trough under the window opening. There, set almost up to its rim in water, was the missing milk in a big can. Debby lifted it out and set it out on the floor, taking off the wire-mesh lid.

'It's one of Jaycott's,' she said. 'Theirs is good milk, Ma'am—a Jersey herd, it is. We get ours from there, too. The milk is always kept in the trough hereabouts—in summer, at any rate. And there's a pat of butter there, too. Mrs Jaycott would send that from their own store. They only make it now and then, when there's danger of the milk not keeping.'

'How very good of her!' exclaimed Mrs Maynard. 'We brought a week's butter and marg. with us; but this will be wonderful for the babies. Thank you so much, Debby. I'll go and get a couple of jugs, for I certainly can't lift that can myself, and Mrs de Bersac and Mrs von Ahlen are putting the wee babies to bed; and the Countess has charge of the rest, with my large niece Sybil to help her. Come in with me and meet them. Then you can see for yourself that we're all quite nice to know.'

Debby smiled grimly, and followed her into the house, which, as she noted, was furnished chiefly with light bamboo furniture. The spotless kitchen had a big table and chairs of deal, and there were two cupboards and a well-polished lino on the floor. Muslin curtains drifted into the room on the summer breeze, and the old-fashioned dresser, which was a fixture, already had a full complement of willow-pattern china on it. Jo led the way through into the hall, and then to the dining-room, where a crowd of small people were seated solemnly round a big table laid with plates and mugs of various kinds. At the head sat a fairy-tale princess with golden hair swung round her head in enormous plaits, and at the foot was a picture-child of ten.

At sight of Mrs Maynard the party set up a cheer, and the lady said eagerly, 'Oh, Joey, have you got the milk?'

'Yes; at the back, in the inner part of the shed. I'll show you later, Marie. Miss Wychcote's maid, Debby—this is her—showed me. Sybs, run and get a couple of big jugs, pet, and we'll soon have everyone served. Debby, this is the Countess Wertheim, one of my friends. Those are her pair,' pointing unashamedly at a boy of seven and a girl of five who were sufficiently like their lovely mother to vouch for the truth of the statement. 'These are my own three,' went on Mrs Maynard, indicating a trio of small girls who bore a close resemblance to each other, though one was very dark, one very fair, and the third brown-haired and grey-eyed. 'This small man,' laying her hand on the shoulder of a fair little lad of nearly three, 'is Louis von Ahlen, whose mother is at present upstairs putting his very new brother to bed. And this,' with a smile at a tiny, dark-haired, dark-eyed maiden, 'is Tessa de Bersac, whose mamma is putting my own small son to bed. I was the only one of us who had cheek enough to beard strangers in search of milk, and I said I'd go if Mrs de Bersac would undress and bath Stephen for me while I did so. And here comes my big niece Sybil with jugs, so we'll go and get that milk we've all heard so much about, and then this pack can get off to bed and leave their elders and betters to do a bit of settling in. It's late enough, goodness knows!'

It was a fine tale Debby had to tell Phoebe when she got back an hour later, since she had insisted on staying to wash up after the small folk. She had met the other two ladies, who proved to be as charming as Mrs Maynard and the Countess. Joey had taken her all over the house, explaining what their ideas with regard to arrangements were, and asking various questions, and saying that they meant to buy The Witchens as a holiday house for them all. The light furniture had come all the way from Tyrol, where they had formerly lived, and would be left in it. There were camp-beds for the small folk, and the grown-ups had beds of cane-work. Mrs Maynard and her small family had the biggest bedroom, which was quite a good size. A wicker-work cot stood by her bed, and in it was a five-months-old baby boy, who gurgled delightedly when he saw his mother. Mrs von Ahlen had the other big bedroom, since she had two small boys with her, the 'very new brother' being only six weeks old. The Countess and her little daughter slept in the room behind Mrs Maynard's, and Mrs de Bersac had the one behind Mrs von Ahlen's, with small Tessa as room-mate. The two attics upstairs were given over to Sybil Russell and young Wolferl Wertheim.

'And now,' concluded Joey, 'I must go to Stephen and settle him for the night—or this part of the night, anyhow. He's had his supper'—she had slipped away to see to it while Debby was helping the Countess to fill the mugs with the rich creamy milk—'but I always tuck him up and so on myself. Goodbye, Debby. Thank you so very much for all your help. I don't know how we should manage if it weren't for all the kind folk there are in the world!'

Debby kept Phoebe thrilled till she went to bed, and it was a very happy girl who finally settled off to sleep in Many Bushes.

Meanwhile, having seen the last of the small fry off, Joey and her friends gathered round the open french window in the drawing-room with their sewing, and discussed the situation.

'I like that—Debby, did you say it was?' said Marie von

Wertheim as she bit off her thread thoughtfully. 'She has an honest look.'

'She's got the strength of a man,' said Jo, who was knitting a jumper for her eldest daughter. 'You should have seen her heave that great can of milk about. And I specially liked that girl, Phoebe Wychcote.'

'Tell us about her, Jo. What is she like?' asked Frieda von Ahlen.

'The image of her father. You saw him, didn't you, Frieda? Of course you did! You went with Jack and me to that last concert he played at at Cardiff. Do you remember?'

Frieda von Ahlen nodded. 'I remember. A giant of a man, with a bush of hair, and eyes that rather reminded me of Corney Flower's. You went round afterwards to see Vanna, but I was tired—it was just before Louis's arrival—and went to the car with Jack. So I never met him.'

'I heard him two or three times over the radio,' said Marie thoughtfully. 'I remember Eugen heard him too, and wanted to know why he was not better known. And this is his daughter? Didn't you say she was a cripple?'

Jo nodded. 'Debby told me that she'd had rheumatic fever when she was a kiddy, and it left her with rheumatism. But—and this is rather awful—she's been in Leaver Mitchell's care. At least, Debby said Dr Mitchell the specialist, and there's only one rheumatic specialist called Mitchell that I know of.'

'But what is so awful about that, my Jo?' asked Mrs de Bersac.

'Why, he died last week, quite suddenly. Heart, I think it was. Jem told me about it when I was up at The Round House. Obviously, these people know nothing about it, and I'm afraid it'll come as a shock to them when they do hear.'

'Wasn't something said about it in the B.B.C. news?' asked Frieda.

'Not that I know of. I didn't hear it if there was.'

'Still, there would certainly be something in the papers if he was so well known,' suggested Marie.

'How many people of our age read obituary notices?' demanded Jo. '*I* don't, for one. Do you, Marie? Or you, Frieda? Or Simone?'

None of them did.

'Very well, then. It's not very likely Phoebe Wychcote does either.'

'What are you going to do about it?' asked Simone.

Jo glanced at her. 'How do you know I'll do anything?'

'I know you, Jo. You won't leave that poor girl to find out just anyhow.'

A faint flush overspread Jo Maynard's healthy creamy pallor. 'Would you do it yourself?' she said defensively.

'I shouldn't want to. But I should feel it a very hard thing to tell.'

'So should I,' Marie chimed in. 'But *you'll* do it, Joey. What was it Dr Jem once called you? A champion butter-in—that was it. Well, you still are. You *know* you're going to break the news gently the first chance you get, so don't deny it.'

'Well, I do feel someone ought to say something. She has such a—such a—*lost* sort of look. I feel her father's death took away the best part of her life. She looked to me as if she was afraid of another blow at any time. I don't know how you people will feel about her; but I just wanted to—to—well, to *mother* her a bit.'

'*Jo!* The girl's much the same age as we are. You said so yourself. You can't go round mothering people the same age as yourself.'

'Oh yes, you can, if they ask for it. There was a hungry sort of look in those great grey eyes of hers. I'd like to find out what it is she wants, and give it to her if I could.'

'If it is her father,' said Simone soberly, 'even your mothering cannot allay that want, Joey.'

'That probably has a good deal to do with it. But I got the impression that there was something else besides. If I can find out what it is, I'll do what I can to help her. So will you three, and you know it!'

'Of course,' said Frieda, beginning to gather up her work. 'We are so happy ourselves, it would be selfish and cruel if we didn't. Oh, I know we have our own troubles. Bruno is away from me, serving in India; André is in the Belgian Congo, and Eugen is hard at it in Italy. But we have so much to console us in our children and our quiet, safe life here. Even you, Jo, during those awful days last year when it seemed as if Jack wouldn't come back to you, it wasn't as bad as it might have been, for you had the girlies. Even if the worst had happened, you wouldn't have been quite alone. But it seems that this girl *is*. And now, I'm going to bed. It's ten o'clock, and by the time I finish up, Gerard will be wanting his second supper. What time will breakfast be?'

They looked at each other. Finally, Marie spoke.

'I don't know about the rest of you; but my family are early birds. We usually have ours at eight. Would that be too soon?'

'So do we,' said Jo. 'The girlies are accustomed to being out by half-past seven at this time of year, and they're famishing when eight o'clock comes. It would suit me all right. But I don't think *you* should get up then, Frieda. You have yours in bed, and one of us will fetch Louis and see to him. You stay put till nine or ten. There won't be anything much to do, and it's been a tiring day.'

The rest backed her up, and, despite Frieda's protests, they insisted that she must rest in the morning. Finally she gave way.

'Oh, very well. I see I shall have no peace if I do not do as you say. But I warn you, this is not to go on. I'm very fit now, and it's only because we had the journey today.'

'All right,' said Jo easily. 'We'll let it go at that for the moment, and settle about other days as they come. Shut these windows, Simone, and I'll go and lock up in the back premises.'

'And I'll go and have a peep at Wolferl and Sybil,' added Marie. 'By the way, Jo, if it continues as hot as this, I think one of your girls should share Sybil's room. There's plenty of room for another bed up there, and five in one room, even if four of them are tinies, isn't too good. You'll have to do it when Jack comes, anyhow.'

They went off to their various tasks, and by eleven o'clock they were all in their own rooms. Marie von Wertheim had slipped in to see that Frieda was all right, and found her just laying a satisfied baby in his cot. In the camp-bed at the far side of the room, Louis was spreadeagled in the deep sleep of healthy childhood. Frieda, with her masses of long fair hair falling over her white nightdress, looked not a day older than when they were all girls at the Chalet School. She turned round to her friend with a smile, and laid a finger on her lips.

'He's just off,' she said in the Tyrolean German that was their native tongue. 'Don't wake him, Marie. I know Jo's children can sleep through anything, but we are very quiet folk at home, and though I don't doubt these eight or nine weeks together will make a difference, I'd rather they were broken in gently.'

Marie laughed, and began to take out the pins and clips that held her golden curls in place. 'On days like this I'm always sorry I never had my hair cut. But Eugen would be furious if I did it, so it's too late now.' She shook out the mane of curls, and ran her fingers through it. 'Ouf! That's better! Frieda, what do you think about Jo's ideas?'

'About this girl, do you mean? Just like Jo, of course. We're all willing to help other people when we find that it's needed. The difference is that it has to be pointed out to us. Jo sees it on the spot, and goes for it.' She paused, drew her hair round, and began to plait it. A sudden mischievous smile curved her lips.

'What are you thinking?' demanded Marie.

'Oh, nothing much. Only, Jo's philanthropy has so frequently led her into the most awful mess. I'm just wondering what this latest crusade will bring.'

'Nothing. Why should it? On other occasions it's nearly always meant Jo going off somewhere. But this time the whole affair lies just across the road. I don't see how even Jo can get into any sort of a mess merely through mothering a lonely girl who is also a cripple. Now I'm going to bed, so good night, Liebchen.' She bent to kiss her friend, and then slipped away to her own room.

Left alone, Frieda finished her hair, drew back the curtains and opened the window as widely as it would go, and then, with a final look at her little sons, got into bed herself when she had said her prayers.

'Marie *may* be right,' she thought as she settled down, 'but I shall be very much surprised if we are not all embroiled in some wild adventure before we're done. It won't be Jo's fault if we're not!'

Chapter III

NEW FRIENDS FOR PHOEBE

'MAY we come in, please? I've brought my family to show you.'

It was another glorious day, and Debby had wheeled Phoebe out to the front lawn at eleven, when she had been brought downstairs and had rested a little in the parlour after the labours of dressing. She had been sitting working at the last spray on her cushion-cover, and had been so buried in her work and her thoughts that she had never noticed the gate of The Witchens open and the little procession cross the road. She looked up at the sound of Jo's voice, and saw her leaning over the gate, a Moses Ark tucked under one arm. Three small girls were clustered round her.

Phoebe dropped her work. 'Oh, come in!' she cried. 'How nice of you to come! Do you know, although I heard the voices coming from The Witchens, and saw the children running about, I was beginning to be afraid that most of it was just a pleasant dream.'

'I say! Did the small fry disturb you?' asked Jo with concern as she came in and dropped on the grass beside the invalid chair. 'We did warn them not to yell; but they're only tiny, most of them, and they forget.'

Phoebe shook her head. 'Oh no! I generally wake early. I roused up at five this morning, and I've been awake ever since. I loved hearing the laughter and chatter. It's funny, but just at this end of the village there isn't a single child. There's plenty at the bottom, but Mrs Tomlin's Maisie is the only one at this end, and

Maisie is twelve now. It was lovely hearing all the very young voices!'

'Well, I hope you're going to think knowing their owners is lovely, too,' said Jo briskly. 'Come here, you three.—Miss Wychcote, may I present my triplet daughters—Len, Con, and Margot.'

'Triplets!' gasped Phoebe. 'Really triplets?'

'Yes; really and truly triplets. Wasn't I lucky? And this is our only boy, so far—Stephen. He'll wake up presently, and then you'll see what a friendly person he is.'

Phoebe smiled wistfully as she held out her hand to the three little girls, who came up without any shyness, but with an enchanting air of courtliness, and shook it very gently, one after the other.

'Which is which?' she asked.

'This is Con,' said one of them. 'This is Margot, and I'm Len. I'm the oldest. *And*,' very impressively, 'I can say my t-h's now. The others can't quite do it yet. They will soon, though. Mamma says so.'

'I expect they will,' agreed Phoebe. 'It's not so easy at first, is it?'

'Can say vem sometimes,' said the dark-eyed little maid Len had named Con. 'Len's older'n us, vat's why she says vem first.'

'How old are you?' asked Phoebe.

'We're free—four in November—Bonfire Night, Mamma says.'

'Do they really call you Mamma?' Phoebe turned to Jo, who had set her son's basket in the shade. 'I thought no one did nowadays.'

'That's why mine do,' said Jo placidly. She suddenly chuckled. 'When people heard it, it only caused a lesser sensation than their arrival.'

'I expect that was a sensation all right.'

'It certainly was. I've done a few weird things in my time; but I must say this was the biggest thrill all round. As for the "Mamma" business, I was tired of hearing "Mummy" and "Daddy" everywhere, and "Father" and "Mother" aren't easy for tiny folk—witness their difficulties with t-h! My husband and I had talked it over, and we decided to be "Papa" and "Mamma."'

'I think I rather like it.' A sudden mischievous gleam came into Phoebe's eyes, and she added, 'The only difficulty is, they may shorten it to "Pa" and "Ma" later on.'

'Mercy! Don't mention such awful ideas before them!' cried Jo. 'Do you hear, you three? Never let me catch you saying that, or there'll be trouble.'

'S'ouldn't, anyhow. Don't like it,' said Len decidedly.

'I do!' Margot's blue eyes were full of wickedness.

'Well, you know what happens to small girls who don't obey,' said Jo.

'It's bed,' explained Con politely to the stranger. 'And if it's *vewy* bad disobey, it *may* be a spanking. But ve only time Mamma had to spank us when we'd been ever so, never so bad, she cwied after. Vat was playin' wif matches when we'd been told not to.'

Jo grimaced at her daughter, and then turned a laughing look at Phoebe. 'I hated doing it; but I had to impress them for safety's sake. It did the trick, too,' she added, as the three, with a sudden shout, darted off after a Scarlet Admiral which came sailing past. 'They've never so much as touched a matchbox since. I don't believe in spanking as a rule, but it seemed the only thing to do when they *wouldn't* remember what I'd said.'

'I think it was,' assented Phoebe. 'If they insisted on playing with matches, you'd never have had a moment's peace about them when they were out of your sight. And spanking isn't half so bad as the punishment *I* got for doing it. Debby struck a match and held it to one finger—only for a moment, of course—but

I've never forgotten the horrible pain and the shock it was. I was a big girl of twelve before I would even take one after that. Before, they had to hide all the matches from me.'

'That was a very drastic treatment,' agreed Jo. 'I don't think I could ever bring myself to do that. Mercifully, the spanking and my idiotic tears after it was over were evidently enough for mine. And when Stephen is old enough to be a worry that way, his sisters will see that he leaves matches alone. Len is quite a motherly little person already. Margot, as you saw just now, is an imp. And Con shows signs of becoming a dreamer. They're all three quite different in character. It's fascinating watching them develop. They're all three truthful, and all three tender-hearted. But they need very different handling. Now there's Stephen. So far, his main characteristics are unbounded good temper and complete obstinacy. He doesn't yell if he doesn't get what he wants. He simply goes on saying "Agh—agh!" which means "I want!" But otherwise, he's far and away the most placid of my four. Now Margot just *dances* when she gets into a rage. But this must be boring for you. Let's talk about you. What lovely work! Do you do it for fun, or do you take orders?'

'I started it when I had to find something to do to pass the time,' said Phoebe, spreading it out to let Jo see the beautifully worked sprays of honeysuckle and wild-rose. 'Later, I was glad to be able to earn a little by taking orders. But I'm handicapped, of course. If the pain comes badly in my hands, I can't do anything. That means that I never dare promise for a certain time, for I couldn't be sure of finishing. I've lost two or three people owing to that. I remember I had a teacloth and napkins to embroider for a wedding-present last year. I got the teacloth done, but only half the napkins, when I had a very bad attack that lasted for a fortnight. The wedding was over three weeks before I was able to send them off to the donor, and she was so angry that she returned them, saying that as they weren't up to time they were no use to her. I might have made her take them, of course, and Debby wanted me to insist; but I couldn't—I'm no good at fighting.'

'What a pig!' cried Jo. 'If she wanted to give the bride her gift dead on time, she could surely have given her the cloth and said the napkins were coming later?'

'I was too ill to think of sending it. And Debby didn't of course. She had the work to see to, and me to nurse. But the worst of it was that two friends of hers had said they would give me orders when the cloth and napkins were done, and she must have told them I wasn't reliable, for the orders never came.'

'How horrid of her!' said Jo hotly. 'But if you do take orders, I wish you'd take one from me. Have you anything else to do when this is finished?'

'No; this is the last of a big order for another bride. I've sent off the other things, and this is to go as soon as it's done—tomorrow, I hope.'

'Oh, then,' said Jo eagerly, 'could you make me a baby frock, do you think? My elder sister, Lady Russell, is expecting her fourth at the end of September, and the baby-clothes are rather worn. I'd like to give her a frock or two for the new arrival. I *am* knitting woollies. But I can't sew—or anyhow, not like you. If you could manage a couple, I'd be thrilled. And so would Madge. I never saw lovelier work, and I was educated abroad among girls who sewed by instinct almost. Do I get you the materials, or do you supply those?'

'I've got plenty in the house. I'd love to make the little frocks if you'll let me, Mrs Maynard.'

'Well, you make them, then, and let me have them as you do them. You'd better make one a little larger than the other. How about coupons?'

'Oh, there'll be no need of coupons. I've had the muslin I'm thinking of for six or seven years. I don't do that sort of thing as a rule, you know. It's mainly table and bed-linen and cushion-covers. Baby frocks would be a lovely change.'

'Very well, then. Let me have a nice, neat bill with them, and I'll present you with an equally nice, neat cheque in exchange.'

'Oh, but—' began Phoebe with a troubled look, but got no further.

With one bound, Jo was on her feet. 'Of course I'll pay for them! What do you take me for? Now, it's no use arguing,' she added cheerfully. 'You said yourself that you couldn't fight, and *I* can when I think it's necessary. If you won't let me pay, I won't have the frocks, and it really would be a boon if you'd do them. Madge would be thrilled to have two really pretty new frocks for her new son—we're all hoping it'll be a boy, you know. David's an only son, so far; and though it doesn't seem to have harmed him, still a brother might be quite a good thing for him. I know when my next baby comes along, I want another boy.'

'Do you mean—' gasped Phoebe, completely diverted from the question, as Jo had meant her to be.

That young lady shook her head. 'Goodness, no! Not yet, my child. Stephen is only five months old. But I'd like him to have a brother by the time he's a year and a half or so, so that they can be chums. Now if Madge gives David one, he'll be so much younger that poor David will be more like a father than a brother to him. There'll be twelve and a half years between them. That's a big difference, you know.'

'Is Sybil who is with you his sister?' asked Phoebe. 'Debby is immensely taken with her. She says she never saw a more lovely little girl.'

'Please warn Debby to say nothing of that kind to Sybil,' said Jo sharply. 'We've had trouble enough with her already, thanks to people discussing her looks *to* her and *before* her. We do want her to realise her beauty. It's as much a gift from God as anything else, and she must be grateful for it. But we don't want her to be conceited. Not,' she added, with a sudden change of tone, 'that I think that's likely to happen now. Sybil has had a lesson against conceit and self-will that she'll never forget. But old habits die hard, and we don't want things made any harder for her than they already are.'

'I'll warn Debby,' said Phoebe, looking, as she felt, rather scared. 'I don't think she would say anything. Praise isn't much in her line. But I'll speak to her, and tell her to say nothing to Sybil.'

'Thank you. You see,' went on Jo, thinking that some sort of explanation was due to Phoebe, 'thanks to Sybil's wilfulness—which was partly the result of silly idiots saying how lovely she is and all that—we nearly lost her little sister, Josette, a few months ago. It's been an awful shock to her; and I don't think she'll ever be as bad again as she was. But it's a struggle for her in any case, and we're all trying to help her.'

'I see,' said Phoebe. 'What a pretty name the little one has!'

'Josephine Mary—after me, really,' said Jo. 'She's nearly five now. She's been terribly ill—she got badly scalded in April—and my sister kept her at home. But I suggested that Sybil should come with me, for Madge isn't too well, and the less she has to worry about the better. David was off with a school-chum of his, so that settled the family. Now I must go, for the rest want to come over and see you, and I think too many of us at once would be too much for you. Where are those girls of mine?' She sent a clear ringing call across the garden, and it was answered by shouts, and then the three little girls came running back. Jo surveyed their crimson faces under the broad-brimmed hats they wore, and shook her head. 'Who looks like a boiled lobster? You bad children, to get yourselves as hot as this! Well, say goodbye to Miss Wychcote and come along now. You shall have a nice nap in the garden, and that will cool you down.' She stooped down and picked up the basket, where Stephen still slumbered sweetly. She laughed as she adjusted it safely. 'I fed him just before we came over, and that's why he's sleeping like this. The next time we come, I'll see he's awake. You haven't really met him properly this time.'

'Come soon,' pleaded Phoebe. 'It's lovely having people like you so near.'

'I'll send the others over now, and probably I'll look in after tea for a moment,' promised Jo, hunting her little girls before her as she went to the gate. 'Goodbye for the present!'

'How kind she is!' mused Phoebe as she leant back against her cushions. 'And how thoughtful! But what a queer mixture! Once or twice I felt as if she were just a schoolgirl on holiday. But when she was talking about the children—and about Sybil—I felt as if she were years older than I.'

Then she sat up again, for the gate opened and a small, dark lady appeared, leading a tiny girl as dark as herself, and followed by a very fair one carrying a baby, and with a little boy rather older than the little girl. She came towards her with shy smiles.

Frieda von Ahlen and Simone de Bersac came forward, and Frieda spoke.

'Please, I am Mrs von Ahlen, and this is Mme de Bersac,' she said. 'Jo said we might come for twenty minutes; but then we are to leave, for Marie—I mean, the Countess von Wertheim—wants to come with her two children. These are ours. Would you like to take Gerard a little? He's very tiny, and not very heavy yet.' And she laid the baby in Phoebe's arms so eagerly outstretched to take him.

'Do you really trust me?' marvelled Phoebe, with a glance up into the apple-blossom face, with its tender blue eyes and aureole of shining hair.

'But of course. Why not? Here is my elder boy, Louis.' And Frieda drew forward the fair-haired boy of two and a half, so like herself.

'Gerard and Louis? What pretty names all your children have!'

'I hope you will think so of my petite,' said Simone, putting the tiny hand into Phoebe's free one. 'She is named Thérèse Élise for a very dear cousin who died some years ago. We call her Tessa, for no one, to us, could bear Cousin Thérèse's name but herself. Tessa, ma petite, salue donc Mademoiselle.'

Tessa lifted her little dark face, such a contrast to Frieda's fair-faced sons, for a kiss, and Phoebe gave it at once.

'Doesn't she speak English?' asked Phoebe. 'I'm afraid my French is a very poor affair nowadays.'

'I 'peak le F'ançais and En'lis' too,' said Tessa for herself. She had a very sweet, clear little voice to match her elf-like frame.

'And both too much at times,' laughed Simone. 'I'm afraid, Miss Wychcote, you'll find that my daughter is a chatterbox. She began trying to talk when she was only eight months old, and she can chatter quite fast now.'

'And Louis is a match for her,' added Frieda, dropping down on the grass. 'If Gerard is as bad when he begins, I shall have to make them talk in turn, Jo says.'

'Jo cannot boast!' Simone chimed in. 'Her own daughters never stop from the time they awake till the time they go to sleep unless she checks them.'

'They are very obedient as a rule, though,' said Frieda; 'and I'm sorry to say that Louis is *not*.' She cast a would-be stern look at the urchin beside her. 'If he is not better soon, I am going to send him to stay with Tante Gisela and Onkel Gottfried for a time. I cannot have him setting Gerard so bad an example.' And she shook her head at him.

Louis's small head sank. 'I will t'y, Mamma,' he lisped.

'There, then. Go and play with Tessa while Tante Simone and I talk with Miss Wychcote,' said his mother with a smile. 'You are not tired of holding Gerard, Miss Wychcote?'

Phoebe looked at her. 'I am almost twenty-three, Mrs von

Ahlen, and this is the first tiny baby I have ever held,' she said. 'Please don't take him from me unless you want him.'

'Of course not.' Frieda sat down on the grass, and pulled Simone down beside her. 'Jo says you do beautiful needlework. Do show us. I am very fond of sewing, but I have so much to do for Louis—and it won't be long after all before Gerard will be trotting about and tearing *his* clothes—that I have no time for embroidery. Oh! that is beautiful!' as Phoebe gave her the cushion-cover with her free hand. 'Look, Simone! I don't think even Bernie ever did anything more exquisite.'

'That is Frieda's sister,' explained Simone as she bent to look at the work. 'She is in America with her husband and children. Kurt von Eschenau is brother to Marie—the Countess, you know. She is coming to see you when we go. Bernie has three little people—Stefan, who is eight; Hilda, who is really Bernhilda after herself, who is five; and Louise, who is four.'

'And,' said Frieda solemnly, 'Francis, who arrived three weeks ago. I forgot to tell you people, Simone. I heard this morning from Kurt. They are delighted to have a second son.'

'You heard that this morning and never told us!' cried Simone reproachfully.

'I meant to; but you know what happened!'

With one accord the two girls began to giggle wildly, and Phoebe felt a deep desire to know what it was that *had* happened.

She was told. Choking back their giggles as well as they could, they made a duet of it.

'It was Jo, of course! It couldn't be anyone else!'

'She said she'd cook breakfast if we would see to the girlies—'

'I took Margot in with me, as Frieda has quite enough to do with her own boys; and Marie had Len and Con, for even Josefa can dress herself once she has been bathed. We teach them to be useful, you see.'

'Breakfast was to be scrambled eggs. Jo can make them beautifully—'

'She got them all mixed, and was stirring them round—'

'And then she thought they looked rather—rather solid, so she wanted more milk, but there wasn't any left in the kitchen.'

'She picked up a jug, and ran out to that trough-place your Debby showed her last night to get it.'

'*Without* moving the pan off the oil-stove! Just like Jo!'

'In the shed she suddenly saw some steps leading up. She'd seen them last night—'

'But there wasn't time then to explore. She forgot the pan, set the jug of milk down on the floor, and went up to find a loft-place—'

'There's a window-place in it, too—just an opening with a door—'

'She leaned out to see, and then she smelt the eggs, which were scorching by that time. She came tearing down the ladder—'

'Leapt down the last few steps—'

'Right into the jug of milk which she'd set at the foot—'

'Slipped, and sat down in the mess—and it *was* a mess!'

'She picked herself up and came rushing into the kitchen—'

'Where I,' said Simone, 'had already smelt burning, and torn down to see what was wrong.'

'Leaving Margot in the bath, too! *And* with the tap running!'

'It was such an awful smell!' said Simone defensively. 'I forgot about the tap. Anyhow, I'd pulled the pan off the fire—with the eggs simply black, and stuck to the bottom and sides, for Jo had turned up the burner to get them done quickly.'

'By that time *I* was down, and there was Jo standing with the back of her clean frock simply dripping with milk, and her hands all filthy with the floor—'

'And at that moment,' said Simone dramatically, 'we heard a

thud—thud, and a yell from Margot. That tap does flow with violence!'

By this time Phoebe was laughing as hard as the girls had done. 'What had happened?' she gasped between her shrieks of merriment.

'Why, the bath had overflowed, and Margot, la mauvaise, was jumping up and down in the water, screaming with joy. Only Marie had rushed to the rescue, turned off the tap, and lifted her out on to the floor with a spank. She knew well enough she should have turned it off.'

'Between all this wetness and burntness,' wound up Frieda, 'do you wonder that I forgot even such news as Bernie's second son?'

Before Phoebe could answer, Gerard, roused by the laughter, set up a wail, and his mother took him from Phoebe. 'He isn't accustomed to noise yet. I have only been at home a fortnight, and we are very quiet in our little house,' she explained as she soothed him. 'I expect, though, that by the time our holiday is ended, both he and Louis will be able to sleep through anything, like Jo's girls and Stephen. There's always so much going on at Plas Gwyn—that is her home—that they have had to learn to sleep and not be disturbed. Jo has a big household, Miss Wychcote. Lady Russell's nieces, Daisy and Primula Venables, live with her in term-time, and so does her adopted sister, Robin. And then she has Highland twins, Flora and Fiona McDonald, living with her as well. And there's nearly always someone coming to stay. Jo sings, of course; and Daisy is developing a voice.'

'I thought Mrs Maynard must sing. Her speaking voice is so lovely,' said Phoebe.

'Oh, she sings—she's had very good lessons. She says that when she has time she means to have more,' said Simone. 'And Daisy has a really lovely soprano. Jo means her to have lessons, now that School Certificate is over. And Frieda plays the violin, too. And Marie is quite good at the piano. I am the only one of us four who can do nothing that way. I love to listen, but I have no voice, and my piano lessons were given up very soon. My young sister, Renée, is very good, though. She was at the Conservatoire in Paris until we left; and since then she has been working at the Royal College of Music. But she is nineteen now, so she is working for her A.R.C.M. When that is over, we hope that she will make a good concert accompanist, for that is what she wants.'

'And here is Marie coming with Wolferl and Josefa, so we must go now,' said Frieda. 'Goodbye, Miss Wychcote. We shall hope to see you again presently. But we must not tire you. Tessa—Louis! Come and bid goodbye.'

The chat with lovely Marie von Wertheim finished what the talk with Jo had begun. And when she took her leave with her children, Phoebe was able to feel that she had added four new friends to her formerly very short list, and that 'That Sodger,' to quote Debby, had not succeeded in interfering, whatever she might try to do in the future.

Chapter IV

Phoebe Seeks Advice

'Mrs Maynard, I wonder if you would give me some advice?'

Jo, stretched full-length on the ground, her hat over her eyes, and her whole attitude rather suggestive of having thoroughly over-eaten, tipped the hat up, and said, 'I don't know.'

'Why not?' demanded Phoebe.

'Firstly, because advice is rarely pleasing to people; secondly, it's hot and I'm lazy; thirdly, if I *do* give it to you, I'm prepared to bet you won't take it, so it's waste of time giving it. What do you want advice about, anyhow? Oh; and by the way, while I remember, we've known each other a full week, and I think it's high time we all left off being so formal. From this moment I propose to call you Phoebe; and I shall refuse to answer to anything but Jo—or Joey, if you're feeling extra affectionate.'

In answer to this tirade Phoebe smiled. 'I'll call you anything you like. I've thought once or twice of suggesting you should make it "Phoebe," but I didn't quite like to. But I really do want advice. In fact, I must have it from somewhere, and I think you can probably give it to me—or at least tell me where to go for it if you can't. You seem to know so many people.'

There was a plaintive note at the end of this that made Jo stop her nonsense. She sat up, transferring her hat to its proper place on her head, and said gravely, 'I'm sorry, Phoebe. I didn't realise you were serious. What can I do to help you?'

'It's about Father's 'cello,' said Phoebe.

'What about it?'

'Well, some months ago I had a letter from a Mr Burthill,

saying that he had a daughter who loves the 'cello. She has been learning for a good many years, and her great ambition is to become a concert performer. She loved Father's playing, and when he died, she begged her father to try to buy his 'cello for her. It seems she isn't getting on as well as she had hoped and she thinks if she had that, it would help her.'

'I think that's nonsense,' said Jo, picking up her knitting. 'There's only one way of becoming an adequate player that I ever heard of. Practise as *hard* as you can *whenever* you can. The greatest genius can't do anything without practice. But I'm interrupting. Carry on, and tell me the rest.'

'As you know,' went on Phoebe, 'I was very ill after Father died, and couldn't attend to anything for ages. In the meantime, this Mr Burthill had found out that Father had left everything to me—his 'cello among the rest; but he didn't know where I was to be found. He got into touch with Mr Avery—that's Father's agent—and finally got him to forward a letter to me. Here it is. Will you read it?' And she gave Jo a letter.

Jo put down her knitting and opened it with some curiosity.

'"DEAR MADAM,"' she read, '"I am sending this under cover by Mr Avery, who was, I understand, your late father's agent, and who, therefore, will be able to communicate with you. He refused to give me your address." I should think so!' observed Jo, looking up from the letter. 'What cheek to ask for it! Well—"I am writing to ask if you are disposed to sell your father's violoncello. I would offer a good price for it. If you preferred we could have a professional to value it. His fee, of course, would have to be my affair; but I am quite willing to pay it.—Yours faithfully, J. GEORGE BURTHILL." Goodness, Phoebe! What did you reply?'

'I wrote to Mr Avery and asked him to tell Mr Burthill that I had no wish to sell the 'cello,' said Phoebe. 'Here is his reply.'

This letter went into more detail. Mr Burthill informed Miss Wychcote that he wanted the 'cello for his only child who had been a warm admirer of Nicholas Wychcote, and was herself a 'cellist. Since he had written his previous letter, he had heard that the instrument in question was a very fine English 'cello, and a genuine Lott. He was prepared to pay £100 down for it if Miss Wychcote would sell.

'What did you say to this?' asked Jo when she had read it.

'I repeated that I had no wish to sell the instrument my father had used whenever he played in public; thanked him for the offer, and refused it,' replied Phoebe. 'He wrote again about three weeks ago. Here you are.' And she handed Jo a third letter in the bold, determined handwriting.

By this time it was clear that Mr Burthill had been making inquiries about Nicholas Wychcote's daughter, for he knew about Phoebe's situation, and reproached her with selfishness in trying to keep to herself an instrument she could use neither at the present time nor later, when a girl who had thought very highly of the musician's playing could use it, and to advantage. He pointed out firmly—there was no false delicacy in Mr J. George Burthill—that, in her financial position, it would be wise in her to make all the money she could. Surely £100 must mean more to her than a 'cello she could never use. He finally requested her to write direct to him, as he preferred doing business that way.

Jo read with growing indignation. 'This is outrageous!' she cried as she finished and threw the letter down. 'What right has he to persecute you like this? The 'cello is yours. You don't wish to sell. You've told him so, and that ought to end it. Besides, how does he know that you'll never be able to use it? There are wonderful cures nowadays. It won't be long before the research people find something to put an end to rheumatism, I'm sure, and once it's discovered, you'll try it, of course, and may be quite well again. Then you *could* use the 'cello. And even if that doesn't happen, why should you be forced to sell, against your will, something that means more to you than anything else you have? It's simply disgraceful!'

Phoebe's lips quivered. Jo was the first person to see just what the 'cello meant to her. She had somehow felt that that young lady would understand; but she had not expected to meet that understanding at the very outset, and it touched a very tender chord in her.

'Have you answered this?' went on Jo. 'What did you say?'

'I haven't answered it. It's so hard to know what to do. I don't want to be selfish, and it's very easy for anyone like me to get selfish, because, you see, everything is arranged for *my* comfort. Debby, bless her, only thinks what will be best for *me*. It's true I can't use the 'cello. I learnt, you know, until my illness. I had a half-size 'cello from the time I was eight. Father taught me himself, and I loved it. He thought—he thought that some day I might do something worth while with it. But then I got ill, and I was ill for months and months, and when I was able to be up again it left me with this form of inflammatory rheumatism which makes it impossible for me to do anything like that. As I told you, there are times when I can't even manage to sew. And with a 'cello you have to have a very free sweep of the right arm, and your fingers must be very supple. Make no mistake, Jo; even if I could be cured, I could never make enough of it now to be a concert performer. It's too late for that.'

'Even so, you would be able to play for your own enjoyment and that of your friends. Why you should be deprived of that, I can't think. And anyhow, what about this girl? Is she such a great wonder as all that?'

'I don't know. But a letter came from her—through Mr Avery, of course—this morning. Here it is. Read it, Joey, and see what you think.'

Jo took the letter, written on handmade paper, with an elaborate monogram at which she made a face. 'What an ostentatious thing! Mercy! Is that the creature's name? Heaven help her! *Zephyr!* I ask you! Her godparents or whoever wished it on to her should have been *guillotined*!'

Jo's scathing remarks drove the tears from Phoebe's eyes; she laughed gently. 'She isn't to blame for that, poor thing. Read her letter, Joey.'

Jo obeyed, and read the letter aloud. '"DEAR MISS WYCHCOTE,—Daddy says that he has heard from you, and you refuse to sell me your father's wonderful 'cello. Oh, please, don't do that! I'm so anxious to have it! I want it more than I ever wanted anything in my life before! Daddy has offered to get me one as good if not better, but I don't want *that*! I want Nicholas Wychcote's!"—If this was one of *my* daughters,' said Jo, looking up, 'I'd spank her every time she said "I want" till she learnt not to say it! It strikes me this girl is the most spoilt object I ever heard of. "I want!" indeed! As if she were the only person to be considered! It's high time someone taught her she's not the only pebble on the beach!'

'I think,' said Phoebe, 'that her parents have tried to give her everything she ever has wanted.'

'Very wrong and unkind of them, then. They surely don't expect to give the girl everything she wants whenever she wants it? She'll come in for some pretty bad shocks before she's through with life, I'm afraid.'

'I suppose, as she's the only one they have, they want to give her everything possible. It didn't work that way with me, of course. But then, Father wasn't a rich man, and this Mr Burthill evidently is.'

'It wouldn't matter how rich we were; I'd *never* give a child every single thing it asked for. I think it's quite wrong. Well, let's see what else this Zephyr person has to say for herself. Where was I? Oh! Here!' And Joey went on reading. '"Daddy says he has heard that you don't play yourself, so it can't be any use to you. I do, and it would be everything to me! Can't you see it? Oh, please, Miss Wychcote, do try to see it with my eyes! I want your father's 'cello more than I've ever wanted anything in my life before. If I had it, I'm sure I should get on so much more quickly. Only think! If you sell it to Daddy, you may be the means of giving a great 'cellist to the world!" Well! upon my word! This young woman does *not* lack for conceit! "Daddy will pay you anything you want for it. I have heard that you aren't very well off. Surely it would be better for you to sell the 'cello and have a nice sum of money, as well as knowing that you are helping me as I'm sure your father would have wished if he had known, than to hold selfishly on to it where it can do no good? Oh, do think of that, Miss Wychcote, and give me my wish! If I knew where you lived, I'd come and beg you for it—on my knees if it would help! If £100 isn't enough Daddy will pay you what you say, as it's for me! He always gives me what I want, and always has. I *must* have it! Please do say yes!—Yours faithfully, ZEPHYR BURTHILL." And that,' added Jo with a grin, as she folded up the letter and put it back in its envelope, 'comes as a complete shock after all the "I want" outpourings. Have you any idea how old this girl is, Phoebe? She writes like a baby of ten. *Ten!* Sybil would be ashamed to write like that! Little Josette wouldn't do it! And has the poor thing ever met with any stop except the exclamation mark?'

'It's all very well,' said Phoebe in a worried tone, 'but I don't know what to do in face of that. If she wants it so badly, ought I to let her have it? Am I being selfish, as she says, in keeping it?'

'Certainly not!' Jo spoke with decision. 'To this girl it only means the instrument a famous man has played on—and a sudden fancy made stronger because she finds she can't get it for the mere asking. To you, it means very much more. I—I don't want to say too much, Phoebe, but it seems to me that the instrument a musician uses and loves must hold a part of—of his—well, his *soul*.'

Phoebe's eyes were wet as she replied, 'I thought you would understand.'

Jo's voice was very gentle as she replied, 'I've lived with musical people, you see. I know what a violin or a 'cello can mean to its owner. And I thank God that He gave me an imagination. That helps me to see just how much that beautiful thing can mean to his daughter now he has left her.'

'Then you don't think I'm selfish and—and not doing what Father would want?'

'No, my dear. I don't for one moment think your father would have wished you to give up the thing that means *him* most of all to you. I feel sure that he would have wished you to keep it until you could either play it yourself, or, if such a thing should ever happen, found someone to whom you really wished to give or sell it. That would be quite another matter. But this girl means nothing to you. From what I can see by her letter, I should say she wasn't the kind of girl you could ever love as much as that. If you want my advice, I should get your father's agent to write to the father saying quite definitely that you have no intention of parting with it. And,' added Jo with a sudden inspiration, 'tell him to say that if this sort of thing goes on, you will be obliged to apply to your solicitor. It's sheer persecution; I'm sure a lawyer could do something about it—get a writ of habeas corpus—no; that isn't what I mean! A—an injunction against the Burthills. And now, don't think any more about it. I've brought you the first half-dozen chapters of my new story, *The Lost Staircase*, to read. Take care of it, my lamb, for it's the fair copy that's going to my publishers. It's a thrilling story, and all true—except that I've altered names and so on. I got it from two girls at the Chalet School—Jesanne Gellibrand and her chum, Lois Bennett. Some day, when you and Debby come to stay with me at Plas Gwyn, you shall meet them. In the meantime, read the story and tell me what you think of it. The truth, mind! I don't want flattery. I prefer good, solid, constructive criticism.'

'Oh, I should never dare to criticise it. I couldn't write a book myself, and I think you're simply wonderful to be able to do it. May I really have it? Thank you so much, Joey! I'll be very careful of it.'

Having bestowed her manuscript on Phoebe, Jo bent to kiss her, and with a hug, repeated, 'Write to the agent. This has got to stop—and at once!'

Phoebe returned the kiss fervently. 'You are *nice*, Joey! And I shall love to read this. Thank you so much! And—and, is it asking too much, will you come over after tea and help me to write that letter? I'm not much good at it, you know, and you'd put it down so clearly.'

'Of course I will! And tomorrow Jack's coming—my husband, you know. I'm going to bring him over to see you. You'll like him,' said Jo, with deep conviction in her tones. 'He's bringing me some things I want—including my precious Rufus. We couldn't bring him with us, for he was rather under the weather, poor dear. But Jack says he's all right now, and will be all the better for the moorland air, as well as being with me again. He always hates to be parted from me. Why don't *you* have a dog, Phoebe? They're such company. You couldn't have a mighty hound like Rufus, of course; but you might have a small one. Debby could take him out when she goes out, and he'd get plenty of exercise in the garden too. Shall I ask Jack to look out for one for you? What breed would you like? A cocker? Or what about a sealyham or a dachshund? They'd be better, perhaps. A cocker's coat needs so much grooming and their long ears can be a nuisance.'

'I'd love a dog,' said Phoebe wistfully. 'It wouldn't be unkind to keep one, would it? I couldn't exercise it properly myself, you see.'

'Ask Debby and see what she says,' advised Jo. 'If she agrees, and you'd really like it, we'll talk it over with Jack while he's here, and he'll see to it. And now I must go and get my family up and ready for tea. I left them all slumbering peacefully. It's been such a hot day. I put them down directly they'd finished dinner, and the girlies can stay up an hour later and play in the cool of the evening.'

'If there is any cool,' put in Phoebe. 'It *has* been hot, hasn't it? Even sitting here in the shade, doing nothing, I've felt boiled all day.'

'I think there's thunder about.' Jo wiped her hot face with her handkerchief. 'I shouldn't be surprised if we had a storm before long.'

'I hope not!' Phoebe shivered. 'I hate thunder. It was a thunderstorm that caused my illness, you know. I was out in it, and I was too frightened to make for home; so I crouched under a hedge and got soaked through. I was there for nearly two hours, and when I did get home, Debby was out looking for me, and I hadn't the sense to take off my wet things, so I was in them for nearly four hours, and that did the mischief.'

'Poor little girl!' said Jo. 'I'm so sorry, dear. But you needn't be frightened now, Phoebe. You won't be out in it; and anyhow, your guardian angel will look after you. And it may be just my fancy; so don't worry. You read those chapters and be prepared to criticise them good and hard when you see me again. Bye-bye for the moment!' And she was off, moving with the swift grace that made so large a part of her charm.

Phoebe looked after her with glowing eyes, and then picked up the two bundles of typescript Jo had laid on her lap. 'How sweet of her! I shall love this, I know. But I should never dare to criticise, even if I thought anything wrong. It would be only my idea, and she's probably right—far more likely to be so than I.'

Chapter V

Dr Maynard Arrives

On the Saturday following, Jack Maynard arrived. Phoebe, lying on a chaise-longue in the garden, saw Jo go past with the children on her way to meet the half-past eleven bus from Garnley. She waved her hand to the invalid as she passed, but made no attempt to stop. Phoebe judged that it would take her all her time to get to the foot of the hill where the bus stopped by a quarter-past twelve. It was a very long hill, winding round and round from the valley up to the moors at the far end of the village. The little girls could not go quickly all the time, and Jo herself had the light folding pram with Stephen in it.

Phoebe smiled as she noted that the triplets were daintily attired in clean frocks and their big Sunday hats. As they were not alike in colouring, Jo made no effort to dress them alike. Today, Len wore wild-rose pink, Con was in daffodil yellow, and Margot's forget-me-not blue frock must match her eyes. Jo herself wore a light cotton of her favourite pale jade, and her hat was an old black one which Simone's clever French fingers had turned into a triumph of millinery. She had used an old jade green scarf to line the brim and make a twist round the crown. The soft colour brought out the faint pink in Jo's cheeks, and suited her exactly. Phoebe thought the five must make a very refreshing sight for the eyes of a father and husband. Then she sighed, and turned again to her sewing.

She had laid it aside, and was eating the light lunch Debby had brought her on the tea-trolley when she heard voices, and knew that the family was returning. Jo's golden laughter trilled out on the summer air, with an accompaniment of a deep bass roar. Margot's shrill treble cried: 'Whyfor does you laugh, Mamma? Papa, whyfor does you laugh?' Then they came in sight, and Jo drew up outside the hedge, leant over it, and cried, 'Phoebe, this is my husband. Jack, this is Phoebe—Miss Wychcote, I mean. Open the gate, Len, my precious! Rufus! Look, Phoebe! This is Rufus!'

Len let go her father's hand to which she had been clinging, ran forward and opened the gate, and a magnificent St Bernard dog walked in, his great tail swinging in a friendly greeting. Phoebe cried out in delight at sight of him, and held out her hand for him to sniff.

'You beautiful creature! Come and make friends!' she cried. Then: 'Can you come in for a minute, Jo? The gong at The Witchens hasn't sounded yet.'

'Come on, Jack! We can spare a moment or two. Here comes Sybil!' And that young lady appeared at the gate of The Witchens, uttered a joyous cry, and tore across the road to fling herself on her uncle. 'Sybs, when you've finished trying to strangle Uncle Jack, take Stephen and the girlies in, will you? And see that the girlies have clean hands and faces for dinner.'

Sybil nodded. 'All right. Auntie Jo. Uncle Jack, it's lovely having you here! How long can you stay? Oh, there's Rufus! *Dear* Rufus!' As Rufus left Phoebe to come and lick her face vigorously. 'Oh, don't! Auntie! Call him off, please! He's knocking me down!'

'Rufus!' called Jo; and the great dog came at once, and fawned on her joyfully. 'Bad lad!' she scolded him tenderly. 'You forget what a weight you are. Take the children, Sybil darling, and tell the others we'll be over in a few minutes. Run along, you people! Shoo! Scat!'

They ran across the road, laughing and calling, and Sybil seized the pram and wheeled it off after them. Then Jo came into the garden, followed by her husband, and with Rufus at her side.

'Here's Jack!' she said, joy in every note. 'Phoebe, you've heard heaps about my very tall husband. This is him!'—with a fine disregard for grammar.

Phoebe lifted her eyes, and looked up into a clear-cut face with a pleasant smile, and keen blue-grey eyes that were looking at her very kindly.

Jack Maynard was, as he would have said himself, 'no film star' for looks. But he was possessed of a fine face, with a firm mouth and chin, and a smile that was a great asset. He came forward, taking Phoebe's hand in a clasp that was gentle but firm, and looking at her with eyes that saw a good deal that was hidden from Jo. He noted the lines about the mouth, the pallid skin, and the strained look in the eyes that told of suffering bravely borne. Certain signs told him yet more,,and he thought to himself that he would like to help this girl to whom his wife had taken such a fancy. Later, he would question her a little. Meantime, he must try to make her feel that in him she had another friend.

'Jo has sung your praises in every letter I've had,' he said genially. 'I hear your needlework is beautiful. I wish you'd make that wife of mine try to take a little more interest in the art.'

'I like that!' cried Jo. 'Don't I do *all* your mending? Do you ever find holes in your socks or buttons missing off your shirts?'

'How much is your work and how much Anna's?' he demanded.

'Anna does very little for you. I admit she helps me a good deal with the children's mending; but I generally do yours myself.'

He chuckled. 'But what about the tablecloths and pin-cushions and all the other little gadgets that women seem to like making? I never see *you* sitting down with a piece of embroidery as Mother used to do.'

'No; and as long as the publishers like my books, you never will, my lad. Granny hadn't so many other jobs. But my time is pretty fully occupied. And if it comes to that, what sort of handyman about the house are you?' demanded Jo, carrying the war into the enemy's country.

'Hush, my child! If you go on like this, you'll be giving Miss Wychcote a most erroneous impression of me. As a good wife, you can't do that.'

'Nothing erroneous about saying you can't even put a washer on a tap.'

'Who says so?'

'Well, I've never seen you. *Have* you ever done it? If so, when?'

'In Tyrol, my love, in Tyrol—over and over again. You can do the washer on the tap business yourself quite nicely, so why should I?'

'To save me the trouble. A good husband always tries to save his wife trouble,' said Jo didactically. She turned to Phoebe. 'I've one thing to be thankful for, anyhow. He's not sawed-off short, is he?' Her eyes dwelt on the six-foot-two of manhood which made even her five-foot-eight seem short, and he returned the look with one that made Phoebe suddenly feel choky. These two might spar as much as they liked. It was quite plain that they were still in love with each other.

The gong at The Witchens suddenly sounded in a wild fantasia that made Jo exclaim, 'That's Sybil performing! Dinner is ready. Come along, Jack. We'll come back later on and you shall get to know Phoebe properly. I'll just run to the house, Phoebe, and tell Debby you're ready for your rest, shall I? You go on ahead, Jack, and say I'm coming at once.'

He nodded. 'All right. Can I make you comfortable before I go, Miss Wychcote? Let me arrange these cushions.'

With deft hands he settled the cushions, and lowered her to an easy position. Phoebe, who had been in pain all night and most of the day, smiled at him gratefully. 'Oh, that is so comfy! I believe

I can sleep a little now. This hot weather is rather trying when it goes on and on.'

'That's the worst of rheumatism. Well, I'll see you later, Miss Wychcote. Goodbye for the present.' He swung off his hat, and then departed, and Jo came racing after him a minute or two later. She had been talking to Debby.

'We'll be over later on,' she said with a smile. 'Try to sleep now, Phoebe, you poor dear. Debby's coming in a moment.' Then she vanished.

She found her husband getting a riotous welcome from the other three, who had known him as long as she had; while all the small folk who could get to him were clinging on to various portions of his anatomy, and shouting, 'Uncle Jack—Uncle Jack!'

'Where's Stephen?' Jo asked.

'In his cot,' said Frieda. 'I've just finished giving him his bottle, and he was nearly asleep when I left him. Go up if you like and look at him; but he's all right.'

'Good!' said Jo. 'What about something to eat?'

'Well, dinner's on the table. I can't say it's getting cold; but the small people are famished, and so am I,' said Marie. 'Let's sit down.'

'You famished, Marie? You look as if you ought to live on rose-leaves and honeydew, an ethereal creature like you,' teased Jack as they made a move. Then, indignantly: 'Here! What's this? You don't make me carver when I'm on holiday, I can assure you!'

'Oh, Jack, do!' pleaded Simone. 'None of us can do it properly. Jo did it yesterday; and *look* at the joint!'

He grinned as he surveyed the wreck. 'What did you do—hack off chunks where they came handiest? Or did you pass it round for people to gnaw at? It looks more like that than anything else.'

'The knife was so blunt. And anyhow, I never could carve,'

said Jo. 'And Simone can't say much. We had a fowl last Sunday, and she cooked it, and volunteered to carve it in the kitchen so that it would be more easily served. I wish you'd seen the bits and pieces that appeared on the dish when it came in! Sit down, my dear, and let's have a decently carved meal for once.'

'You've put that beyond my reach with your own performance. However, I'll do my best for once. But I'm not going to continue, so don't any of you think it,' he informed them as he took up the carvers and began running the knife down the steel. 'There, that ought to be all right. Who says grace? Sybil—you? Go ahead, then.'

Sybil said grace as they stood round the table with bowed heads, and then they sat down and the meal began. It was hardly a quiet meal. Jack had always loved tormenting Jo and her chums, and they gave him as good as they got, though the palm went to Marie on this occasion.

She had had to put up with a good deal of teasing about her fragile appearance and her very healthy appetite, and she resolved to have her revenge. Just as dinner was ending, she said sweetly, 'Oh, Jack, I am so sorry! What are you doing about it?'

He looked at her sharply, but there was nothing in her violet eyes but the most limpid sympathy and concern. 'Doing about what?' he asked.

'Your hair. Have you tried anything for it?'

'My hair? What's the matter with it?' he demanded, looking round for a mirror, while Jo, after a quick look at the thick crop of light brown hair that covered his head, glanced at her friend, and then fell silent, though she had been on the point of protesting that there was *nothing* the matter.

'I always think baldness is such a pity,' went on Marie placidly. 'Even the tiniest patch seems to make a man look so much older than he really is. What have you tried for it?'

Completely taken in—none of the girls looked anything but

sorry—Jack put up his hand and felt his head. 'I'm not bald,' he protested.

'I suppose you can't see it yourself,' said Marie gently. 'Jo, you must really see that Jack does something about it. Don't they say that if you take it at the very beginning it can be cured? I should try something as soon as possible if I were you. What about violet rays?'

Jack said no more, but he looked worried. Len piped up. 'What is "bald," Auntie Marie? An' why is Papa feelin' his head like that?'

'It means that your hair is beginning to come off,' said wicked Marie gravely. 'You know what Father Edmund's head is like? Well, like that.'

The triplets surveyed their father with horror in their faces.

'Don't want Papa to get a head like Farver Edmund's!' said Margot decidedly.

'Oh, but that's only when it's very bad,' said Sybil. 'And men do go like that when they get old. I heard Daddy say one day to Mother that he thought he was beginning to get thin on the top and he'd heard a good idea was to rub the place with a raw onion, and would she get him one?'

'This is news to me,' said Jo, sitting up. 'What did your mother say, Syb?'

'She said, "Not if you go completely bald, my dear! Try something else. And who's been telling you old wives' tales?" What *are* old wives' tales, Uncle Jack?'

'Oh, things like—well, if you have whooping-cough, tie a red stocking round your neck. And that a bowl of celery soup set by your bedside for you to inhale at night will cure rheumatism,' he said. 'What did your father do about it, Sybil? I can't say that I've noticed any thinning of his ambrosial locks.'

'What's ambrosial locks?' Len wanted to know.

'Very thick hair.'

'Vewy thick hair? Oh, Mamma! How simply *howwid*!'

'Horrid? What *do* you mean?' asked Jo, fogged for once, though generally she was able to follow her daughters' trains of thoughts.

'Why, you said that the Gweek gods *ate* it,' said Con with a shudder.

Jo collapsed in fits of laughter. '*Ambrosia*, my child! That's got nothing to do with ambrosial locks—Or, wait a minute! It has! It helped them to have very thick, curling hair. That's all. Do you see, pet?'

Con nodded. 'I see. But why has Uncle Jem am—am—'

'Ambrosial locks? You must ask Papa that. *He* said; *I* didn't.'

'Why, Papa?'

'It's just a saying, Con. But Sybs hasn't answered my question. What did Daddy do about it, Sybs? Do you know?'

'I don't think he's done anything,' said Sybil gravely. 'But the next day I heard Mother telling him he was the worst tease in creation, so I *think* it was only a leg-pull. His hair looks just the same to me, anyhow.'

Jack laughed. 'How like Jem!'

'Well, don't you try the same trick on me, for it won't work,' said Jo thoughtlessly. '*You're* not bald nor likely to be so for years to come.'

There was a dead silence. Then Marie wailed: 'Oh, *Jo*! How could you?'

Before Jo could answer, Jack spoke. 'So you were trying it on *me*?'

'Yes; and you fell for it!' retorted Marie. 'Don't try to pretend you didn't, for you *did*! And now, perhaps, you'll leave off teasing me about my appetite!'

'It's time the little ones had their nap,' said Frieda, rising. 'Say grace for us, Margot, and then Louis, at least, must go to his hammock.'

That ended it; but Jack vowed vengeance on Marie sooner or later. Jo took her daughters off to the garden where they cuddled down on mattresses, and Simone put Tessa down beside them. Jack began to clear the table, helped by Marie, who chuckled at intervals. Then she suddenly sobered.

'Jack, have you seen Phoebe? What do you think of her?'

He looked at her. 'Why do you ask that, Marie?'

'I went to see her early this morning, and was horrified—she looked so ill. I'm afraid she suffers very badly at times, Jack. She was in Leaver Mitchell's care. Jo had to tell her he had died, and she doesn't know what to do now. Couldn't you or Sir Jem take her on?'

'Yes, if she asks us. We can't just go round drumming up patients, you know, Marie. What were her symptoms this morning? Can you tell me?'

'She was white—no; she was *grey*! Her eyes were black underneath. Even Jo never looked like that at her worst; and you know what she *can* look like when she is really worn out.'

'I know,' said Jack gravely. 'Go on, Marie. What else can you tell me?'

'Well, her lips were such a queer colour—almost purple. She begged me not to touch her—not even to kiss her. I could see she was in agonies of pain. Jack! Can't you do anything for her? It doesn't seem right that anyone just our age should suffer like that.' And Marie's eyes filled with tears. 'Isn't there *anything* to be done?'

'I don't know, dear. I should have to have her under observation for a time before I could say. And I'm not a rheumatics specialist, Marie.'

'No; but you are very clever, Jack. What, exactly, would you want?'

'Well, she ought to go into the San.—and there isn't a bed to spare at the present. We're full up. If she went, then I should ask two or three of our men to watch her symptoms—see how she reacted to diet or drugs of various kinds—that sort of thing. I can't go into detail. Jo told me in one of her letters that this state of things had gone on since she was a child. That means that it's got a thorough hold on her system. I doubt if we could do more than alleviate the pain when it was very bad. How old is she now, do you know? Jo didn't say when she wrote.'

'I think she's about twenty-three. It began when she was twelve.'

'That means eleven years of it.' He turned away, frowning. Marie watched him as she put peppers and salts and other sundries into the sideboard, folded up the cloth, and laid it in its drawer with napkins and bibs. Then she came to where he stood by the window.

'Jack,' she said, her face full of a sweet seriousness, 'we all love Phoebe. She's so brave—so good—so sweet. You must have felt something of it yourself even in the few minutes you were with her. We all did. Is all that courage and sweetness and goodness to be wasted? Can *nothing* be done for her? Must she go on suffering like this all her days?'

Jack Maynard looked at her again. 'I said we might be able to *alleviate* the pain. There is continual research going on, Marie. Some time someone is going to find a cure for it. But it's slow work, and hard work.'

'And, meanwhile, Phoebe must just suffer?'

Jo came into the room in time to hear this. 'Oh, Marie, are you telling Jack what we want? Jack, you *will* do what we want, won't you? I know Phoebe would like it. She said to me once that she wondered if you or Jem—and then she stopped. You'll take her on, won't you, dear?'

'Yes; if she wishes it. And if she fully understands first that I am not a specialist in her particular disease—nor is Jem. But, Joey, I have just been telling Marie that I am afraid we can do little but use alleviative measures. From all I can hear, it is a very bad form from which she suffers. And it has gone on for eleven years. I cannot say we could cure her, my darling.'

'But will you try? Oh, Jack, will you *try*?'

He nodded. 'Yes; if the conditions are as I have just stated, we would try. But don't hope for too much, Joey.' Then with a sudden passion he added, 'You two don't know what it means to *want* to bring relief to pain and to know yourself to be helpless! So don't hope too much, either of you. Only pray that we may be able to help her.'

Very low in her beautiful tones, Jo quoted, '"More things are wrought by prayer than this world dreams of." Yes, Jack; we will all pray. And you and Jem and the rest will do your best.' She glanced round, but Marie had slipped out. So Jo flung her arms round his neck and said, 'Thank God once more for you, Jack! I feel that now there may be a little hope for Phoebe.'

Chapter VI

Storm and Stress

'Jack! Was that thunder?' Jo had sat up in bed and was gazing out of the open window. She could see very little, for the sky was completely overcast. The hot day had been succeeded by a hotter evening, part of which they had all spent with Phoebe. When they had made a move at about eight o'clock, Jack had insisted that among them they must carry her in her chair to the bedroom, and then he had helped Debby to move her gently from it to her bed, for she was in severe pain. He had gone back later and mixed her a draught from her own medicaments which, he hoped, would bring her a little ease. But he had looked very grave as he returned to The Witchens.

At his wife's words he stirred, and then sat up. 'What's the matter?'

'It's thunder,' said Jo tensely. 'Listen!' And she held up her hand as a very distant growl sounded.

'What's the matter with you?' he asked. 'You aren't afraid of it, surely? You never used to be.'

'Afraid of thunder? Me—I mean I? Talk sense! Of course I'm not. But if it's going to be a storm we'll have to shut the windows. We don't want the place flooded out. And if it gets very bad, someone ought to go over and see if Debby wants any help. I know that Phoebe is terrified of it. Go up and see that the girlies and Sybil and Wolfram are all right, will you, dear?'

Jack groaned. 'I did think I should get an uninterrupted night for once! All right; I'm going. I'd better draw the curtains again. You'll want the light on.'

'No, I shan't. And it might wake Stephen and Margot. Here's a torch for you. Don't switch on if you can help it. And go quietly. We don't want the children to rouse if we can help it.' Jo pressed a torch into his hand, armed herself with another, and left the room to visit those of her friends.

Jack went upstairs to the attics, where Wolfram slept in a small one at the back, while in the larger one were Sybil and, since their father had come, Len and Con. Jack slipped in quietly, and found all four children sleeping soundly. He closed the lattice windows, drew the dark curtains in case the lightning should disturb them, and left them still sleeping.

Downstairs, Jo had found Frieda and Marie awake, and Frieda was already closing her windows and drawing her curtains. Marie was lying placidly in bed, Josefa in her camp-bed at the far side of the room in a deep slumber.

'Better close the windows in case of floods,' advised Jo. 'It sounds as if it might be going to be bad. It's coming up pretty quickly, I think. That growl was much nearer. Will Josefa waken?'

'I don't expect so. She can generally sleep through anything—like your own family,' said Marie. 'I heard Jack go upstairs, so I suppose he'll see to Wolfram. All right, Jo; I'll shut the windows. What about the others?'

'Frieda's awake. I haven't been in to Simone yet.'

'Shall I go and make us some tea or coffee?'

'It would be quite a good idea. If it's really bad, I shall send Jack across the road. Debby may need help. Phoebe was ill this evening, and I know she has a horror of thunder. I'll keep an eye on Josefa if you'll do that. I have an idea we're in for something outsize in the way of storms that even she and my infants won't sleep through. I'll just pop in and see what Simone is after, though.' And Jo went across the landing to the room where Simone and her small daughter lay placidly wrapped in slumber. She hesitated for a moment as to whether she should rouse her friend or not.

Then she decided that it would be better. If the storm were a bad one, Tessa would certainly wake, and it would be better for her if her mother was beside her then, for she was a nervous little soul. Jo laid a hand against Simone's cheek, and drew it firmly down. It was an old signal, dating from the time when the four of them had been wicked Middles at school, and was guaranteed to wake up any one of them at once. Simone opened her eyes immediately, stared up at Jo who, with her long pigtails, looked a mere schoolgirl, and then murmured—they had long ago learnt that whispers carried much further than very low tones—'What is it, Jo?'

'A storm coming up—fairly quickly, too. I thought you'd better be awake on Tessa's account,' replied Jo softly.

Simone sat up with a low giggle. 'I must have been very deeply asleep,' she said in the French both were speaking, 'for I thought for the moment that we were at school and Bill might hear if we weren't careful. You know what ears she always had!'

Jo chuckled. 'My child, you must have been dead to the world! It's a good many years since we planned misdeeds in the dead of night; and as for school, we shall have to be thinking of that for our own daughters before so very many years are up. Draw your curtains when you've closed your windows. I must go back in case Stephen or Margot wakes. Marie's gone downstairs to make tea or coffee, and if it's really bad, I'm going to send Jack over to Many Bushes to see if they're all right there … I say!' she added in a different tone. 'That was a bright flash! It's coming up quickly.' Simone was out of bed and tackling the windows. The crash of thunder that followed the lightning caused Tessa to stir and murmur in her sleep, and Jo fled back to her own room where her pair were still slumbering sweetly. Jack had gone downstairs to help Marie with the milky coffee she was making, and across the landing she could hear Gerard whimpering.

Having made certain that the two tinies were still safely asleep, she slipped to the foot of the attic stairs and listened, but no sound came from there, so she looked in on Josefa, who had never stirred, and then went back to her own room where she turned up the bedside lamp, as they could scarcely manage with just torches.

The storm *was* coming up rapidly. The lightning could not penetrate the thick curtains; but the crashes of thunder were growing louder and more frequent. It was evidently going to be what Jack would call 'a snorter.' A frightened voice from the top of the attic stairs called her: 'Auntie Jo!'

Jo ran out. 'That you, Sybil? Are you all right? Are Len and Con awake?'

'Yes, Auntie. We're all right, but may we come down to your room while it is so noisy? Wolfram says he's going in beside Auntie Marie.'

'Come along, then. But Wolfram had better come here with you. Auntie Marie is downstairs, and Josefa is still asleep—though she certainly won't be for long if this goes on,' she added, as the thunder pealed out.

A whimper from her room took her back there, to find Stephen sitting up in his cot, his yellow hair standing up in a tuft on top of his head, his eyes wide and frightened. Margot had rolled out on to the floor, and as Jo entered, she picked herself up and darted to the side of the cot with an eager 'It's all wight, Steve. Mamma will be here soon. Don't cwy!'

Jo smiled to herself at this fruit of her teaching that the little girls must look after their brother because he was so much smaller than they. Then she went forward and picked up her son. 'Silly boy! What's the matter with you? Frightened of a loud noise? Oh, come! This won't do! My Stephen must be a brave boy.' She smiled down at Margot. 'Thank you, darling, for looking after him. You are a good little girl. Len and Con and Sybil and Wolfram are all coming down beside us. Won't that be fun?'

Margot's wide blue eyes lost their look of fear, and she

chuckled. 'It's a party—a late-night party! What fun! Can we have milk an' biscuits, Mamma? Oh, Stephen is goin' to cwy!'

'He's too little to understand,' said Jo, rocking him in her arms. 'Here come the others, and Sybil shall run down to the kitchen with Wolfram and ask Auntie Marie for biscuits and milk for all of you. There, there. Mamma's little man! Don't cry, my pet. It won't hurt you.'

But though Stephen was accustomed to the noise of voices and music, he had never heard such awful crashes before, and he yelled his disapproval at the full strength of a pair of excellent lungs. In vain Jo rocked him, and talked soothingly. He was thoroughly frightened, and he intended that all his world should know it. His howls did what the thunder had failed to do—woke up Josefa, who, finding herself in a world of crashes, with no mother flying to her aid, added hers; and as Gerard was wailing, and Tessa also sobbing, the noise they made almost drowned the noise of the thunder.

Jo sent Wolfram to bring Josefa to her, and Sybil with the same message for Frieda and her sons. 'If we're going to have all this yelling, we may as well have it all in the same room as scattered everywhere in the house,' she thought desperately. Then, as Wolfram appeared with his weeping sister, she held out her hand. 'Come along, Josefa. Mamma will be here soon, and she's bringing milk and biscuits for you people. We're going to have a midnight feast. Won't that be fun? What—frightened? Why, my precious, there's nothing to be frightened about. It's God Who is sending the thunder, and He won't let it hurt us. Dry your eyes, pet, and stop crying. Can't you and Sybil, our two *big* girls, clear the bedside table ready for the trays when they come? That's right! Wolfram, you go and help Mamma and Uncle Jack to carry the things upstairs, will you?'

'Me, too!' cried Len. 'Me cawwy the biscuit-box, Mamma!'

'Very well; you go too. Con can go and bring the sugar. And

no helping yourself to sly spoonfuls, my lady!'

Con giggled, and the three children ran off downstairs to where their elders were packing china on to a tray. They were thankful for the reinforcements, and in ten minutes' time everyone was sitting down to what Jack called 'A midnight snack'—'And very welcome too,' he added. 'What are you giving Stephen, Jo?'

'Just a rusk to keep him quiet. He's been very frightened, poor little man. And Margot was such a good, brave girl, Papa. I was out of the room when he woke up, and she was trying to comfort him.'

'Good girl, Margot. I'm very pleased with you,' he said, with a smile at his youngest daughter who was perched on the bed beside him. He put his arm round her and gave her a hug. 'And what have the others done?'

'Len and Con came to help you with Wolfram, and Sybil and Josefa got the table ready,' said Frieda. 'I'm afraid my own small men are too small to help; but Louis was very good, Uncle Jack. Gerard, like Stephen, is too little to understand, so he just yelled.'

'Tessa tried hard to be brave,' put in Simone. 'She hates thunder, but she only cried a little, and she did try to stop, so I think she was quite brave for her. It's a bad storm—almost the worst I've known in England.'

Before anyone could reply to her, there came a resounding knock at the front door, and Jo, since Stephen was nodding drowsily over his rusk, hurried to answer it. Debby stood there, a big shawl flung over her head and shoulders. Jo saw her clearly in the light of a streak of lightning that seemed to stab the ground only a few paces to the right of her. A terrific peal of thunder followed on it almost at once, and Jo would have dragged her into the shelter of the little hall, but Debby resisted fiercely.

'I've come for the doctor, Mrs Maynard. Miss Phoebe's downright ill, and I can do nowt with her. She's in terrible pain, and she's that frightened she's neether to hold nor to bind. Tell him to come, will you? I must get right back. I scurcely durst come as it was.' And she whisked away, even as Jack, who had come to the head of the stairs, called down, 'I'll be over in a minute. Tell Miss Wychcote not to be afraid. I'm coming.'

Jo shut the door after her, for the rain was coming down in torrents and her dressing-gown was quite damp with standing the few seconds at the door. She ran back upstairs, to find Jack dragging on his trousers and jacket over his pyjamas. She brought his raincoat with her, and helped him into it.

'Get the children back to bed as soon as you can,' he said hurriedly. 'They'll be all right now. They're all nearly asleep, and will probably be off as soon as they lie down. You girls wait a little. I may need help.'

The girls looked at each other as he vanished. The slam of the front door roused them to action, and Marie whisked away her pair to tuck them up in Josefa's bed. She stayed in her own room long enough to dress, and then went back to Jo's. Frieda, by Jo's advice, had gone back to bed.

'You're not so very strong yet,' urged Jo. 'And you don't want to be worn out tomorrow—or is it today? What's the time, anyone? My watch has stopped as usual.'

'It's half-past two,' said Simone, who was stooping over a sleeping Tessa. 'Jo, I'll just pop Tessa into your bed if I may, and we could put Sybil and Con with her, and Len can go in with Margot for once. If we are not wanted, you can come in with me. But Jo is right, Frieda. I'll just settle Tessa, and then I'll carry Louis in for you. You go on with Gerard.'

Thus persuaded, Frieda went, and when Marie returned, twisting up her golden curls into a great fat knob at the back of her head, she found only Jo, who was dressing as fast as she could. Of the children, only Sybil was sufficiently awake to murmur, 'Good night, Auntie Marie.' The rest were all sound asleep. Jo had opened the lattices again as the rain was not beating on the windows, and the fresh, cool air blew in through the closed curtains.

'Have the others gone to dress?' asked Marie. 'Wolfram and Josefa are safely over. He has her cuddled up in his arms, so she will be quite all right, even if she wakes again—which I don't think she will.'

'We've sent Frieda to bed,' said Jo, pulling her frock over her head. 'She's not strong yet, and in any case, she couldn't leave Gerard.'

'No,' agreed Marie. 'If anyone goes, it must be me, Joey. You oughtn't to leave Stephen, either. If Jack wants anyone, Simone or I had better go. I see you've got Tessa here, so she will be all right. What a fearful storm it is! I only wonder the children have been so brave about it.'

'Well, we've never let them be frightened of such things,' said Jo as she unwound her long plaits and began to brush them out. 'They know that God sends it, and that He loves them all too well to harm them. Isn't the faith of little children beautiful, Marie? If one could only keep it!'

'We can all pray for it,' said Marie, a sweet gravity in her lovely face. 'But I know what you mean. You are thinking of Phoebe.'

'I was. I cannot see the reason for all her sufferings.' She suddenly gave a little, ashamed laugh. 'Con heard me say something of the kind a day or two ago to Frieda. I didn't know she was listening, but she was. She said, "But, Mamma, you said God gave pain to Miss Wychcote. And you always say He never gives us what isn't good for us. So won't it be good for her as He sent it?" I had nothing to say.'

The sound of the key in the front door broke into their talk, and a minute later Jack Maynard was with them. One look at his face told them it was serious. He gave them no time for questions, however.

'Marie, go and put on a raincoat and take an umbrella and go across to Many Bushes,' he barked at her.

Marie scuttled off on the words, and then he turned to his wife. 'I'm going to Garnley, Jo. Can't telephone—the wires are down. Something must have been struck. Dr Palmer at the end of the village is out in the country and not expected home before morning, if then. That poor girl is desperately ill, and I haven't the things at hand that I want. Nothing for it but to go and get them myself.'

'Jack! It's about fourteen miles—and in *this* weather! You'll be killed!' began Jo; but he hushed her peremptorily. 'I've sent up to the farm to borrow Fenner's hunter. He can't go himself, for Debby tells me he had a fall from a rick and broke his leg a fortnight ago, and there isn't anyone else near. I can't send that young girl of theirs at this hour—just after three! Luckily, it'll be light soon. The thunder's passing, and once the sky clears it'll be easy enough to see the road.' Then, as Jo's face was still mutinous, he took her by the shoulders. 'Joey, it is serious for your friend. Her heart's bad. She can't go on too long like this. Do you understand?'

'Yes,' said Jo. 'Very well, Jack. But—be careful, won't you? I mean, the roads aren't too good till you get to the main road, and it won't help anyone if your horse puts its foot into a pothole and flings you, and you—you break something.' Her lips were quivering, though she tried to speak lightly.

'I'll be careful all right,' he said. 'And remember, Jo, you're a doctor's wife. It's a life of sacrifice in many ways, and you know it. You knew it when you married me. Don't fail me now, dear.'

'No, Jack; I won't. Only—after last autumn—when I thought for so long I had lost you—' She stopped, and he bent and kissed her.

'That's over, Jo, my darling. Try not to hark back to it. Now here's Marie, and we must both go. Lie down on the lounge and try to get some sleep, Joey, or you'll be all in later on when I expect I shall need you.'

'Very well, Jack,' she said meekly. 'Come back as soon as you can. Marie, stay as long as Debby wants you. I'll see to Wolfram and Josefa.'

'They won't need any seeing to,' said Marie briskly, 'so long as you wash Josefa's neck and ears for her. She can manage the rest herself.'

'Ready?' asked Jack. 'Come along, then. Don't worry, Joey.'

She smiled at him, but said no more, and when she had heard the slam of the gate, she extinguished the lamp, and opened the curtains before lying down as he had told her. It was still pouring with rain, but it seemed to her that the clouds were beginning to lift a little, and the darkness was paling. She was so tired that she fell asleep almost at once, and when she woke it was broad daylight, the sun was pouring in at the window, and Stephen was beginning to make sounds that warned her she was late with his first breakfast.

Once that was seen to, he settled down again in his cot with a little grunt of satisfaction, and Jo saw that he would soon be asleep again. She glanced at the other children, but they were still slumbering soundly, so she went along to the bathroom, took a bath, and then dressed rapidly with many a glance over the way. The curtains were still drawn, and there was no sign of life about the cottage, though the rest of the village seemed to be up and doing. Presently she went downstairs, where she lit the kitchen fire, put the kettle on, and began to cut the enormous plates of bread that their small fry demanded. She took them to the dining-room, filled up the mugs with milk, and then went out. The air was cool and fresh after the storm, and everything looked green. The birds were singing, bees were already buzzing about the flowers, and as she stood at the gate in the early morning sunshine Joey felt hope springing up in her heart. She turned, after another look at Many Bushes, and went in, glancing up at the grandfather clock in the hall as she passed it. It was eight o'clock. High time they were up. However, she had no idea of calling anyone after their broken night. The kettle was boiling, so she made herself a cup of tea, and felt better again when she had had it. Then, as she could wait no longer, she found some paper and a purple crayon of Josefa's. With this she scribbled a note which she propped up on the kitchen mantelpiece, and then left the house and ran across the road, followed by Rufus, who had been sleeping beside the kitchen settle when she came down and had been out in the garden since.

'No barking!' she warned him as they left The Witchens. 'Now to see if anyone is about. On the grass, old man. She may be sleeping.'

They went round the house to the kitchen, where Jo pressed her nose against the window-pane. It was tidy as usual, but in a big armchair by the fireplace, where a small fire still burned, was Debby, sleeping heavily. Her face was pale and lined, and her hair was tumbling down. As she watched her, Jo realized that Debby was an old woman—too old to carry the burdens she was carrying. But even as she watched, Debby suddenly opened her eyes and sat up. She saw the face at the window, and got up to come to it with a threatening gesture. When she realised who it was, her face changed, and she flung open the casement.

'I thought it were that young rip, Reg Entwistle,' she said. 'Come yer ways in, Mrs Maynard. I'll open the door for you.'

'How is Miss Phoebe?' asked Jo anxiously.

'Sleeping now—or she was when the doctor sent me down to rest. A grand man he is, Ma'am. "You go and get a nap, Debby," he says. "The Countess and me'll watch by her for a bit, but you're tired out." And him just off from the gallop to Garnley and back! He said she was better, or I couldn't have left her. But come in, and I'll go up and tell Doctor you're here.'

'No, don't do that,' said Jo quickly. 'It might disturb Miss Phoebe. I just slipped over to ask how she was. I'm afraid you've had a bad time with her, Debby. I wish I could help you.'

'So you do, Ma'am; so you do. Miss Phoebe has been that happy since you came, being so friendly and kind to her. This is just one of her bad turns, and the storm made it worse. She'll be better in a few days now. I've seen her like this before, Ma'am, in such pain she can scurcely bear a foot on the floor near her. I don't know what the doctor give her, but it seemed to ease her, like, and then she went to sleep, and Doctor, he sent me down. What's the time, Ma'am, for I forgot to wind up me clock last night, as I should ha' done, for she only goes the eight days. But there; Miss Phoebe was that ill, I couldn't think of nowt else.'

'There's the church clock,' said Jo. 'That's nine. I'm going back to see if anyone's thinking of stirring yet. There wasn't a soul awake when I came over. Don't bother to cook today, Debby. We'll send something across for you. I'm so glad Miss Phoebe is better; but my husband will give me the news when he comes home again, so I won't keep you now. I'll be over again later on. Let me know if there's anything we can do, won't you?'

She departed, to find that the grown-ups were moving, and Sybil and Wolfram were up and dressed. They demanded breakfast, so she set them down to eggs, milk, and bread-and-butter, with a promise of stewed raspberries to follow. Then she ran upstairs, where her own trio were all out of bed, and also their sleeping suits. Len had managed to get into her vest, but Con was only halfway into hers, and Margot was turning hers round and round, murmuring, '*Where* does I go in?' with a worried look.

It was the work of ten minutes to wash and dress them, and then she heard their prayers before chasing them off downstairs, where Frieda was seeing to the eggs. She went to see what Josefa was doing, but Simone had taken charge of the young lady, and was just putting the finishing touches to her curls with a big bow. Tessa, already dressed, was standing near, saying delightedly, '*Pwetty* bow!'

'Whose—yours or Josefa's?' demanded Jo, picking her up for a good-morning kiss. 'Simone, I've been across the road, and Phoebe is sleeping, so that's good news. No; I didn't see Jack. He was upstairs with her, and I couldn't let Debby go and rout him out in case it disturbed her. And now, I'm ravenous, so let's go and get something to eat. You look very nice and tidy, Josefa. Have you said your prayers yet?'

'Said them while Tante Simone dressed Tessa,' said Josefa. 'Come on, Auntie Jo! What's for breakfast?'

'Eggs and rasps, so you're in luck, aren't you?'

'Ooh! Goody! Where's Wolferl?'

'Getting his. He and Sybil were both down when I got back, so I started them off at once. Come along; I expect yours are waiting for you.'

After breakfast, the three girls cleared up, and Jo made a pilgrimage to the butcher's to try to coax a calf's foot from him.

'I've never made calf's-foot jelly, but we've got "Mrs Beeton," and it's only a question of following her recipe,' she said hopefully.

However, Jo was fated to make no jelly that day, for the butcher was closed, and when she came to read the recipe and found out what she would require, she got such a shock that she renounced all idea of making it. Jack must send them some from the San., she said—Matron would be sure to have jars and jars of it—and then she was informed that Phoebe must have nothing of a meaty kind for some days yet.

Jack himself returned at ten. He said that Phoebe had roused, and was a little stronger; but it had been a very bad attack, and she was still in great pain, though he hoped this would pass by degrees. Jo gave him breakfast, and then coaxed him to go to bed for a couple of hours, while Simone went to relieve Marie for a while. Marie said almost as little as the doctor. But she did tell them that never, in all her life, had she seen anyone suffer as Phoebe had done during the hours when they had waited for his return from Garnley.

'It was terrible!' she said as she climbed into bed. 'Jo, Jack and Sir Jem must try to do something for her. We must insist on it. Debby wants Jack to take Phoebe on as a patient, and Phoebe herself wishes it. She managed to tell me so when I was sitting with her. "Ask him to help me!" she said. "I want him for my doctor." I told her I knew he would do all he could for her, and she smiled a very little.'

'They'll do what they can, I know. Now lie down and go to sleep, Marie, for you look all in. We're taking the whole tribe off to the meadow for a picnic tea, so you and Jack will have the house to yourselves and be able to rest in peace. Goodbye, Liebchen. I'll see you at the babies' bedtime, and not before. You stay where you are till you're called.' Jo stopped short there. She was speaking to deaf ears, for Marie was sound asleep, and Jack, when she visited him, was also lost to the world.

Chapter VII

Zephyr

Jo Maynard was sitting on top of the gate at The Witchens when the car arrived. It was a most reprehensible act for anyone who was not only a wife but a mother; but it is to be feared that a good many of Jo's habits were inclined that way. Rufus lay on the grass near her, his wistful eyes fixed on her with deepest adoration in them. Simone had taken all the small folk off to a convenient meadow where they would play about happily, and Jo herself had arranged to stroll along at about four o'clock with the tea-baskets. Marie had gone to Garnley to do some shopping, and Frieda had gone with her, leaving Gerard in Simone's care. Therefore Mrs Maynard was to all intents and purposes alone when she was roused from a day-dream by the hooting of a super-magnificent horn. She looked up, and her eyes widened when she saw the equally magnificent car to which it belonged. Even as she looked, an elderly man in chauffeur's uniform got out and came round to open the door. Out stepped a Vision.

She was tall and very slim, clad in the latest freak of fashion, a tiny hat perched on the top of a head where the light, flaxen hair had been swept up in stiff curls. Her summer frock and short coat were the very latest mode, and the face she turned to Jo's interested gaze was made up so that she had about as much expression as an Easter egg.

She turned away and looked round. Then she glanced back again at Jo, whose frock of pink gingham was four years old, and faded in streaks though it was scrupulously clean, and whose mane of straight black hair was worn with a fringe cut across her brows, and then parted down the centre and twisted in wide whorls at either side of her head. The stranger's gaze fell on the name of the house, which was painted across the top bar of the gate, and she swung forward at once.

'Is this where Mrs Maynard is staying?' she demanded imperiously.

'It is,' said Jo calmly.

'Is she in?'

Jo slipped off the gate. 'She is. Why?'

'I want to see her. Please go and tell her at once.'

The imperative tone annoyed Jo, but she replied: 'No need. She's here.'

'Here?' The Vision stared round the little front garden and then came back to tall Jo, who was looking at her with a steady gaze. 'What do you mean? Please tell your mistress I wish to see her at once.'

'I haven't got a mistress,' returned Jo blandly. 'And if you want to see Mrs Maynard I'm afraid you'll have to put up with me. I'm the only one here at the moment, you see.'

The Vision stared again, disbelief in her eyes. '*You* are Mrs Maynard? But Mrs Maynard is the wife of a doctor—a lady.'

'Sorry I don't come up to your requirements of ladyhood,' quoth Jo. 'I'm Mrs Maynard, just the same. Perhaps you'll tell me what you want?'

The Vision looked again. Then she said grudgingly, 'Oh, well, I'm sorry if I've made a mistake. I'm Zephyr Burthill.'

Now Jo knew where she was. At Phoebe's request she had written to the agent, asking him to inform Miss Burthill that the 'cello was not for sale and that Miss Wychcote would be compelled to ask her lawyer to intervene if any further attempts to approach her on the subject were made. She had written as from her own home, so she guessed that Miss Burthill must have been there—though how she had got hold of The Witchens address was a puzzle to Jo—and found out where she was. She stiffened inwardly, but all she said was: 'I think you had better come in for a few minutes. I am unable to spare you much time, as I have an engagement which I must fulfil presently.'

She opened the gate, big Rufus rising and coming to her side, and the girl with a careless 'You can wait, Jones!' tossed over her shoulder to the chauffeur, entered. Jo turned to him. 'The car will be safe enough where it is,' she said courteously. 'If you care to go round to the left of the house, you will find a comfortable bench under the trees.'

Zephyr Burthill stared again. 'Jones would be all right here,' she said abruptly. Then she stopped as abruptly, silenced by the expression in Jo's eyes. It was a blazing hot summer afternoon, the white road was dusty and glaring; even seated in the car, the man in his uniform must have suffered discomfort that, in the circumstances, was unnecessary.

All this and more Miss Burthill read on Jo's face. Quite meekly for her she added, 'If Mrs Maynard allows it, you had better find the garden bench.' And then she turned and followed Jo who was leading her to the other side of the house, to the orchard that bounded it there, running from the high wall by the road to the thick hedge at the bottom of the back garden. Here they had made an encampment with deck-chairs and hammocks among the trees, and here Jo led her uninvited guest, and established her in a canvas chair under a big pear-tree, while she herself took another near at hand. Then there was silence. Jo guessed what Zephyr had come for and she had no intention of easing things for her.

As for Zephyr Burthill, she felt unaccountably ill at ease. The rather delicate only child of a wealthy man who had indulged her to the top of her bent all her life, she had never been at school, and had never undergone the healthy process of finding her own level among other girls. Governesses had been employed to educate her; but as any complaint on her part brought about the dismissal of any governess who tried to do her good, her education was practically nil. Her chief god was Zephyr Burthill. Wealth came second. Nothing else mattered. Her father, a self-made man, had encouraged her attitude, and her mother, poor lady, was too weak-willed to stand up to the pair of them. She had married Mr Burthill when she was thirty-five and he was forty. She was 'a lady,' the youngest daughter of an impoverished baronet whose long pedigree was his chief asset. Zephyr had been born nine years later, the last of a family of four of whom none of the others had lived more than a week or two. So the girl had had no brothers or sisters to share things. As for cousins, which can often take their place, the baronet's family had scattered to various parts of the globe at his death, only the eldest son remaining. He had three boys, but all were years older than Zephyr, even the youngest being now a man of thirty with a wife and two children of his own. None of them had cared for their cousin or their aunt's vulgar, purse-proud husband, and except for letters at Christmas none of them had attempted to keep up any connection with the Burthills. So Zephyr had grown up with an exaggerated idea of her own importance, and a wrong sense of values. She was to learn a thing or two from her connection with Joey Maynard, but neither of them knew this at the present moment.

It was Zephyr who opened the conversation. 'I got your letter, Mrs Maynard,' she said.

'How was that?' asked Jo. 'It was addressed to Mr Avery.'

'I know it was. But Daddy went to him when he wrote and got it from him, and gave it to me. I asked him to do so, so he did, of course.'

'Oh?' Jo's voice was polite, but there was something in it that brought a faint flush of natural pink to Zephyr's cheeks.

'I'm the only one. He always tries to get me what I want,' she said defensively.

'What a pity!' ejaculated Jo.

Zephyr's brows, plucked till they resembled a thin pencil-line on her forehead, drew together in a frown. 'What do you mean?' she demanded.

'What I say. I have three little girls and a boy, and I hope I may always be kept from trying to give them everything they want. I can't imagine a more cruel thing to do to a child,' said Jo soberly.

'*Cruel?*'

'Yes—cruel. It's given you a totally wrong idea of life. Don't you call that a cruel thing to do to a child?'

'But how can that be a *wrong* idea of life? If you can pay for anything, why should you not have it? I don't see it at all.'

'Ah, but that's just what you can't do—pay for everything, I mean. Money won't buy you good health, for instance. It can't buy you happiness—not the happiness that lasts,' said Jo gently. 'It can't give you genius if you haven't got it already. All it can give you are the things one can touch and see and handle. You, for instance, can pay to go long voyages to all the famous beauty-spots of the earth. But unless you have the seeing eye that recognises beauty, they will mean little to you.'

Zephyr stared. Never in all her life had anyone spoken to her like this. She was not sure that she liked it. This tall, graceful woman with the clever, sensitive face and lovely voice seemed to be pitying her—*her*—Zephyr Burthill, whose every want had been gratified as soon as it had been spoken. This business of Nicholas Wychcote's 'cello was the first time she had ever come up against a flat denial. She rose from her seat with an air of hauteur.

'I don't in the least understand you,' she said, 'and I think you have a good nerve to lecture me like this. I came to talk to Miss Wychcote about her father's 'cello, and all I want from *you* is her address. If you will be kind enough to give it to me, I'll go.'

Jo shook her head. 'I am sorry, Miss Burthill, but I cannot give you Miss Wychcote's address.'

'Cannot? Do you mean that? Or do you mean you won't?'

'Both,' said Jo promptly. 'You've been told once that Miss Wychcote refuses to sell, so I won't expose her to any more persecution from you or your father. And as for "cannot," naturally I can't, when I know she doesn't wish you to have it. So there it is!'

Zephyr Burthill's face suddenly flushed under its paint. 'How dare you talk of persecution like that. I'm not trying to get her to *give* the thing to me. We're prepared to pay any sum in reason for it. And I must say,' she went on in injured tones, 'I think she's behaving in a thoroughly dog-in-the-mangerish way about it. She can't use it herself—it's no use to her. I can, and she won't let me have it. It's downright selfish and mean of her.'

Jo was boiling inwardly at this, but she made a big effort and managed to restrain the flood of words that rushed to her tongue. 'I'm sorry you look at it like that,' she said. 'You are all wrong, you know. But you can take my word for it that no power on earth will induce Miss Wychcote to sell, and if you insist on worrying her about it she will put the matter into the hands of her lawyer. I can assure you of that.'

Zephyr Burthill shut her lips till they were a thin straight line of scarlet across her face. Then she swung round and made for the road, calling the chauffeur as she went with an imperiousness that brought him off the comfortable garden seat where he had been enjoying the coolness of the shady trees. She flung herself into the car, and he hastened to get into the driver's seat after closing the door. Jo followed them to the gate, and Zephyr leaned out of the open window to fling a last word at her.

'You can tell that girl,' she hissed, 'that I'll find out where she lives, and if she won't agree to sell me that 'cello, then I'll get it some other way. I've *got* to have it, and I'm going to!'

'And I tell *you*,' retorted Jo, thoroughly roused by this, 'that if you do, you'll probably find yourself in the nearest police court. So put *that* on your needles and knit it!'

At this point Jones evidently thought it advisable to get away before any further exchange of incivilities. But as he drove off Jo saw a wide grin on his face at her last remark.

Left alone, she returned to her chair and sat down to think. She had known from Zephyr's own letter to Phoebe that she wanted the 'cello badly, but she had not realised that the girl was so set on it as her words today showed. Clearly, she would stick at little or nothing to get her way, and Jo was seriously concerned as to the extra trouble that might come to Phoebe from it. She must think of some way of safeguarding the 'cello.

'I don't think she'd even shy at a little gentle burglary,' mused Jo as she lay in her chair. 'Shall I invite Phoebe and Debby to come here for a few days? I don't think it would do Phoebe any good if the house were broken into in the small hours of the morning.'

She could come to no decision, so she finally glanced at her watch, uttered a loud squawk of dismay on finding that it was past four, and the small fry would certainly be wanting their tea, rushed off for her hat and the baskets, and presently set off for the meadow, where she found the entire flock rolling on the short turf—haymaking was a thing of the past, and in the next field the tractor was reaping the golden wheat—and waiting impatiently for her coming.

'How late you are, Joey!' cried Simone. 'I began to think you were not coming after all. Is it a new adventure in the story?'

'No; I had an unexpected visitor,' replied Jo, as she set the baskets down and mopped her hot face. 'Tell you about it later when the others get back. Meanwhile, what about tea?'

'I'll lay the cloth.' And Sybil pulled it off the top of one basket and began to spread it. 'Josefa, you get the mugs, and Len can put out the sandwiches. Con, you are not to eat the sugar!'

Con chuckled wickedly, but put down the spoon with which she had been helping herself from the tin, and went to assist Josefa in setting forth the array of mugs. Simone nodded to the big double pram in which Stephen and tiny Gerard were lying.

'Gerard has had his bottle,' she said. 'You see to Stephen, and I'll see to tea. You can tell us the news after supper tonight.'

Thus adjured, Jo got up from her seat on the grass, picked up her placid son and saw to his wants, while Simone saw to the laying of the cloth. Presently she called to her friend to give an eye to the children, and Jo, glancing up, saw her racing down the meadow and out through the gate.

'What's the matter with Tante Simone?' she demanded of Len, who appeared at that moment.

'You forgot the milk,' said Len sweetly. 'She's gone to get it.'

Jo nearly dropped Stephen as she clutched at her hair. 'So I did! How stupid of me! But why didn't Sybs go and get it with one of you three or Josefa?'

'Tante Simone said it would be quicker if she went herself,' explained Len, squatting down beside her mother. 'Mamma, may I bath myself tonight?'

Jo chuckled. 'What for? Besides, I'm afraid you wouldn't get all the corners clean. Just look at you!'

'I can't. There isn't a glass,' said Len reasonably. 'Why couldn't I, Mamma? I'm a big girl now.'

Jo's eyes softened as she looked at the grey-eyed mite beside her. 'You are getting a big girl, but hardly big enough for that, pet. Even Josefa doesn't bath herself yet. You must wait a little, precious.'

Len set her elbows on her knees and buried her chin in her hands. 'Papa said when he went home that I was to help you 'cos you had such lots to do. There's four of us to bath. I thought if I did myself it would help,' she explained.

Her mother bent down and kissed the hot and dirty little face. 'Mamma loves bathing you, sweetheart. I'm not ready to give up that job yet. Besides, if I let you try, Connie and Margot would want to as well. I should have to spend half the night cleaning up the bathroom after that, as you very well know. And you do help me ever so much as it is. No; I don't think you may try bathing yourselves yet. But I'll let you three try to brush each other's hair to-night—all at once, just as Tante Simone and Aunties Frieda and Marie and I used to do at school.' And she chuckled again as she recalled the lively scenes they had had over that same hair-brushing.

'All at once? How?' Len's interest was roused at once.

'You'll see when bedtime comes. Now hold out your arms for Stephen while I tidy my hair. He's pulled it all over the place.' And she laid the bonny boy on the small lap, and Len sat hugging her burden for the two or three minutes it took her mother to make herself tidy.

Simone appeared by the time Jo had put him back into the pram, and they set to work to give the small folk their tea. When it was over, they packed up and made for home. Stephen was sleeping, and Jo put Gerard, also asleep, at his side, so that they could pop Tessa in at the end. Then, laden, and—in the case of the children—very grimy, they strolled homewards, where baths and bed were at once the order of the day.

'You see to Gerard, and I'll get Stephen done,' said Jo to Simone.

'And if Sybil could help Tessa and Louis, we could get them packed off too,' agreed Simone. 'Run upstairs, you two. What about the others, Jo?'

'We'll wash their hands and faces, and they can sit quietly in the garden till we're ready for them,' said Jo, as she lifted the babies out of the pram and started off up the stairs, a baby under each arm. 'Wolferl can help Louis, and Josefa can see to Tessa.

Get their clothes off, you two, and put them into their dressing-gowns till we're ready for them. Sybs, you spread the table for supper, will you, darling? The Aunties will be ready for it by the time they get back. It's been hot enough up here. What it will have been like in the town I shudder to think.'

Sybil nodded, and went off with the triplets to the kitchen, where she washed herself, washed their hands and faces, and then, with them to help her, laid the table for supper, so that by the time the four tinies were all safely in bed, everything was ready for Simone's attention. Jo saw to her own daughters, showing them how to stand in a little circle, each brushing the hair of the one in front of her, while she finished off Josefa's 'corners' in the bath. Then she gave them their milk and biscuits before she saw to toothbrush drill. Prayers followed, and then she put them into their beds with a goodnight kiss and a special blessing for each one.

'Bless my guardian angel, Mamma,' demanded Margot suddenly.

'Angels don't need blessing—not human blessing,' said Jo.

'You isn't human—you's Mamma,' returned Margot sleepily. 'Say "God bless Margot's guardian angel" quick, please. I'm so sleepy.'

Jo knew her daughter. Meekly she repeated the blessing, and then retired convulsed with laughter. 'I'd like to know what Margot thinks a human is,' she told Simone as she helped that young lady to prepare a salad. 'I couldn't ask her tonight. I wanted her to go to sleep. But I'll find out tomorrow, or my name's not Jo Maynard.'

Simone laughed. 'D'you remember how Janie Lucy once told us that when Julian was hearing Betsy's prayers when she was very small, he was stroking her hair, and she suddenly stopped in the middle and told him she wasn't a pussy? They are funny sometimes, aren't they?' Then she gave a quick little sigh.

Jo glanced at her. 'What is it, Simone?'

'Oh, silly of me. But I do wish André were not missing all Tessa's baby days. He's never seen her since she was six months old. She was so tiny then, and now she is running all over, and chatters so much.'

'But she's only eighteen months old,' said Jo, putting an arm round the slim shoulders. 'Perhaps he'll be sent home soon.'

'I wish I could think so.' A tear hung on Simone's long lashes.

'Well, Julian hasn't been home for two years,' said Jo gently. 'Try not to fret, Simone chérie.'

'Oh, I try. But it is not easy, Jo. If anything should happen—'

'I know.' Jo's voice was very tender.

Simone dashed her hand across her eyes. 'I'm silly. I think I must be tired. Truly, Jo, I try to trust that all will be well. It is only sometimes—and mostly at night when I am in bed and cannot sleep—then I begin to wonder what I should do if—if—'

Jo nodded. 'I know,' she said again. 'I went through it when Jack was away. I used to wonder how I should manage with the three girlies if I were left to be father as well as mother to them. But back of my mind I always knew I shouldn't be alone, even if it came to that. Thank God it didn't!' And her mind went back to the awful days of the previous year when Jack had been reported drowned, and for some time she had believed herself to be a widow.

Simone glanced up at her. 'I *am* selfish!' she cried. 'I've made you remember. Joey, mon chou, ma bien-aimée, *don't*! It is over now. Jack is safely at home.'

'Yes,' said Jo. Then she added passionately, 'I can never be grateful enough to God that He saved me from that worst of all losses! But because I owe so much to Him, I always feel if I *can* help people I *must*. That's one reason why I want to help Phoebe.'

'Only one reason, though. Even if it weren't for that, you would try to help her, because that is you, my Jo,' said Simone.

'No need to shake your head! Even when you were a little girl of twelve you tried to help people.'

'And got into some horrid messes as a result,' said Jo, a quiver in her laughter. 'Here comes Rufus. Want your supper, old man? Come along, then. You shall have it. How late the others are, Simone. It's eight o'clock. I must go and tell Sybs to put her book away and lie down now.' And after giving big Rufus his supper, she ran upstairs to tell Sybil to get off to sleep, and peep in at the others. They were all asleep, as she reported when she came down to find Simone carrying in glasses of rich milk from the shed.

'And Marie and Frieda are coming up the bank,' she added. 'I saw them from Wolferl's window. Set the window wider, Simone. I believe there's a breeze springing up. It feels cooler already. Then, when we're all comfy at supper, I've got *such* a tale to unfold!'

Chapter VIII

'What Shall We Do?'

Simone put the finishing touches to the table while Jo set the chairs, and when the two wanderers arrived, hot, sticky, and tired, everything was ready for them. In the kitchen, a bowl of cool water, soap, and a towel awaited them, and while they sponged their faces and washed their hands, the other two unpacked the parcels and put their contents away. Twenty minutes later they were all sitting round the table which Jo had pushed to the open lattices, enjoying their meal, and chatting about the shopping expedition, the babies—Frieda had slipped upstairs to assure herself that her pair were safely asleep—and Jo's lamentable lapse of memory in regard to the milk.

'But it's no wonder, you know,' said the culprit calmly. 'I only wonder that I ever put in an appearance at all, all things considered.'

'What *do* you mean?' asked Marie. 'What has been happening here? Simone, do *you* know anything about it?'

Simone shook her head. 'All I know is that Jo says she has an awful tale to unfold, and so far she has refused to unfold it. She had a mysterious visitor this afternoon, so I suppose it has something to do with that?' She ended on a note of query, and three pairs of eyes were turned on Jo.

'You're right there,' admitted Jo. 'Who do you think turned up, complete with uniformed chauffeur, swagger car, and the very latest fashions?'

'I have no idea,' said Frieda. 'Do get on, Jo, and don't be so maddening! There are times when I could shake you well.'

'It's too hot for such violent exercise,' murmured wicked Jo. 'Now, keep calm!' as Frieda jumped to her feet. 'I mean to tell you everything. I want your advice, you people, and you'll have to think hard. So let's get this débris,' she indicated the table, 'cleared off to the kitchen, and we'll take chairs on the lawn where we can hear if anyone wakes up, and you shall have the whole tale. Come on! Forward the Light Brigade!' And she set the example by picking up the salad bowl and cheese-dish and making for the kitchen. The others knew they would get nothing from her until she was ready, so they made the best of it, and in a very few minutes the table was cleared. Simone slipped off upstairs to make sure that all was well with the sleepers, while the other three washed up, laid the table for breakfast, and then tidied themselves. It was twilight by the time they were lying in their deck-chairs on the front lawn where they could hear any noise from the house, and they relaxed with sighs of relief as they felt the cool, evening breezes blowing over them.

'Now for your tale, Jo,' said Marie. 'No, thanks; I'm not smoking this weather. It's too hot. Put that case away, Simone, and listen. Come on, Jo. Who was your mysterious visitor? Get on with the story.'

'It was Zephyr Burthill,' said Jo.

'Zephyr Burthill? You mean the girl that wants Phoebe's 'cello? But why on earth should she come to *you*?'

'To get Phoebe's address—if she could,' said Jo simply.

'But didn't you write from Plas Gwyn? How on earth did she find out where you are?'

'Ask me another. I should guess—but it's only guessing, mind—that she turned up at Plas Gwyn, saw Anna, and bullied her into giving this address. It's rather the sort of thing she would do, I think.'

'It's a pity she didn't see Jack,' said Marie. 'He would have let her know what he thought of her manners. What a horrid thing to do!'

'Very ill-bred,' put in Frieda. 'Well, go on and tell us what happened. I hope,' in anxious afterthought, 'that you kept your temper, Jo. You can be so very—well—rude yourself, when you are roused.'

'I was calm—and pitying—and lecturious,' replied Jo sweetly.

'And—*what*? I never heard that last word of yours before. What d'you mean?'

'Well, she said so, anyway. She said I had a nerve to lecture her. Now sit back and lend me your ears, and you shall hear the whole tale.'

They did as she said, and she gave them an unvarnished account of all that had happened that afternoon. They shrieked with laughter at the end of her story, so that Rufus, who had been stretched out in the orchard, heard them, and came to see what was happening. Jo laid a hand on his head as he flumped down with a contented grunt beside her, and he lay there, adoring eyes fixed on her. Jo rubbed his ears.

'Poor old man! It's too hot for the likes of you, isn't it? But I pity that unlucky chauffeur of hers in his heavy uniform. The selfish little pig was actually going to leave the poor man in the car, with the sun blazing down on the road. You know,' went on Jo seriously, 'I don't believe she has an idea in her head that doesn't relate to Zephyr Burthill and her comforts and likes. Honestly, she goes on about "I want" just like a baby—and a very spoilt baby at that. It's time someone showed her that she isn't the only pebble on the beach. I wouldn't allow any of mine to think that way, I can tell you. She may be the only child of her family, but she's a long way from being the only person on earth; and so she'll have to find out before she's much older. But what I want to consult you three about is what we are to do about Many Bushes and the 'cello. You know, I wouldn't put even burglary past her.'

'Nonsense!' said Marie crisply. 'If she is as you say, she certainly won't run any risk of trouble with the police. Too cautious!'

'Oh, I don't think she'd try to do it herself. But there *are* people who would do anything for money these days, and she may get hold of some of them to do it. Quite a lot of that sort of thing goes on, I believe.'

'It mustn't be allowed,' said Frieda quickly. 'Phoebe could never stand such a shock as that would be. Didn't Jack say her heart was still in a bad state?'

'He's still a little worried about it,' agreed Jo. 'When he was over on Wednesday he said that she was gaining ground steadily now, but it was slow work, and she must not be worried or excited about anything. That's one reason why I think we'd better not say anything to the police.'

'I don't see how you could in any case,' said Simone. 'You have only your own ideas, and what Zephyr herself said about it, to go on, and I don't think they would take any notice of that.' Then she added, 'I wish it were possible to get Phoebe into the San. at once. Then Debby could come here—'

'And where would she sleep?' asked Jo blandly. 'We're chock-a-block as it is. I don't see where we could edge another bed in anywhere.'

'Wolferl could come in with me,' said Marie. 'It wouldn't matter for a week or two, and I think that whatever that Zephyr child does will be done soon. From what you say, she isn't inclined to wait for anything.'

'Then would you bring the 'cello over here, too?' asked Frieda.

'Yes; I think so. Don't you?'

'I don't know. Do you think they'd bring people here to steal it just that one night? Wouldn't they make some inquiries first? Then, if they heard that Phoebe was in San., and Debby with us, they'd probably guess where the 'cello was and try to break in here. We don't want the children frightened, you know. And you could scarcely leave Debby alone over there. She's old. Any trouble of that kind might make her ill, and that would be another worry for poor Phoebe.'

'I don't think we had better try to do anything ourselves,' said Simone. 'At least, it would be better to tell Jack about it and see what he says.'

'And anyway, he said they were full at the San.,' added Jo. 'What about having Debby *and* Phoebe over here? They could have my room, and I'd take Stephen, who's too little to be frightened, and Rufus, and sleep over there. How about that for an idea?'

'A complete wash-out,' declared Marie. 'Jack would never allow it.'

'Jack wouldn't be asked. Don't be silly, Marie. What harm could come to me if I had Rufus? He'd make short work of anyone trying to harm us.'

'Well, we won't allow it, either,' said Simone firmly. 'I never heard of anything so mad. Now don't argue, Jo. No one is going to hear of it. If you try it on, I'll wire Jack myself, or get him on long-distance.'

As the other two agreed with this, Jo subsided. Frieda suddenly looked up. 'Jo, you say you didn't give Phoebe's address. Then how could Zephyr know where she was? She evidently had no idea that it was just over the road or she wouldn't have bothered with you, but gone to Many Bushes at once.'

'She'd find out soon enough if she chose. She had only to ask the first child she met. They all know Phoebe now.'

'Yes; that's true,' agreed Frieda. 'But, on the other hand, she might not think of it. She has no idea that you did not know Phoebe till just a week or two ago. For all she knows, you may have been friends for years.'

'And that's true, too, though it doesn't seem possible,' said Jo wonderingly. 'Can you believe, you three, that six weeks ago we didn't know her at all? I knew she existed, of course, for Vanna di Ricci told me of her; but I'd really forgotten all about it. Well, there's ten o'clock, so we'd better lock up and go to bed. I'll just slip across and see if they are all right for the night. You get on with the work. I shan't be ten minutes. Coming, Rufus?' And she got up and went across the road, followed by big Rufus, who was ready for a walk now that it was cooler.

She was back by the time the others had put away the chairs, locked up the back premises, and seen that all was safe. Phoebe was asleep, she told them, and Debby just going off to bed herself. She fastened the front door, and they were just mounting the stairs, when the telephone bell rang. The Witchens had been already wired for it, and Jack had succeeded in getting the instrument put in. Marie, who was last, ran back and lifted the receiver. Then she called Jo.

'Jo! It's Jack. He says he has some important news for you.'

'*Madge!*' Jo turned and tore down the narrow stairs, almost upsetting Frieda and Simone on the way, for she had been leading. She clutched the receiver from Marie, and cried, 'Jack! It's Jo! What's wrong?'

'Nothing this end,' came back the answer. 'Only, there's a bed vacant tomorrow, quite unexpectedly. I want you to go over to Many Bushes first thing in the morning and tell them that the ambulance will be here for Miss Wychcote in the afternoon. All she wants is nighties and washing things. She might add a brush and comb, perhaps! Someone can bring over anything else later on. But she must be ready for us when we arrive.'

Jo drew a long breath. 'How you frightened me! I thought something had gone wrong with Madge. All right, Jack. I'll pop over at nine tomorrow and help Debby get things ready. What time will the ambulance be here?'

'Oh, about three, I suppose. As for Madge, she's perfectly all right. You needn't worry about her now. Jem kept her in bed for ten days, and she's as fit as can be. How are the children? All well?'

'Oh, fit as fiddles. Steve's beginning to dribble a little, so I'm keeping an eye on him. But he's in splendid condition. They all are.'

'Good! I'm coming myself to get Phoebe, so I'll have half an hour or so with you tomorrow.' At which point they were cut off.

Jo hung up and turned to the others. 'They're coming for Phoebe tomorrow, as a bed has fallen vacant, so that's *one* difficulty disposed of. We'll have Debby over here, if you think you can really manage with Wolferl as well as Josefa, Marie. And as for the 'cello, I've had a great idea. Jack shall take it back with him and park it at the Round House in case the Burthill mind runs on burgling our place. They'll never think that Sir James and Lady Russell would have it. Now would they?'

'It's a brain-wave!' said Marie. 'Of course I can manage, Jo. Josefa can come in with me, and Wolferl can have her bed. Then Debby can sleep in his attic. And if you get the 'cello away, that ought to settle things.'

However, in part of this they reckoned without their host. Debby declared that nothing would make her sleep out of her own house. She was glad enough to know that Phoebe was to go to the Sanatorium, for she had hopes that there her mistress would be helped. Jack Maynard had explained to her that complete cure could hardly be hoped for; but he thought they could mitigate her pain, and even, perhaps, relieve her helplessness. If there was anything that could help Phoebe, Debby was not going to lift a finger to prevent it. As soon as she knew that the ambulance was coming for the sick girl that afternoon, she set to work to pack for her.

Jo, meanwhile, accompanied by Simone, went up to Phoebe

herself, who lay against her pillows, nearly as white as they. The hot weather tried her, and her room was so stifling that Jo nearly gasped when she entered it, though the window was pushed open as far as it would go, and a thin green curtain darkened the brilliant sunshine. Phoebe smiled at them. She was still in a good deal of pain, but she was accustomed to that, poor girl, and this last attack, severe as it had been at the time, had yielded much more readily than others had done.

'How nice of you both to come in,' she said. 'Sit down, won't you? Pull that curtain back a little, Jo. Then I can see you.'

Jo drew back the curtain, and then came over to the bed. 'Phoebe,' she said gently, 'Jack rang me up last night to tell me that a bed has become vacant quite unexpectedly, and he is coming with an ambulance this afternoon to take you to the San.'

'This afternoon?' Phoebe's eyes opened widely. 'But—how can I ever be ready in time? This is Sunday. We can't buy a thing, and I need a good many—well, one or two, anyhow.'

'Jack said all you would need would be nighties, washing things, and perhaps, a brush and comb. Perhaps, indeed!' Jo spoke with mock indignation. 'I wonder how he imagines you could keep your hair tidy without! But you must have a cool dressing-gown, and a few other things. Your work, for instance. You're much better now, and you'll be able to use your hands again in a few days. Debby is washing through a couple of nighties and some hankies for you, so we came to get your other things while she is busy. Tell us what you want, and we'll put them out. Don't worry about anything, dear. We'll see to everything.'

Phoebe's eyes shone. 'How good you all are to me!' she said. 'Oh, Jo! When Dr Maynard was here on Wednesday, he said he wanted to get me to the Sanatorium, and he thought that a month or two there would help me more than anything else. I know I can't be cured. It's too late for that now. But he says there's some wonderful new treatment they would try which had helped other people, and he feels sure it would do me good.'

'I've heard of it,' said Jo. 'It's injections of some kind. You remember that Dr Peters who came about six months ago, Simone? You met him at dinner at our place at Easter, didn't you? Well, he's studied in America, and this is some marvellous treatment they've been trying there. I believe it's done endless good already.'

Simone screwed up her face in thought. 'I remember,' she said. 'A short, rather ugly little man with very blue eyes that seemed to look through one. He was sweet with the children, I remember.'

'That's him,' said Jo, who was a great stickler for grammar in writing but on occasion apt to be careless when speaking 'Now, Phoebe, tell us where to find your things, and we'll begin. Marie is seeing to the dinner, and Sybil will bring over yours and Debby's because Debby certainly won't have time to see to anything until we've got you off. Where are your nighties?'

Phoebe told them, and they took from the drawer nightdress after nightdress adorned with her own lovely embroidery. The two exclaimed over them as they worked, and Phoebe smiled at their praise.

'I knew your work was wonderful, but I never even imagined anything so fairylike,' said Jo, as she gloated over one of white crêpe-de-chine, with sprays of lilac embroidered on the shoulders and the edge of the short sleeves. 'Will those be enough? What next?'

'Woollen vests in the next drawer,' said Phoebe. 'I have to wear them under these, you know. I must always wear wool next my skin.'

The fine, woollen vests were as dainty as the nightdresses, embroidered like them, but with fine darning patterns. Handkerchiefs, dressing-gown, bedjacket, all were alike. Jo laughingly protested that they were fit for a bride's trousseau.

'Not that I had a trousseau anything in the least like them,' she added. 'Jack married me very shortly after we'd escaped from the Gestapo. We got into awful trouble with them, you know, for trying to defend a little Jewish watch-maker we knew in Spärtz—that's the little town at the foot of the mountain railway up to the Tiernsee where we used to live. My adopted sister, Robin Humphries, and quite a number more of us had to fly for our lives. Jack had to go too. He was under suspicion for more than one reason. He and I were engaged shortly before Hitler walked into Austria, and we married almost as soon as we got to Guernsey. Then Frieda was engaged to Bruno von Ahlen who was a doctor at the San. when it was at the Sonnalpe on the east side of the Tiernsee. *He* was caught, poor lamb, and spent some time in a concentration camp. As for Marie, she and Eugen von Wertheim have lost every stick they had in Austria. They were in America at the time, visiting Eugen's American relatives. The Nazis ordered him to return to Austria, and he took no notice of them, so they sequestrated everything—the beautiful old castle, with all its pictures and tapestries and everything. Whether he'll ever get them back again, goodness knows.'

'And for me,' said Simone, as she counted handkerchiefs, 'André and I were friends. We did not become engaged till some time after. And we were married long after the rest of us.' She began to laugh, and Phoebe asked why. 'Oh, because when we were at school, Jo used to say that she would never marry, but be a nice, old-maid aunt. Marie wedded first. But Jo was the second.'

Jo grimaced at her. 'I was young and silly. And I didn't know what a solid lump of comfort Jack could be until we had that awful flight from the Gestapo. I decided then that I'd make sure of him, so I did.'

Phoebe laughed, but she knew all the same that Jo's feeling for her husband was very much more than her words said.

They got the things together, and at twelve o'clock Sybil came across the road carrying a daintily laid tray very carefully. Phoebe tried to do justice to Marie's cookery, but she was too excited to make much of a meal. Simone saw it, and checked Jo when that young lady would have urged the invalid. She made Phoebe lie down, darkened the room again, and took Jo off to The Witchens for their own meal. In the kitchen at Many Bushes Debby was sitting down to one as good, and the girls promised to return in an hour. Meanwhile, they hoped that Phoebe would get a nap. Excited as she was, she was still too weak to lie awake, and when the faithful maid tiptoed upstairs a little later, she found her mistress fast asleep.

Simone undertook to look after the children for the afternoon, so the other three ran over to Many Bushes and packed the two suit-cases with Phoebe's possessions, only pausing to enjoy the cup of tea Debby made for them halfway through. By half-past two everything was ready, and Jo and Marie went upstairs with Debby to help to prepare Phoebe for her journey. The dressing was simple. They put her into a clean nightdress and a dressing-gown, after Debby had sponged her hot face and hands and done her hair. Jo knew that she would be wrapped in a blanket on the stretcher, and they could do nothing more. Then the two girls went down to the garden to watch for the ambulance, leaving Debby alone with her nursling. Jo had put the precious 'cello into its canvas bag, ready to go with the ambulance, and it was in the little sitting-room, close at hand. From the open window they could hear the low murmur of Phoebe's voice and Debby's harsher North-country tones drifting out on the still summer air. The only other sounds were the humming of bees and wasps in the phlox clumps down the border, the song of birds, and, from the bottom of the village where the church stood, the light voices of children as they went to Sunday School.

Frieda looked round with a smile. 'What peace!' she said in the soft Tyrolean German they often spoke together. 'England on a summer Sunday! Jo, this is a beautiful country of yours, as well as kind. For some things,' she went on, 'I like your quiet Sundays better than our gayer ones.'

'They *are* restful,' agreed Jo. 'But I shouldn't like to think I'd never known another Tyrolean one. Do you remember the Tzigane bands that used to come to play at the Kron Prinz Karl? Poor little Herr Braun! I wonder what has happened to him? And Gretchen, and all the others too?'

'We shall find out one day—and not so long now,' said Marie. 'I love England—how could I help it?—but Austria is my country. Josefa has never seen her own land; and Wolferl cannot remember it either. Keferl is the only one of our little people who can, for even Maria Ileana was too tiny.'

But Jo was paying no attention. 'I hear a motor,' she said. 'Listen!'

The others listened, and then Frieda nodded. 'It's at the bottom of Tedder's Bank. It will soon be here. Run and tell Phoebe and Debby, Jo.'

'I'll bring the cases,' said Marie, forgetting her dreams of her homeland at once, and becoming brisk and practical. 'Jack will have people to help him lift Phoebe, won't he, Jo? Then go and pop on a kettle. They won't say "No" to tea or coffee on a hot day. Bring that tray, Frieda. I left it on the kitchen table.'

They scattered, and when the ambulance drew up before Many Bushes Jo had tea waiting for them, and Phoebe, her hand clasped in Debby's hard, work-worn one, was leaning against her pillows, a faint pink born of excitement in her cheeks, her eyes starry.

Jack Maynard had come in his own car, which followed the ambulance, and Jo was at the gate to welcome him as he came round, followed by a much shorter man, not even as tall as herself, whose clever, ugly face was lighted by a pair of such vividly blue eyes that most people forgot the rest of his appearance once they had met them. She knew him at once.

'Dr Peters!' she cried, giving him her hand. 'How good of you to come too! Come in and have some coffee. It's all ready, and so must you be after motoring on such a dusty day as this.'

'We can't spare more than a minute, Jo,' said her husband quickly. 'We are later than I meant to be, but we got held up twice on the road. No; no coffee for me, thanks. Marie, take Dr Peters up to see Miss Wychcote while I have a look at the babies. I want to see Steve's gums, Jo.'

'He's all right so far,' said Jo, going across the road with him. 'He only began dribbling the day before yesterday. But I think the teeth are ready to come through any time now. And as for the girlies, they couldn't be fitter if they tried. They have huge appetites, sleep from the time they're put to bed till half-past six next morning, and are the sturdiest trio I've ever seen. They make Simone's Tessa look fairy-like beside them.'

Jack laughed. 'Yes; we've a healthy family. Margot is the only one who has given us any real anxiety so far, isn't she?'

'She looks far stronger now,' said Jo. 'And you people always said she would outgrow her delicacy as she got older. Here we are! I expect they are all in the orchard. Simone offered to stay with them while we saw to Phoebe.'

But Simone, hearing voices, was already at the corner of the house and greeting them with a finger on her lips. 'Be quiet,' she said softly. 'Everyone is asleep but Sybil and me, and I'm not too sure about her.'

She led the way to the orchard, and there they found themselves in a real Garden of Sleep, for the two babies were lying on rugs under a huge sunshade; the triplets and her own little Tessa slept sweetly on mattresses beneath the apple-trees. Wolferl and Josefa were in hammocks slung between two pear-trees; and little Louis was cuddled down on a light bamboo lounge close at hand. Sybil, spread-eagled on a rug, looked up, and jumped to her feet with a muffled cry of delight on seeing her uncle. He gave her a hug and a kiss, peeped at his daughters, and then turned to Jo, who had lifted Stephen quietly and was holding him, still sound asleep, in her arms.

'Bring him into the house, Jo,' he said. 'No, Sybs. You stay here, pet. Mummy sent her love to you, and so did Daddy. He's going to try to come and see you all one day next week. Josette is very well now and running about all over. David seems to be having a great time, and says he will write to you soon. Now let me go, for we must get Miss Wychcote off as soon as possible, and I just want to look at Stephen.'

Sybil released him obediently, and went back to her rug and the book she had been devouring, and the Maynards went into the house where Jack soon satisfied himself that Stephen's teeth were well on the way, gave Jo a few simple directions, and then went back to Many Bushes whither she followed him, once she had given her son into Simone's charge.

They were bringing the stretcher downstairs when she got there, and she had only time to kiss Phoebe and promise to let her know how everything went on at Many Bushes, and then she stepped back. Dr Peters came up to her, while Jack saw to the settling of the sick girl.

'We'll do our best for her, Mrs Maynard,' he said.

'Can you really help her?' Jo knew too much to ask if they could cure her.

'I think so,' he said. 'It is of long standing, of course, and a cure in present conditions would be impossible. But I think we can give her much relief. And now, we want to get her back as soon as possible. She will not suffer on the road. I have given her an injection to make her drowsy, so as to save her pain in movement. You shall hear regularly. I expect your husband will write. Are these her cases? I'll put them in the car. Goodbye! We shall hope to have good news for you before very long.' And he picked up the cases and hurried to the car.

Jack had been speaking to Marie and Frieda. Now he turned to his wife and took her in his arms. 'Goodbye, my Joey. Remember what I told you about Stephen, and take care of yourself. Jem will be over during the week some time, and I hope to get off for a week after that—first week in September, I expect. And you'll be home at the end of the next fortnight. Anna has finished her cleaning, thank heaven! Now I must go.'

He kissed her, and was off. The three girls and Debby stood gazing after the two vehicles until they swung round the curve of the road and were out of sight. Then Jo turned to the old woman.

'Now for a cup of tea! I'm parched! I'll help you wash these cups, Debby, and we'll have tea in the sitting-room where it'll be cool. Then we must go home and claim our families. You're coming over to us tonight, aren't you? We shan't feel happy about you unless you do.' She turned into the sitting-room as she spoke, and her gaze fell on the 'cello in its case. 'Mercy! The 'cello! We forgot all about it! Frieda! Marie! We forgot to give Jack the 'cello to take to the Round House and it's still here! What *shall* we do?'

Chapter IX

STEPHEN TAKES A HAND

THE other two joined in Jo's outcry. Debby looked from one to another, puzzled as to the cause for all this fuss about the 'cello. Jo explained. She gave a brief outline of her interview with Zephyr Burthill, and told of their fears lest, in her great desire for the instrument, Zephyr might manage somehow to get it by foul means since fair ones were useless. As she listened, honest indignation swelled up in the old woman. She was quite unable to understand Phoebe's love for the thing, but she was furious at the thought of what harm might have been done to her mistress.

'So now you see, Debby,' wound up Jo, 'why we want you to come to us. We all think that whatever may be done will be done quickly. I'm more thankful than I can say that your Miss Phoebe is well out of it. But I don't think you ought to stay here alone. I know she would say so if she knew about it. You'll be safe enough in the daytime. There are too many people about for them to attempt anything like burglary then. You could be over here then. But I do think you ought to come to us at night. Unless,' she added, 'you'll let some of us come over here to sleep.'

Debby looked round for a chair which Frieda promptly pushed towards her, and she sat down heavily. 'You must let me think, Mrs Maynard, Ma'am.'

'I'll go and make the tea,' said Marie. 'Don't worry, Debby. We will all help you. And when Sir Jem comes along, we'll make him take it back with him, so it'll be safe enough then.'

A shadow fell across the open doorway, making them all look up. There stood Reg Entwistle in all the glory of his Sunday suit, well-slicked hair, and shoes gleaming with polish. Sunday School was over, and he had heard some news from Mrs Purvis as he left the church that sent him post-haste to Many Bushes. As she saw him Jo's eyes sparkled, and she called to him to come in at once. It had flashed across her quick brain that Reg would make an ideal scout for them. Holidays had begun for him a fortnight ago. He was an inquisitive youngster, who would note every stranger who came to the village. They must take him into their confidence and enlist his aid. She felt sure of getting it.

But Reg was full of his own grievance, and he was scarcely inside the room before he gave vent to it. 'Is it true Miss Phoebe's gone away?' he demanded. 'Why'nt some on you told me? … I s'pose,' with heavy sarcasm, 'you just didn't think on.'

'That was exactly it,' said Jo calmly. 'We only knew late last night that they were coming today to take her to the San., and then, in all the hurry of getting her ready, no one thought of telling you. I'm sorry, Reg.'

'That's a lot o' use! An' why'd they take her away, any-road?'

'To try a new treatment that they hope will make her much better,' said Frieda, who always lived up to her name's meaning, and tried to make peace wherever she went. 'You knew there was talk of her going some time, didn't you? They could take her now, so they came for her at once.'

'Some time ain't *now*—an' not without a word to me,' growled Reg. He was, secretly, desperately jealous of Phoebe's friendship with these newcomers. Under Reg's stolid exterior there flamed a heart full of knight-errantry which Phoebe's helplessness and pain had roused. He had been inclined to look on her as his; but these laughing women had been taking her from him. Now he glowered round at them, miserable to think that she had gone away; and without saying goodbye to him.

Jo understood at once. 'I'll be going to see her in a week or two, when they let her have visitors,' she said gently. 'Would you come with me, Reg? She'd love to see you, I know. And you'd like to see where she is and what it's like, wouldn't you? I'll ask your auntie if you can come. We'd have to take Stephen and stay one night at my home in Howells Village, for we couldn't manage the journey there and back in one day.'

Reg's miserable eyes lightened a little. But he was not yet prepared for a truce. 'An' who's to say they'll let *me* in? It's different for you. You're a lady. I'm a lad, an' a village lad, too. Likely they'd say she couldn't have more'n one visitor, an' they'd choose you.'

'I don't think they will,' said Jo simply, 'but if they do, then you will be the one to see her. It's your right. You're a much older friend than I am. Debby must be first, of course,' with a smile at the old woman, 'but I promise that you shall be the next.' Then she changed her tone. 'Come, Reg! Shake hands and be friends. There's something we want you to do for Miss Phoebe, and only you can do it.'

'Let's hear what 'tis, then.' But though Reg's tone was still sulky, and he took no notice of the slim hand held out for his, he was coming round. He sat down on the edge of the sofa and looked at Jo.

Once more that young lady told the story of her meeting with Zephyr Burthill the previous day. Then she explained quickly that they were afraid of the means the Burthills might use to get the 'cello, and wound up by asking him to keep his eyes open and let them know if any strangers came to the district during the next week or so. The sulkiness left his face as he listened; and when Marie brought in the tea-tray, he was full of enthusiasm about his part of the plan. Yes; he would keep his eyes open. His aunt was a kindly, easy-going soul, who never minded what he did in his holidays so long as he was in time for meals and did not destroy his clothes unduly. He made a good tea with them, and finally went off to tell his aunt where he had been before he returned to the church for evensong. He had to go, for he was in the choir, and had been entrusted with six bars of treble solo in the anthem. When he had gone, the girls turned to Debby. But she had made up her mind. She would sleep at The Witchens, since she knew it was what Phoebe would have wished; she would help with the work there till eleven, and then go back to Many Bushes for the rest of the day.

'And as for the 'cello,' said Marie, as she helped Debby to wash up, 'we'll take that with us, and it can go into one of our rooms. It'll be safe enough there until Sir James comes, and he can take it to the Round House. There; that's the last of the china. I must go and see to my family now'—Jo and Frieda had already departed to seek theirs—'and you can tidy up and lock up and come over to us when you like. Only, don't be later than about eight o'clock, will you?'

Debby agreed, and Marie left her to go and see what her son and daughter had been up to while she had been gone. She found them sitting in the orchard listening while Sybil told them of school doings which lost nothing of excitement in her tale. Marie collected Josefa, since it was now after six, and bore her off to bed, leaving the elder two alone. In the bathroom she found Jo tubbing Stephen, while Simone saw to Tessa. The triplets were undressing in their mother's room with shrieks of laughter, and Frieda was putting tiny Gerard into his cot.

'You dear, Simone!' said her friend. 'Thank you for looking after my bad family. I hope they've been good?'

'Good as gold and twice as precious,' said Simone with a smile. 'One of us had to be with the children. It was me this time. Another time, someone else will do it. There! Tessa is done, so you can have the bath.' And she lifted her little daughter on to her lap and began to dry her tenderly, while Marie slipped off the frock, knickers, and vest which formed Josefa's attire, and then popped her into the bath and began to scrub her well.

The girls were unable to talk privately until all the smaller folk were safely in bed. Simone finished Tessa, heard her prayers, and put her down. Then she went to see what was happening in Jo's room, and found the triplets capering gaily about in their vests, while their other garments strewed the floor in all directions.

'Oh, méchantes!' she exclaimed. 'Pick up your things quickly or Mamma will be so cross with you. Where are your dressing-gowns? Put them on, and get your sleeping-suits. Here comes Mamma with Stephen, so I will take you to the bathroom while she finishes him and puts him into his cot. Come along, quickly.'

Jo, burdened by a Stephen who was inclined to be cross, gave her a grateful smile as she chased the little girls out of the room, picking up their towels as she went. 'Thank you, Simone. I'm afraid Stephen is beginning to feel his teeth, he's so crotchety this evening. I'm longing to get down for a chat with you people, but I must see him safely asleep before I leave him. I only hope he isn't going to make a night of it!' Simone laughed and went out, shutting the door behind her.

'How Simone has changed,' Jo mused, as she sat, nursing the baby. 'When I remember what she was like those first years at school, and see her as she is now, I can scarcely believe it's the same girl!' And her mind went back to schooldays, when Simone, very shy, sentimentally fond of herself, and desperately jealous of every other friend she had, caused both of them a good deal of trouble by frequent scenes. It *was* hard to believe that the jealous, emotional child had grown into this quiet, self-controlled, helpful woman who rarely seemed to think of herself, but generally saw the next thing to do and did it without fuss or remark. 'It was partly school, of course,' she went on, 'but I think it was also Mademoiselle's death, and then her own marriage and Tessa's coming.' And again she thought back to the days when the school had been ruled by Simone's cousin, Mademoiselle Lepattre. After her own sister had married Jem Russell, Mademoiselle had been

Head of the school until six years ago, when her serious illness had ended that.

Mademoiselle had been an invalid when Hitler had marched into Austria, and she and Simone's parents, M. and Mme Lecoutier, had left the Sonnalpe where they had been living. The long journey back to Paris had ended what the illness had begun; and Mademoiselle had died during the first term the school had reopened in Guernsey. So she had never lived to see what the Nazis had made of her beloved France. M. and Mme Lecoutier had escaped to England at the beginning of the war, and then had got to Canada where a sister of hers lived in Quebec. But Simone was mathematics mistress at the school, and besides, was engaged to André de Bersac, so she had remained. Sitting there, Jo smiled again to herself as she traced the changes in Simone. Then she found that Stephen was drowsing, so she rose, carried him over to his cot and laid him in it, and then, when she felt sure that he was practically asleep, changed from the morning cotton she was still wearing into something rather more appropriate to the time of day, and began to tidy the room. The triplets came in, sweet and fresh from their baths. Len and Con were both sleeping upstairs in Sybil's room, but Margot had the camp-bed at the far side of her mother's. Jo looked at her doubtfully.

'I—wonder. Simone, would you let Margot sleep upstairs, do you think? Stephen's quiet at the moment, but his poor little gums are hot and I'm afraid we may have a disturbed night. I don't want Margot wakened up halfway through. When Stephen yells, he *yells*!'

'It will be very hot with four of them up there,' said Simone. 'Why not let Margot come in with Tessa and me? We can put her at the foot of the bed. Tessa is still awake. I peeped in at her when I brought your girls along. Let Margot come to us for once, Jo.'

Margot was delighted at the idea. 'Oooh, Mamma! Do let me

sleep wif Tessa! Please do! I'll be everso, neverso good if you will!'

'Good—you?' teased Jo. 'Why, you couldn't.'

'Oh, Mamma, I could—I could! I pwomise you!' Margot's eyes were very pleading. 'Tante Simone, I won't 'sturb Tessa. Ask Mamma! Please do!'

'Let her come, Jo,' urged Simone. 'If Stephen is likely to be restless he'll certainly wake Margot. I know he's a placid baby as a rule, but I also know what he's like when he *does* cry. Far better let her come in with us. She'll be no trouble. I've often felt I ought to have one of them with us in any case, as I have only Tessa.'

Jo laughed. 'You haven't given me much chance to do anything but say "Yes," have you?' she said. 'Very well, Margot. But remember, precious, you must be very good if I do let you go. I'll hear their prayers, Simone, and then bring Margot along in case Tessa drops off soon. We don't want her disturbed. I only hope Stephen doesn't rouse the entire house.'

'He seems to be all right now,' said Simone, bending over the cot. 'What a lovely boy he is, Jo! Well, I'll go along to Tessa, and you bring Margot when she's said her prayers.' She went out, and Jo, sitting down again at the window, collected her daughters round her for prayers and their good-night talk. This was the time when the little girls always confessed to any small sins during the day, and they talked them over seriously. Tonight, there was very little. Con informed her mother that she had stolen two spoonfuls of sugar when Tante Simone's back was turned, and Len had to confess to calling Sybil 'You pig!' which drew from Jo the remark that if she said such things again her mouth would be soaped out. Len looked very serious at this, but said no more, and it was Margot's turn.

'I stamped my foot at Sybs,' she said. 'An'—an' I called Auntie Mawie a howwid old fing 'cos she scolded 'bout the sugar.'

'Oh, Margot! That was very naughty. You must try to keep your temper, darling. Do you want to grieve the little Christ Child?'

'No, Mamma. But when vere's such lots an' *lots* of little girls an' boys can He hear just *me*?'

'Yes, my pet. He always knows when we do wrong because He is God. So we must try with all our might not to do things that will hurt Him. Now, Margot, you were rude to Auntie Marie as well. What must you do?'

Margot's small face went red. She was a proud little person who hated saying she was sorry, and her quick temper forced her to it a good many times in the week. But she knew there was no help for it. If *she* didn't do it, Mamma would—*for* her and in front of her, which would be worse.

'I'll tell Auntie I'm sowwy,' she said meekly.

Jo bent and kissed her. 'That's right, pet. And Len must not call names, either. And Con, if you don't leave the sugar alone, something very unpleasant will happen to you. And now, my darlings, kiss Mamma, and then we'll have our prayers. Tomorrow is a new day, and we'll all try to keep it a good one.'

They clung round her a moment. Then they knelt down and said their prayers, and after more kisses Jo escorted Margot along to Simone's room, where she was tucked up at the foot of Tessa's bed, and the other two were taken upstairs, and then Jo, feeling her labours over for the present, ran downstairs to see to supper, for Frieda was still busy with Louis, and Marie was out in the orchard to bring Wolferl in. Simone, having bidden Tessa and Margot not to talk, presently joined her, and by the time the other two were ready, and Sybil had been called into the kitchen for her milk and bread-and-butter, supper was ready. Sybil was despatched bedwards with her book, and permission to read till half-past eight. Then the four friends settled down for a cosy chat which mainly centred round Phoebe and the 'cello. They discussed the questions in all their bearings, and were still at it when they saw Debby coming up the path. Simone ran to open the front door, and they asked if she had had her supper. Independent Debby had had all she wanted, thank you. If the ladies had done, she would just clear away, and then, if they would excuse her, she would go to bed.

'We'll clear, Debby. You're too tired,' said Jo, with a pitying eye on Debby's rather drawn face. She could see that the old woman had been shedding tears, and she thought that bed would be the best cure for her troubles; but Debby was adamant. If she came to The Witchens to sleep, then she was going to do certain things for them. They gave in, for they all saw that she was not fit for an argument; but each one of them vowed to herself to have a word or two to say on the morrow. So Debby washed up, laid the breakfast table, and then Marie showed her to her room, and after seeing that she had all she needed, and looking in on Sybil on the way down to bid her put her book away and go to sleep, returned yawning to suggest that bed would be a good idea for themselves after the scrambled day they had had.

'Jack won't ring up tonight, will he, Jo?' she asked.

Jo shook her head. 'No; he said he would send me a card to let us know how Phoebe got on, and write a long letter tomorrow when they'd had a chance to examine her. Well, if Stephen is going to wake up later on, I suppose it would be as well to get what sleep I can. We'll lock up, and go up. I only hope that son of mine will behave himself.'

They laughed as they went to see to the locking-up, and by half-past nine the house was silent.

It was half-past one before Stephen, who had slept quietly up till then, stirred, and began to whimper. Jo sat up at once, and turned up the little hand-lamp she kept burning all night on the bedside table. The boy was moving uneasily on his pillow, and his cheeks were flushed. She tried to make him comfortable, but his teeth were bothering him and he refused to be pacified. She gave him a sip of boiled water, turned his pillow, then she laid him back, and waited to see what would happen. For about ten minutes he lay quiet, the coolness and change of position bringing him a little relief. But that was all. He started whimpering again, and the whimper rose louder. Jo got up, put on her slippers, and taking the baby from his cot, laid him across her shoulder, and began to move up and down the room, patting his shoulder gently and murmuring lovingly to him. After twenty minutes of this, he seemed inclined to doze off again, and she went to the cot. But the moment she moved his position, he started again. Jo sighed, for she was tired; but she seemed to have no choice in the matter. Either she must sit up with him, or she must be prepared for his whimpers to become roars which would certainly rouse most of the household, and that was not to be thought of for a moment.

'Poor little man,' she said softly, laying her own cool cheek against the small head with its yellow fluff. 'Mamma's poor little man. Come and sit down and Mamma will rub his gums a little.'

She sat down, turning down the lamp again, and pulling the curtains apart. Very gently, she began to rub the hot, swollen gum. It seemed to bring him relief, for he began to drowse off, the undried tears still on his hot cheeks. But the moment she tried to withdraw her finger, the wail started. For two solid hours Jo sat there, trying one simple remedy after another. Nothing did any good till, just as the grandfather clock in the hall chimed the unearthly hour of four, Stephen gave a sudden gulp, turned his head to her, and fell into a quiet sleep.

Jo sat where she was a little longer. Then, as the pain seemed to have ended for the time being, she got up, laid the boy in his cot and covered him up, and stood watching him for a few minutes. He gave a little grunt, and snuggled into his cool pillow, but that was all. He was well and truly over. Jo was just about to get into bed, when a sound sent her to the window. Rufus, who slept in the kitchen, had growled, a deep growl of disapproval and warning, from the foot of the stairs. Jo was at the window in a flash, and was just in time to see a very tall man turn away from the gate and enter a car standing a little distance away. From the way it started, with scarcely any noise, and certainly none to disturb anyone who was asleep, she argued that it was an expensive car, and therefore, the intruder was Mr Burthill himself. But Rufus was growling again, and she must stop him. Not for worlds would she have had Stephen roused again. She slipped out of the room, and downstairs to Rufus, who wagged his tail, but still kept looking at the door warily. There was only one thing to do. Jo did it. Very quietly, and with one ear listening for any sounds from Stephen, she unfastened the door, and was about to let the dog out when her eye was caught by a dark blotch on the grass near the gate. Regardless of the fact that she was not wearing a dressing-gown, she sped down and picked it up. It was a huge lump of raw meat!

For a moment she was so furious that she could scarcely see. Then she carried it in, locked it up in the kitchen cupboard, and went out again and searched the entire lawn before she allowed Rufus to come out with her. He was satisfied in a very few minutes that the invader had gone, and came back with her. She took him up to her own room, where her boy had not stirred. Rufus went over to the window and dropped down. Jo, at long last, got back into bed, turning the lamp out, for the dawn was now flushing the sky. But before she lay down, she hung over the side of the cot for a moment.

'Thanks, sonny boy,' she said below her breath. 'If you hadn't put a finger in the pie—and a most definite finger too, bless you!—we might have lost our precious old Rufus. The *brute*!—the *cad*!' Then she lay down, and in five minutes was sleeping as soundly as her son.

Chapter X

THE NEXT STEP

'Jo—Jo! Wake up! *Joey!* Do you hear? We want the key of the kitchen cupboard! Oh, someone else try! The girl's in a trance!' And Marie threw up her hands and turned away from the bed where Jo lay sleeping.

Simone chuckled. 'Have you forgotten, Marie? See here!' And she stroked Jo's cheek, and that lady's long black lashes lifted, and she stared up foggily at the two standing on either side of her bed.

'What *have* you been doing overnight?' demanded Marie. 'And do you know where the key of the kitchen cupboard is?'

Jo sat up. 'Where's Rufus?' she demanded in her turn.

'In the garden, of course. I heard him thumping at your door, so I came— Goodness, Jo! What's wrong with you?' For with one bound Jo was out of the bed and hanging out of the window, calling Rufus urgently.

At this point, Stephen, who had been making little noises for the last ten minutes or so without getting any satisfaction, made up his mind to let his mother know that he was hungry, and roared. Jo left the window and ran to pick him up. 'What's the time? Oh, poor little man! It's half an hour after his time. There—there, my lamb!' She sat on the side of the bed, Stephen soothed at once, and looked at the other two with wide, serious eyes. 'I've had a night of it, I can tell you! The key is under my pillow, Marie. Take it, but don't interfere with the chunk of meat you'll find in the cupboard. That's going straight to the police.'

'Meat? Straight to the police?' repeated Marie dazedly. 'What *are* you talking about? Are you having nightmare with your eyes open, by any chance?'

'That brute of a man tried to poison my Rufus during the night!' said Jo, her voice shaking with anger at the bare thought.

'*What?*' The other two were agog at once. 'How do you know?'

'I saw him at it!'

'YOU SAW HIM AT IT? Jo!' Marie's eyes looked ready to fall out of her head, and Simone's were not a whit better. The key was forgotten as they plumped down, one on each side of Jo, and demanded the story.

Jo needed no urging. She told the tale with all the drama possible when her hands were very occupied with a big baby, and the others listened with exclamations of horror and anger as she proceeded. She had just finished when Frieda came in to see what was wrong, and she, too, had to be told. Finally, Frieda got the key and went off, promising that the meat should be untouched, and warning Jo that breakfast would be ready shortly.

'Was Margot good?' asked Jo, as she finally laid a satisfied Stephen back in his cot and began to gather her towels together.

'Good as could be. We rather thought you might have had a bad night with Stephen, so did not disturb you till we wanted the coffee from the cupboard and could not find the key,' said Simone. 'They are all downstairs and having their fruit-juice. Breakfast will be ready shortly.'

'Thanks very much, whoever helped the girlies,' called Jo as she vanished into the bathroom, whence she presently emerged, looking and feeling much fresher for a cold splash. She hurried into her clothes, and arrived downstairs shortly after the rest had sat down with the news that Stephen was sleeping again, and seemed much cooler. 'So I hope he will be able to get whatever tooth is bothering him cut without much more trouble,' she concluded. 'And now, what are we going to do about this attempt to poison my Rufus?'

'Take the meat to the police and see what they've used,' advised Marie. 'But I should like to know why they should try to get him out of the way.'

Later, they were to discover that Zephyr had stopped the car outside the village to make inquiries of a passer-by about Mrs Maynard. A chance word had told her that Phoebe, too, lived in the village, and on reaching home she had gone straight to her father and told him her story with tears of wounded vanity as she thought of Jo's words to her.

Mr Burthill listened with fury rising in his heart. 'Don't cry, my darling,' he said, pulling her on to his knee. 'It's not worth spoiling those pretty eyes over. You shall have the 'cello, I promise you. Daddy will get it for you somehow. You'll make yourself ill if you fret so, and then what shall I do? Here, take my handkerchief and dry your eyes. You shall have it, if I have to break into the house myself. I promise you that. So don't cry.'

Zephyr dried her eyes, and then, mindful of what tears did to her make-up, went off to repair the damage, sure that the 'cello would be hers before long; and '*that* would show that horrid woman!'

Later on her father had called her to his study again and asked her to tell him all she had learned about The Witchens and Many Bushes. He had made a face when he heard of Rufus. He did not wish to harm the dog, but there was no doubt that he would be a danger. But he had passed his word to his girl, and she should have the thing since her heart was so set on it. The chances were that he would have tried to get the Crown jewels for her if she had wanted them, and such a thing were possible. If ever a girl was adored by a parent to the point of sheer folly, that girl was Zephyr Burthill!

It was a piece of luck that she had found out that Phoebe Wychcote lived in the same village. He knew of one or two people unscrupulous enough to do as he wanted, and he thought the 'cello would soon be Zephyr's now. He set off for the big city near which they lived after he had had his dinner, to seek those who would help him. When it was all over and they had the instrument safely, he would manage somehow to send Phoebe the money he had offered for it, then they would be quits.

All this was hidden from Jo and the rest at the moment, however, and once they had had breakfast, and the children were all out playing in the orchard, while Jo and Frieda bathed and dressed their babies they discussed the night's big event with vim.

'I don't think I should trouble the police,' said Marie at last. 'Not Bert Trinder, anyhow. If you must see them, I should go to Garnley and see the head there. Bert Trinder may be all right for little things, but I don't think he would be much good in an affair like this.'

'I'm not going to the police at all,' declared Jo, as she slipped Stephen's frock over his head with a deftness born of much practice. 'I'm going to the vet. He's the best man. If we go to the police there may be all sorts of fusses, and we don't want that. I'll see what Mr Grey says, and talk it over with him. In the meantime, someone must keep an eye on Rufus. There, my lad! That's done for the day!'

And she held the baby up away from her, and eyed his clean frock approvingly.

'Is the tooth nearly through?' asked Marie. 'Let me feel.'

Cautiously she slipped a finger into Stephen's mouth, to withdraw it with a yell. That young man, resenting the liberty, had bitten her well and truly. Jo, nearly choking with laughter, turned him back on her arm, and, warned by Marie's mishap, felt the gum gingerly. A tiny point was just through the gum, and the gums themselves were as hard as could be.

'It's through,' she announced. 'I can just feel the point.'

'So did I,' Marie assured her ruefully, rubbing her finger. 'You'd better give him rusks, Jo, to help them through. There's a tinful in my room. I'll get them for him. And if you're going into Garnley, you'd better see if you can get a bone ring for him.'

'I've got the old corals here,' said Jo cheerfully. 'When we came away Jack said he thought the teeth might begin at any time. Give me one of those bibs, Frieda. He's dribbling badly. And I'm not going to Garnley. What have we got a 'phone for? I'll ring him up and ask him to come here. Then we can tell him the whole tale, and give him the meat for analysis. Thanks, Frieda. Now, my lad, lift up your chin, and let Mamma tie this. Oh, where's the oilsilk one, first? He'll soon have this soaked at the present rate he's going. Thanks, Marie. There; that's better. Now I'll take him down and lay him in the pram outside. Is Gerard ready, Frieda?'

'Just,' said Frieda with a smile. 'Come along. We'll put them down, and then get the beds done. Have you got the coral thing, Jo?'

'No; it's in the top drawer. Simone, you're nearest.'

Simone found the old silver bells and coral on which the last five generations of Maynard babies had cut their teeth, and Jo tucked it into the pocket of her overall. The babies were put down in the big double pram and left under a lime-tree in the front garden, and then Jo went to the telephone while the others scattered upstairs to make beds and tidy up the bedrooms. Sybil made her own bed, and so did Wolferl with a little help from her; but the tinies were not much use as yet, though Marie called Josefa to come and help her. The four had decided to bring up their families to be useful, and all the children who were three or over had their own little chores to do each day.

The vet duly called during the morning, and after examining the meat took it away, promising to send a report as soon as possible. He looked at Rufus, pronounced him a fine specimen and in grand condition, and then departed. The rest of the day passed without incident, and so did the night. Stephen, having got the tooth through, slept in his usual whole-hearted way, but in his waking hours they noticed that his fists went to his mouth a good deal, and Jo felt certain that there were more wakeful nights before her.

No message came from the Sanatorium that day; but early the next afternoon Jo was called to the 'phone, when Jack told her that Phoebe was reacting to treatment very well. The worst of her pain was over, and she was sitting up in bed with her work and books.

'Does Dr Peters think there can be a real cure after all?' asked Jo.

'He doesn't say so, and I doubt it,' replied her husband. 'Don't be silly, Jo. It's far too soon to tell yet. What we all think is that her worst attacks can be relieved; and Jem thinks we can strengthen the heart. But that's all at present. You won't get anything more for some weeks or even months to come. How are the small fry?'

'Very well. Stephen gave me a night of it on Monday, but the tooth is through. He's dribbling a lot, though, so I'm prepared for more of it. How is Madge?'

'Very well. Jem will be over on Friday if nothing occurs, so he can give you all the news then. Let him look at Stephen while he's there.'

'Of course. I say, Jack—' But at that point they were rung off, and Jo hung up the receiver without saying anything about the further excitements of Monday night as she had suddenly meant to do. She turned away, and went to sit in the garden where the rest were reading, toying with mending, or just chatting. She gave them the news about Phoebe, and then, calling Rufus, went across to Many Bushes to tell Debby too. The 'cello was safely tucked away in the little boxroom at The Witchens, and

Reg had reported only that morning that the only strangers were people who had cycled over from Garnley to get to the moors, and they had gone straight through the village. They were laden with baskets, and he had scouted after them and seen them sitting among the purple heather, picnicking.

Debby was delighted to hear the good news. A postcard from Phoebe had been waiting for her at Many Bushes, and the old woman had begun to hope that a cure might be made. In her joy she was turning out the little sitting-room, and Jo strolled up the path between chairs, tables, and piles of books, music, magazines, and papers. Debby herself was out in the little courtyard at the back, beating the rugs with might and main.

'You bad old thing!' cried Jo when she found her. 'It's far too hot for work like this! What *would* Phoebe say if she saw you?'

'The place has got to be kept clean,' returned Debby, leaning on her stick. 'When young Reg comes along, I'll get him to help me take the carpet up and beat that too.'

'You'll do no such thing! It's blazing hot and going to be hotter. Give me a broom and I'll have a go at it. But take it up and beat it on a day like this you shall *not*!' And Jo sounded very fierce.

Debby looked at her, saw she meant what she said, and gave in, though she flatly refused to let Jo do the sweeping. That young lady had to be satisfied with what she had got, and finally went back to the family, where she found Reg showing Sybil, Josefa, and Wolferl how to make whistles by removing the pith from willow-stems. The noise they made when whistles for everyone had been finished was deafening, and woke the four tinies who had all been asleep. Easy-going Jo laughed, and soon hushed her son's roars, while Frieda did the same for Gerard. But Marie ordered the noisy crowd to the far end of the orchard where they could make all the noise they pleased, and Rufus departed with them.

At twelve o'clock, when Reg had gone to seek his dinner, and the triplets had been sent to lie down for a nap, the vet arrived with his report.

'Not poison,' he said. 'It was something guaranteed to make him distinctly under the weather for a few days, but it wouldn't have killed him. Now, Mrs Maynard, what do you want to do? Will you inform the police?'

Jo thought. 'No, I don't think so,' she said at last. 'Trinder here couldn't do much, and it would mean sending to Garnley. I could send Rufus home, of course, but I don't want to do that. He always frets so when he isn't with me. I think he'll be safe enough. He won't touch food as a rule unless one of us gives it to him. We'll keep him with us, and I think he'll be safe enough then.'

'But what is the meaning of it all?' demanded the vet. He glanced round the room with its pretty but inexpensive furnishings. 'You haven't any valuable jewellery or anything of that kind here, have you?'

'Do we look like it?' laughed Jo, who certainly did *not*, in her old cotton frock which had started life pale blue, but was now greyish in tone.

'Then what is the meaning of it? There's something behind this, Mrs Maynard, and even if you won't get the police, I'm none so sure that I ought not to see to it myself.'

'You can't if I refuse you permission,' flashed Jo.

'Oh, yes, I can. Or else I can write to your husband. Come, Mrs Maynard. I don't want to seem rude; but you are four women with a crowd of small children, and the dog is your best defence. Plainly someone wants to put him out of action. Now, why? I must know.'

Seeing no help for it, Jo gave him the bare bones of the story, adding, 'But my brother-in-law is coming to see us on Friday, and he will take the 'cello back with him, and once it's gone I intend to tell everyone that it's been taken away, so that will put a stop to any hanky-panky tricks here. They haven't done anything since Monday night, and Reg Entwistle is keeping an eye open for any strangers. He's all there, and he'll soon let us know if anyone does turn up. Please, Mr Grey, I'd rather you didn't do anything more about it. And I don't want my husband worried at present, because he's worked off his head at the San. just now. And you can see for yourself how little we have to go on. The police would most likely just laugh at us.'

'They would not—not after the attempt to upset the dog. That's proof positive that there's some sort of mischief going on. I won't write to Dr Maynard, but I must report the affair at the police station.'

From this stand he was not to be moved, so Jo gave in with none too good a grace, and he went off, fully intending to call in at the Garnley police station on his way home. But halfway there, he was summoned by a wild-eyed small boy to come to a mare who had had a serious accident, and he was held up for several hours at the farm. He called in at his house on his way into Garnley, and found three urgent messages awaiting him, so that he had barely time to swallow a cup of coffee before he had to go off in the other direction. He tried to get the police on the 'phone, but the number was engaged, and though he gave his housekeeper a message for them she forgot all about it, and with the press of work the whole thing passed out of his mind.

Meanwhile a telephone message from home told Jo that her brother-in-law was coming the next day, and would stay till the Saturday, so they had to decide where to sleep him for the two nights. Debby finally came to the rescue by offering Phoebe's room, and they accepted the offer with thanks. The rest of the day was spent in putting the room ready, and once more they passed a peaceful night.

Sir James Russell arrived next day, bringing with him sundry belongings for them all, and messages by the score. All was well at home, and Phoebe had been allowed to sit up in a chair the day before, and seemed fairly well again. They had not yet begun the injections, but would do so in a week's time. He told the girls frankly that complete cure could not be looked for, save by a miracle. But everyone at the Sanatorium felt that her condition could be greatly alleviated. He exclaimed at the tanned creatures who greeted him, examined Stephen, and said he thought the teeth were well on the way, and would soon be through. Then they took him over to Many Bushes and introduced him to Debby.

Debby looked at the great doctor with awe, a little tempered by finding him such a young man. She had expected to see an elderly gentleman, but there was nothing elderly about Jem Russell, who looked a good ten years less than the forty-eight he laid claim to, and who was determined to enjoy his brief holiday. He teased the girls, romped with the children, and generally conducted himself, as Jo told him, as if he were no older than his own son.

'You are the limit!' she said indignantly as she sat down to recoil the long plaits that had tumbled down as a result of the merciless tickling he had treated her to in return for much teasing about his proposed cure for baldness. 'Another time, Jem Russell, I'll wear a net.'

'Not you. You'll never remember where you've put it,' he told her.

'Never mind that,' said Marie, coming from the kitchen where she had been preparing supper. 'Come and help to carry in. Everything's ready, and the coffee is only to heat up.'

After supper they sat talking quietly in the garden till half-past nine, when they went off to bed. Jem was taken over to Many Bushes, and left there, and the girls, having locked up, retired quickly. They were all tired with the hot day and Jem's teasing. By ten every light was out, and the only sounds at The Witchens were occasional cries from little Margot, who was given to talking in her sleep, and Debby's heavy snoring.

Chapter XI

THAT NIGHT!

JEM RUSSELL was as tired as the girls. He tossed off his clothes, and was speedily in bed and asleep. But, doctor fashion, he slept with one ear open, and when a rising breeze began to swing the gate backwards and forwards to a melancholy tune of squeaky hinges, he roused up, cursed the gate, and got out of bed. If he were to get any more sleep he must shut the wretched thing safely. Yawning widely, he pulled on his jacket, shoved his feet into his carpet slippers, and padded downstairs. The door took some opening, for the lock was an old-fashioned one, and the key turned stiffly. At last it was done, and he stepped out quietly on to the narrow, flagged path. The flags struck chill to his slippered feet, and they were rough besides, so he got off them on to the grass. He had just reached the hedge when a great car swept almost silently round the turn and drew up a little way away from The Witchens. Two men got out, and stood for a moment or two at the far side. One of them must have got back again, for only one appeared beyond the bonnet. He went quietly, almost stealthily, it seemed to Jem, who was staring with all his eyes at the proceedings. He had ducked down behind the hedge, but there were breaks in it, and he could see what was going on fairly well. The man reached the stone wall of The Witchens garden, looked carefully round, and then clambered over it with the utmost precaution. He reached the other side, walked across the lawn, and disappeared round the side of the house. Presently he reappeared at the other side, and made a beckoning sign. A second man left the car and joined him, again climbing over the wall. By this time the stupefied Jem had come to his senses, and was crawling on all-fours back to Many Bushes to see if they had a telephone.

In the meantime, at The Witchens, Rufus, sleeping on the landing outside Jo's door, lifted an uneasy head and listened. There was no sound beyond the accustomed ones, so he dropped back and went to sleep again. Margot suddenly began struggling in the throes of nightmare, and muttered violently. Jo roused almost at once, and getting out of bed went across the room and turned her on to her side, murmuring to herself, 'I thought so many apples would upset her. She'd better have something tomorrow.' She glanced at Stephen, but he was fast asleep. Then she decided that she was thirsty and could do with a drink of water. No; tea! Nice tea! It would be the work of a few minutes to light the Primus in the kitchen and she need wake nobody if she took her torch.

With Jo, to think was to act. She picked up her torch, tossed her dressing-gown round her, and after a last look to make sure that both the children were all right, slipped out of the room—nearly falling over Rufus as she did so—and went downstairs, followed by her faithful hound, as she said later when telling the story, and leaving the bedroom door open.

'Quiet, old man,' she murmured to the dog as they went. 'For goodness' sake don't disturb anyone, or they'll think we're being well and truly burgled after all.' And she chuckled to herself as she thought of the sensation they would cause. She led the way to the kitchen, lit the Primus, and went to the cupboard to get a cup and saucer.

At the same time she set the tap running to give Rufus a cold drink. Therefore neither of them heard any sound till the door leading to the courtyard suddenly opened, and a little, thin man with a rat-like face appeared at it. He was followed by a big, burly fellow. Both wore rough clothes, and both had handkerchiefs tied round the lower part of the face. It was a dramatic moment!

Rufus, who was in the scullery, heard his mistress gasp, and appeared at the door. He uttered a deep growl, and Jo, rousing from the trance of surprise which had held her till then, snatched up the first thing that came handy—the big frying-pan, in which Debby had put the rashers of bacon for the morning, carefully covering them from flies with a large enamel plate—and hurled the whole lot, frying-pan, plate, and rashers, straight at the intruders. For a girl she had a remarkably straight aim. The pan hit the taller man squarely on the side of the head and he dropped where he stood, stunned, for being made of iron it was heavy. The smaller man got the plate on his mouth, and the flying rashers were strewn over his head. At almost the same moment he received the full weight of Rufus's bulk as that wise animal hurtled across the kitchen like a war-horse, and landed on his chest. Jo's shriek as she flung her missile would have outdone anything the worst banshee ever known to Ireland could have produced. The noise caused by all this naturally woke the children and the other sleepers. The little ones set up wails of protest, and the rest came tumbling pell-mell down the stairs to the kitchen. There they found Jo struggling to keep Rufus from hurting anyone, two terrified men on the floor, one still looking dazed, and Jem Russell just irrupting through the doorway with angry demands to know what all this meant.

By degrees the tumult was quelled. Simone and Frieda raced upstairs again to calm the babies. Rufus was dragged off his victim, who rose declaiming bitterly that his new 'plate' was broken with the force of Jo's effort—and held out a handful of cracked plate and loose teeth as proof. Bert Trinder, the village constable, drawn to the spot by the noise, promptly arrested the pair, and, aided by Jem, haled them off to the outside shed where they were shut into the inner half, since they could not hope to escape from there. Then he commandeered the telephone, and by four o'clock the intruders were well on their way to Garnley gaol. Meanwhile, Marie had slipped on a piece of fat bacon and measured her length, bumping her head against the corner of the dresser. Jem ministered to her, and Debby, snatching the kettle off the Primus just in time to prevent its boiling dry, refilled it, and made preparations for tea for everyone.

'You'll have a nice black eye, I'm afraid, Marie,' said Sir James as he finished with her. 'Jo, are you hurt anywhere?'

But Jo was past speaking. Rocking backwards and forwards on the settle in a positive agony of laughter, she only waved her hands feebly, and went off again. Jem decided that it was a case for strong measures. He snatched a cup from the tray, filled it with water, and advanced on his sister-in-law, grim determination on his face.

'Now then, young Jo,' he said, 'stop these hysterics at once, or you'll get a good shower-bath to cool you down.'

Jo made a wild effort to pull herself together. 'I'm not—hysterical,' she managed to gasp. 'I'm—only—*laughing*!' Then off she went again.

Jem shook her slightly. 'Stop it, you silly creature! You're actually crying with laughter! Jo! do you hear me? Stop it, I say!'

Thus adjured, Jo contrived to control herself, and a good strong cup of Debby's tea helped her, though she made faces as she swallowed the bitter compound. Debby had made it to her own taste.

'And now,' said Marie when she was sober again, 'perhaps you'll tell us what was so funny. Now don't begin again! Jem's got that water handy still, and if you start, I'd advise him to use it at once. But in the meantime, we'd all like to know what the joke of being burgled is.'

'It wasn't that, exactly.' Jo's voice wobbled ominously, but she managed to steady it. 'It was the whole thing. That man's face when the plate hit him in the mouth—and his false teeth all smashed up—and the bacon everywhere. But Trinder was the last straw. Did you *see* him? He must have heard the noise and been wakened by it. He—he had on—pyjamas—and his—*helmet*!' She stopped, unable to continue as the picture of the stolid village constable as she had last seen him rose before her eyes.

The rest laughed unrestrainedly. Bert Trinder in pyjamas of violent orange and yellow stripes, with his helmet perched on top of his head and his feet in a pair of purple slippers embroidered by Mrs Trinder, was, as Jem agreed, enough to make a cat laugh. But they had had a very broken night, so he suggested that it would be advisable to get back to bed for what was left of it. Jo, at any rate, had to go to Garnley in the morning to be interviewed by the police, and it was now five.

'Off to bed, all of you,' he said. 'You can get three hours' sleep if you go at once. We'll have to get off early tonight to make up for what we've lost. And I should recommend a nap this afternoon, as well. Goodbye. I'm going. I'll be over for breakfast about half-past eight, when you can tell me the whole story. So far, all I know is that Miss Wychcote's 'cello is at the bottom of all this. Jo, take that dog of yours to the hall. Frieda, you're not to get up till I've seen you. You're as white as chalk at the moment. Goodbye!' And he departed, leaving them to obey him meekly.

It was nearly nine before anyone got downstairs again, for, once in bed, they all slept heavily after the excitement. But at ten to nine Marie slipped down to fill the big kettle and put it on before she had her bath. Then, moving quietly, she dressed and came down again, and by the time Simone, who was next to awaken, had appeared, the kettle was boiling, fresh bacon was sizzling in the pan, and Marie was putting the finishing touches to the table. Debby then came and took charge, and Jo, accompanied by Rufus, was the last. The children, needless to state, had risen at their usual early hour, and were all out in the garden. They had washed and dressed themselves, Sybil and Wolferl lending assistance where necessary. Jem, having overslept himself considerably, came in at half-past nine to find the others dawdling over the end of their meal, while the little ones were all out in the orchard again.

'The *late* Sir James Russell,' said Jo as he entered. 'Mourned by all who knew him! Aren't you afraid you may make yourself ill with all this early rising, my love? You should be careful, you know.'

He chuckled as he sat down. 'It doesn't look as though any of you people had much to boast about in that line. Frieda still in bed? Good girl! Marie, I'll look at that eye after I've fed. It's better than I thought it would be. Did you all sleep after I left you?'

'Like the dead,' said Jo, bringing in his coffee. 'At least, I did. I know nothing about the rest. Stephen woke me at half-past six for his breakfast, and I shoved his bottle in beside him—in my sleep, I think. However, he was all right when I finally woke. Here's Simone with your bacon. It's the last we have unless I can get any in Garnley. But I don't want to stay. I want to get the one o'clock bus. So if they keep me too long at the police station, there'll be no bacon for tomorrow unless anyone can wangle some out of Mrs Jaycott. Simone, she loves you best. What about taking the family along there and seeing what she can do for us?'

'I will go with pleasure,' said Simone. 'Frieda had better stay in bed, I suppose. She seemed worn out when I looked in for Louis. You'll leave Rufus with us, won't you, Jo? I'd like to know he was here. Though,' she added, 'I scarcely think there will be any further attempt to burgle us after last night's failure.'

'Oh, Rufus must stay,' agreed Jo. 'He's too big for the bus. What time is it? Twenty to ten! Good gracious! I must fly or I shall miss the bus, and there isn't another till something past two.

I should think that police sergeant—or superintendent, or whatever he is—would simply chatter with rage if I didn't turn up at eleven as I was told. Goodbye, everyone!' And she fled upstairs to powder her nose and get her hat and gloves. Jem was ready for her when she came down, and they set off by a short cut over the fields, having left themselves barely time to catch the bus.

It was after three when they returned, having had to endure close questioning on the events of the night. Jo had been very proper, Jem told the girls, and very much Mrs Maynard. As for the men, they had refused to say why they had broken into The Witchens, and when Jo flatly accused them of trying to steal the 'cello, they denied it. They had seen the place, and wanted food, they said. That was what they had come for. They did not know anything about any 'cello.

Jo opened her lips to confute this. Then she closed them again. Finally, the men had been taken back to the cells, to be brought before the magistrates next morning, when the police would apply for a remand to make further investigations.

'So that means trailing in to Garnley again tomorrow,' complained Jo. 'Well, I can get the bacon then. Did you have any luck with Mrs Jaycott, Simone? No? Oh, well, I can get it tomorrow, and we must do with toast and marmalade for once. And I can see you off, Jem, so it's all to the good.'

'I'm not going,' returned her brother-in-law calmly. 'I'm going to ring up the Round House presently, and tell Madge I'm staying till Monday. In the meantime, I think it would be as well if you people packed up and prepared to come back with me. I don't want to leave you girls here without a man to look after you.'

'Oh no, my dear, we don't do that!' retorted Jo. 'On the contrary, you can take the 'cello back with you. And I'll tell you what!' with a sudden inspiration, 'you can take it to the San. and park it there. No one in his senses would go hunting through that mammoth of a place to look for anything, so it'll be safe enough.

And, once it's gone, we shall be safe too. I intend to spread it abroad that the thing's gone. As for Mr Burthill, I should think he'll tell his precious Zephyr to cry her eyes out if she must, but he won't have any more shots at giving her her own way about this.'

'Jo, will you hold your tongue about Mr Burthill?' said Sir James. 'We have no direct proof that he hired these men to steal the 'cello, and unless we can find any, you'll be landed with a slander action if you talk like that. But unless the police can unearth any evidence to connect him with this, I don't see what we can do about it if both they and he choose to deny the whole thing.'

'But—the attempt to hurt Rufus?' exclaimed Marie.

'Again there is, at present, at any rate, no proof that he was connected with that. Jo says she only saw the silhouette of the man who did it. It might have been anyone. Oh, I don't doubt that he was at the bottom of everything; but unless you can get hold of direct proof, I'm afraid there's nothing in it. Now give the subject a rest, there's good girls. I've had more than enough of it for today. Where's my Sybil? I haven't had a chance to talk to her. In the orchard? All right. I'll go and hunt her up, and after tea I'm taking her for a walk by herself.' He got up as he spoke and went in search of his daughter, and presently they saw the pair strolling off down the village, Sybil hanging on to her father's arm, and her tongue going hard about all the fun they were having.

Jo got up. 'I'm going to write some letters,' she said. 'And please note, everyone, that I'm just as sick of the whole affair as Jem is. You heard all that happened today, and we'll tell you tomorrow's story when it's happened. But otherwise, I don't want to hear any more about it at the moment. Oh, by the way, I forgot to tell you that Phoebe may have visitors. Jem is going to take Debby back with him on Monday. She'll sleep at the Round House, and come back again next day. Then I must go later on in the week and take young Reg as I promised.' She went into the house, and the others looked at each other in silence for a moment.

'She means it,' said Marie. 'Well, I think I'll see to tea, and the rest of you can call the family to get ready. I see Jem coming back with Sybs.'

Tea was a cheerful meal. Jo, with one letter, to her sister, just begun, was rather distrait, but the others made up for her silence, and when Sir James took his daughter off for a walk, he told them he hoped they would have got through the last of their excitement by the time he got back. They took the hint, and when he brought back a tired Sybil, they were in the garden with books and sewing, and the evening passed with quiet talk about general subjects, till Marie suddenly heaved a deep sigh.

'What's wrong?' asked Jo, glancing up from her book.

'I was just thinking of Tyrol,' said her friend with another sigh. 'Jem, when things are quiet again, will the San. go back to the Sonnalpe?'

'I expect so. We shall probably keep our present building going, and also run the old one. We'll have to see what's left of it first, though.'

'And the school?' asked Frieda. 'Will the same thing happen there?'

'I can't tell you about the school,' he said. 'To begin with, Ernest Howell will want his house back again, so it can't stay at Plas Howell anyhow. I don't know whether we shall keep an English branch going or not. Naturally, if the San. returns, the school must. They've been run in conjunction so long. But we shall certainly have to find somewhere if we intend to keep the English place going as well.'

'Perhaps Ernest Howell won't be able to afford to run Plas Howell,' suggested Jo. 'Jack says we'll all be as poor as charity when things are settled up. He might be glad to lease Plas Howell to us for a few years.'

Jem smiled. 'I can say nothing about that as yet. We must wait.'

Simone suddenly turned to Jo. 'Are you going back to Tyrol to live, Jo, if we go back there?'

'We'll be there part of every year, of course,' said Jo. 'I don't know if it will be altogether, though. Jem must go to the Sonnalpe, of course. But Jack may be tied here to a certain extent.'

'Jo! What can you mean?' cried Frieda in dismay. 'I never thought but that you would return with the rest of us. Oh, Joey! We've been together so long, we can't part now! Jack will be wanted at the Sonnalpe as much as anyone. Of course you must be there!'

'If Jack is at the Sonnalpe, I shall, of course,' replied Jo quietly. 'But we aren't sure yet if he will be.'

'Why not?' demanded Marie. 'What is there to prevent it?'

For reply, Jo bent down to the writing-case at her feet and fished out a letter. 'I heard from Jack this morning. Bob—his brother, you know—died from wounds two days ago. Jack was Bob's heir, as poor Rolf was killed. That means that Pretty Maids is his now. What will happen, I don't quite know. He's going to see if Bob's widow would like to stay on there for the present, as we can't leave Plas Gwyn. But later on, we shall have to see. Lydia may not want to stay. She's never been very fond of the Forest. She prefers London. At present, she'll stay, I know. But later on, she'll probably want to live in Town. If that happens—though I most sincerely hope it won't—Jack would have to go home.'

'I see.' There was silence for a minute or two. Then Simone said, 'But who will see to the business side of it all?'

'Bob had a very good agent—Mr Tingle. Yes,' as the girls cried out at this; 'it sounds like Dickens, I know; but that really is his name. He's seen to all the estate business while Bob was away. But he's not a young man by any means. If he would stay on for the next five or six years, we should be thankful. Jack doesn't want to give up his work, and that's what going to Pretty Maids would mean. And I don't want to live there, either. Hampshire always makes me feel so tired. It's at the bottom of a hill, you know, and we're all accustomed to such bracing air, I don't know how it would suit the children, either. We've only had odd fortnights there since Grandpa died.'

The rest nodded. They knew that Jo and her sister-in-law did not get on well. Mrs Robert Maynard could never forgive Jo for having four children all well and healthy while her only child, Rolf, had been killed as a little chap of thirteen through the disobedience she had never tried to control when he was tiny. The Major had been fond of his sister-in-law whom he had known as a schoolgirl; and he was devoted to her babies. But his wife had made things difficult. The visits the Jack Maynard family had paid to Pretty Maids, the beautiful old home, had been few and far between since the death of old Mr Maynard.

'Well, I hope things can be arranged so that you and Jack can come with us to Tyrol,' said Marie at last. 'You *must* be there when the school begins again, Jo. Why, you're one of the foundation stones! You were the first pupil—you and Simone, and Grizel Cochrane. Even Frieda came later.'

Jo nodded. 'What fun it all was, beginning like that, and in such a beautiful place, too! Oh, I shall be there for the reopening—D.V., of course. And as soon as my girls are old enough they will go there. But I'm not sure we can live there as we had hoped.'

'In the meantime,' said Sir James, getting up, 'may I suggest that it is after nine, and quite time we cleared up and went to bed? I hope we'll have a quiet night. After all the excitement of last night I could do with a sleep. Collect your things, girls, and come along. Jo, I'll take Rufus down the village while you tidy up. I'll be back in half an hour or so. Come on, old man!' And he strolled off, big Rufus at his heels.

By the time they got back the girls had everything ready. He handed Rufus over to Jo and departed to Many Bushes, while the four, having seen to locking up, retired to bed, where they were soon all sleeping the sleep of the just and weary.

Forty miles away, Zephyr Burthill was crying herself to sleep because her father had told her that he was afraid that the ’cello would never be hers now.

Chapter XII

Jo Visits Phoebe

The rest of that week-end passed off quietly. They had no other midnight alarm. Stephen, having got the one tooth through, settled down to his usual placid self. The other children went on as before, and there was, as Marie said, perfect peace, little things like Sybil falling off the fence into the horse-pond and being rescued a regular mud-maiden, or Margot finding the end of a used can of green paint and adorning the shed wall at The Witchens—and herself!—with it, being merely everyday affairs. A bath put Sybil right, and Jo washed her frock; while Jem cleaned up his sinful niece with some mixture of his own. Margot returned to her family looking as if she had been parboiled, and quite subdued for the time being by her uncle's severe lecture. On the Monday Jem departed, taking Debby and the precious 'cello with him, and on the Friday Jo set off with Stephen and an enraptured Reg. The rest all escorted them to the train, and when they had gone Marie suggested coffee for the grown-ups and milk for the small folk at Garnley's old coaching inn, the King's Arms.

Meanwhile Jo settled herself comfortably, and proceeded to tell Reg something about the place he was going to see shortly. As she had to go back to the beginning of the Sanatorium in Tyrol to answer all his questions, her story lasted them till they reached Armiford, the cathedral city near which they lived. Here they were met by Jack Maynard, who told them that Phoebe was making steady improvement, and was looking forward to seeing them. He whisked them off for a meal, and then packed them into the car and drove them away up the winding roads, between orchards where apples and pears were ripening, and fields where reaping was in full swing. Then he turned west, and they drove through the great hills, up and up, till they turned in at a wide gateway; and ten minutes later they were drawing up outside the huge gaunt building where sick folk from all over England came to seek health. Reg looked at it with awe, and Jo with a sigh for the graceful buildings they had left at the Sonnalpe. Then they were out of the car, and Jack was leading them in through the big entrance, and up the stairs to the little private ward where Phoebe was waiting for them.

At the door Jo stopped, and gave Reg a push. 'You run along in,' she said. 'I just want to see to Stephen for a moment.'

Reg gave her a look of unbelief. Then, seeing she meant what she said, he tapped at the door. Phoebe's well-known voice called, 'Come in!' and he went in on tiptoe, leaving Jo and her husband outside.

'What do you want to do for Steve?' demanded her husband. 'He's all right, isn't he?'

'Jack, you ninny! Don't you *know* that Reg simply worships Phoebe, and has been suffering agonies of jealousy, poor kid, because of us? We'll give him a few minutes alone with her first. In the meantime, you can admire your son. Doesn't he look fit?' And Jo thrust the boy into his father's arms. 'There! How's that for weight for not quite seven months?'

'I'd rather carry him one mile than five,' said Jack. 'Rum little beggar, isn't he? Always chuckling. Hi, young man! What's the joke about?'

Stephen gurgled, and thrust his fist into his mouth while he battered aimlessly with the other at his father's broad chest.

'Here! That's me!' protested Jack. 'You don't seem to have given him any sense of respect for his papa, Jo, my girl. How are the girls, by the way?'

'Full of beans, as usual. And *growing*! I'll have to let down all their last year's winter frocks. They'll be frills round their waists, I should think. Jack, have you heard from Lydia again?'

'Yes; I'll give you the letter later. It's at home. She wants to stay on at present, which will suit us very well. Tingle has the work well in hand. There are some repairs poor Bob was going to see to when he got back. I'll have to go to Pretty Maids some time, but I'm waiting till you get back. Then I vote we leave the girls with Anna and young Rob to see to them, take Steve, and go down and see what's happening.'

'It'll have to be soon, then, if you want us to leave Rob in charge. She goes to Oxford early in October. How long do you want to be there?'

'Oh, about a week or ten days—not more. And, Jo, what about asking Lydia to come to us for Christmas?'

Jo made a face. 'I don't want to do it, but I suppose we must. She probably won't come. But we can ask her. By the way, Jack, it won't be too unkind to take Steve, will it? I mean—poor Rolf, you know.'

'Well, you can't leave him behind yet. I'd rather we went while Rob was there to see to the girls. Anna can't manage them as she can. But we'll think it over. And now, if you think we've given Phoebe's young friend long enough alone with her, we'd better go in. Time's not waiting, and it's just on four. You may have half an hour with her, and then I'll run you home.'

'One moment, Jack! How is Phoebe exactly?'

'Better than we expected. Oh, it won't be a cure, Jo. Don't hope for that for a moment. The thing's of too long standing. But there's no doubt that she's reacting to this treatment very well, and I believe we can make life a great deal easier for her. But when she's able to be worried about such things, I want you to talk to her about leaving Many Bushes and coming somewhere close at hand. Then, if she needs attention at any time, she can get it with the least possible delay. But that can wait for a month or two.'

Jo nodded, and then they went into the room where Phoebe was sitting up in a big chair, propped up with cushions. She greeted Jo with a cry of delight, and even as Jo bent to kiss this new friend of hers, she noted the really wonderful improvement. Phoebe's cheeks were faintly pink. Her eyes were smiling, and she had lost the drawn look about the mouth. Even her hair seemed to have more spring in it.

'Phoebe, you're a marvel!' cried Jo as, holding the thin hands in hers, she took in all these details with eager eyes. 'You don't look like the same girl! I hope,' teasingly, 'that that colour is *real*, and not out of a box! But seriously, my child, the improvement is amazing.'

'It is,' agreed Phoebe happily. 'And I can move with much less pain. Of course, I have to go very slow; but I can use my hands much more freely than I've done for years. They won't let me try to walk yet; but I do believe that when they do I'll find that easier too. It seems a miracle that so much could have been done in such a short time.'

'And you're growing pretty,' added Jo, as she sat down and took her boy on her knee. 'Don't blush like that, my child. It's true.'

Phoebe laughed. 'It couldn't be. But I'm glad I'm not quite the scarecrow I used to be. Today Nurse said she thought I was beginning to put on a little flesh. Do you know, Jo,' she leaned forward, 'I feel as if one of my very private dreams might be going to come true.'

'Oh? What's that?' queried Jo with interest.

'Jo, forgive me interrupting you,' put in Jack, 'but I'm just going to take Reg to have a look at the X-ray room. We'll come back presently. You and Phoebe must make the most of your time, as I'm taking you away soon. We've got to get back to Plas Gwyn, and you don't want that imp of ours up till all hours, I imagine.'

'I don't. All right. You two men trot off and see the machines and what-not, and Phoebe and I will have a feminine chat while you're away.'

The two went out, and then Jo turned to Phoebe to ask, 'What's the dream?'

Phoebe blushed again as she said shyly, 'When I was little I had dimples, but, of course, when I was so ill I lost them, and they've never come back. It's silly of me, but I've always hoped that some day they would. Then she added, 'Father's pet name for me when I was tiny was "Dimples." That's why.'

'They're beginning to come back already, I believe,' said Jo, squinting vilely as she stared intently at Phoebe's face. 'Weren't they there and there,' touching the thin cheeks with a gentle finger.

'Yes; do you really think you see them, Jo? Father would have been so pleased if he could have known.' Phoebe's voice shook a little.

'Well, either your face hasn't been properly washed, or it's their shadows,' declared Jo; which made Phoebe laugh.

'I've been thoroughly well washed, I can assure you. So it must be them. Do stop squinting like that, Jo! You may stick that way, and what would your family say then?'

'They'd have several fits.' Jo sat back in her chair. 'Here's Steve come to show Auntie Phoebe his first tooth. Don't try exploring with your finger, my love, or you may regret it. But it's coming along nicely now. What a dance he led me over it last week, poor little man!'

'Poor pet!' Phoebe tickled the baby under his chin. 'What a jolly boy he is, Jo! He always seems to be laughing. Were your girls like him?'

Jo shook her head. 'Con was the most solemn thing you ever saw. And Margot was an imp from the first. Oh, what fits of fury she used to have! Still does, at times. Len was more like Steve.

But he really is the most placid infant I've ever encountered.' Then she changed the subject. 'You've got the 'cello here, I see. I'm glad. We thought you'd like to have it.'

'Oh, I *do*!' Phoebe laughed. 'When Sir James brought it in, I couldn't believe my eyes at first. It was good of you people to think of it.'

Jo went pink. 'Oh, we—we thought it would make this place more homey for you,' she said hurriedly. 'And now, have you done any sewing yet?'

'Not a great deal. They won't let me have it for very long at a time. But I've got one of the little frocks finished, and I've begun the other. You'd better have the one to take with you, Jo. Will you get it? It's in that case under the window.'

Jo got up, dumping her son down on the bed, while she brought the case to its owner. Phoebe opened it, and produced a baby's gown of such fairylike loveliness that Jo cried out when she saw it.

'Oh, Phoebe! That's exquisite! What wonderful work! And I love the wee white violets round the neck and sleeves. Madge will be thrilled when she sees it. Has she been up to see you, by the way?'

'Lady Russell, do you mean? No, Sir James says it's too far for her just now. She sent me a dear letter, though, and said she'd come as soon as she could, and bring me the new baby to see, as well. Jo! What makes all you people so kind? I'm almost a total stranger, and you are all doing all you can for me. Why?'

'Why shouldn't we? Did you expect us to be *un*kind to you?'

'Jo, I'm serious.'

'So'm I.' Then Jo's eyes suddenly softened. 'Phoebe, just think for a moment. Look at all we have—our husbands, and children, and dozens of friends, and our happy homes. If we didn't try to share, do you really think we'd deserve all we've got? For I don't! And then, we like you, you know. It isn't all unselfishness or sharing by any manner of means. I don't say we wouldn't have done what we could if you were a grumpy old thing, always growling, without a civil word for anyone. But when we see how plucky you are; how you try to think of other people—like that little pig Zephyr even—we couldn't help getting fond of you. So now you know.—Hi! Don't do that, you monkey!' And Jo jumped up to grab her son who was within an ace of rolling off the bed; rather thankful for the interruption, for Phoebe's eyes had filled at her words.

She sat down again, and busied herself with pulling the boy's clothes straight. Then she went on: 'I don't talk much of these things, Phoebe. I never do about things that go deep. But—we all try to be Christians, not only in name but also in fact. We all want our children to grow up feeling the same way. If we don't set them the example, how can they?'

'I—see.' Phoebe spoke slowly. 'Thank you, Jo. You know,' she continued, 'I felt that, somehow, with all of you. It wasn't only me, either. You've been good to Debby. Oh, I know what you've done for her. She told me when she was here on Monday. And then Reg—sending him in first today, and giving us that few minutes alone together. Reg is a very lonely boy in some ways. His aunt is good to him, but she's really his mother's aunt, and she's elderly. She gives him good food, and sees that he has good clothes and all he wants that way. But he's not just like the village boys. His mother married above her station, and I think Reg has a good deal of his father in him. He's ambitious, and wants to get somewhere in life. His father was a master at Garnley Grammar School, and a doctor's son. He fell in love with Reg's mother—she was a very pretty girl, they tell me—and married her, and she died when the baby was born. A sister of his kept house for him, but he was killed in a motor-bus accident when Reg was seven, and the sister got married, and her husband didn't want Reg, so old Mrs Thirtle took him. He had to go to the village school, and he didn't like it. We made friends when I came, and I've lent him books, and tried to help him to speak nicely as I'm sure his father did. The aunt is no use, you know. When she married, they went out to Canada, to Vancouver, and she writes very rarely. She has two little girls of her own now, and I rather think from her letters that they have a struggle to make both ends meet. So Reg can't look for help there.'

'I see,' said Jo. 'Oh, Reg was furious when he found you'd gone! He thought we had done it on purpose to annoy him, I believe. But look here, Phoebe. Aren't there free places at the Garnley Grammar School? Why hasn't he tried for one of those?'

'He was in hospital having adenoids and tonsils out when the exam was held,' explained Phoebe. 'The next year he was too old. There were about twenty-five places, and seventy-odd boys in for it. He's thirteen now, and will leave school next year, I'm afraid. His aunt is talking of finding him a job somewhere already. He doesn't want it. He wants to go on and try to get a scholarship at one of the universities. Then he could teach, like his father. But Mrs Thirtle won't pay out the money, and there's no one else to do it. The little his father left him brings in something like twenty-five or thirty pounds a year.'

'Is it necessary for him to work?' asked Jo.

'I don't know. I don't think so. Mr Thirtle was what they call a "warm" man, and she got everything. Her cottage and the land with it is her own. She has a couple of cows, and a pig, and some poultry as well. And she's not the spending kind. The Vicar once told me that she could quite well afford to send Reg to the Grammar. But she says she has no use for education. So there you are.'

Jo thought a minute. Then she suddenly sat up as her quick ear caught footfalls outside. 'Here they come! They mustn't think we've been discussing Reg. At least, Reg mustn't. Don't worry, Phoebe. Something will turn up. It always does if you want it badly enough.' Then, as the door opened, she flashed a smile at Reg. 'Well, what do you think of it all?'

'Eh, it's wonderful, Mrs Maynard.' Reg's eyes were glowing, and he was flushed. 'Wonderful it is.' Then, wistfully, 'Guess I'd like to be a doctor like the doctor here.'

'Well,' said Jo briskly, 'there's no saying what may happen in the years to come. George Stephenson who invented the railway engine was just the son of a collier, and could neither read nor write at your age. You can do that and more, so you've an even better chance than he. But we mustn't stay here talking. It's time to move, or Steve will be late to bed, and when that happens, cross isn't the word for him.' She got up, and bent to kiss Phoebe. 'Goodbye, Phoebe. It won't be so long before we come home now, and then you'll be having visitors as often as they'll let you.'

'I'll look forward to it,' said Phoebe. 'Give them all my love, and say I'm longing to see them.—Reg, old man, you'll have to go now, but you are coming again to see me, aren't you? Perhaps Mrs Maynard will bring you with her again.' She held out her hand, and Reg took it awkwardly. 'I'll write to you, now I can use my hands. And you must write to me. See; here's the address on these envelopes. You can use them, and I'll send you some more when I think you need them. Tell me all the news of Garnham—every single thing. Debby doesn't tell me much; she doesn't like writing. But you always get full marks for compositions, don't you?'

'I'll write,' said Reg briefly. 'Goodbye, Miss Phoebe. Be seeing you.' And with a wag of his head he followed Jack Maynard from the room.

Jo followed after another kiss, and they were soon flying down the steep road to Howells Village, where Jo's home was. Jo, after a rapturous greeting from Anna, her faithful Tyrolean maid, went up to the nursery with Stephen, while Jack took the guest to the bathroom to wash, and then brought him down to the little morning-room, where a good tea with scrambled eggs and ham awaited them. Jo appeared later, and joined them with the remark that she was famished, and proceeded to prove it with such goodwill that even Reg's sharpened appetite passed unnoticed. After tea, while the hostess went to put her son to bed, the doctor did the honours of Plas Gwyn, and when Reg finally tumbled into his own nest he was the doctor's sworn hench-man. Also, he made up his mind firmly that somehow, some time, he too would be a doctor and do what he could towards lessening the pain in the world.

Next day Jo returned with the two boys to Garnham, and promptly became embroiled in Debby's feud with the Vicar's wife, with some funny results and at least one startling consequence.

Chapter XIII

'THAT SODGER!'

ONE thing and another had kept the Vicar's wife from meeting the newcomers at The Witchens. To begin with, she had been called to the help of a sister with three small children, who had all gone down with mumps, while their mother was in hospital having an operation. When the attack of mumps was over, her husband, who had already arranged his holiday so that it began the week before she was free, went off to the North Wales farmhouse where they had taken rooms, and she joined him there for three weeks. But they had returned in the afternoon of the Saturday after Phoebe had gone to the San., and she was soon on the hunt for all news. As the Vicarage was at the far end of the village, she had not known that The Witchens was occupied, nor did she learn it until, after the evening service on Sunday, the butcher, who was also Vicar's warden, happened to mention it. Then the lady pricked up her ears with a vengeance.

'The Witchens taken?' she exclaimed. 'Who is it, Mr Foster? I trust they are nice people? I don't think I saw any strangers in church.'

'Well,' said Mr Foster in his slow way, 'seeing they have a mort o' little children it isn't like they'd be there. Nine quite little 'uns there are, and a girl of ten or so. But they don't go to church, only the little Russell girl. They go into Garnley of a Sunday with Mrs Barnes. Likely they go to the Parish. But they ain't said.'

'This must be seen to,' replied the lady. 'Nine little children!'

'Aye; there's Mrs Maynard has four; and Mrs de Bersac, she

has one; and the Countess has a boy and a girl; and Mrs Ahlen has two little boys.'

'Then it is a *party* of people? Dear me! And all those children, you say? I must go and call on them as soon as possible.'

However, she was unable to do so for some days. Indeed, it was not till the Saturday that she found herself free enough in the afternoon to pay her call. The weather had changed, and they had had two or three days of heavy rain which had kept the children in the house, or she might have seen something of them. As it was, even hardy Sybil was weatherbound from the Tuesday till the Friday. In the meantime, Mrs Hart had heard about the friendship which had sprung up between Phoebe and the newcomers, and also how Phoebe had gone, and Debby was living at The Witchens for the present. The lady felt that she must delay no longer in putting the Countess, Mrs Maynard and the rest right about the Wychcotes and their belongings. Strangely enough, nothing had got out about the burglars at The Witchens. The local newspaper only came out once a week, on the Saturday, and the morning after it had all happened Bert Trinder had sustained a compound fracture of his left leg, which had tied him up safely in hospital at Garnley; and Mrs Trinder had shut up her cottage and gone to stay with a sister in the town so that she could be on the spot. The man sent over from Garnley to take Trinder's place was so far from talkative that his mates called him 'Silent Joe,' and he had said nothing about the events to anyone. Therefore Mrs Hart felt that she had two good reasons for calling at The Witchens. She must know exactly what had happened. And it really was quite exciting to think that the great Sir James Russell—she knew Jem well enough by reputation—should be a friend of these people.

When she reached the gate, the family were all out on the lawn, the babies rolling on rugs, and the others playing games under Marie's supervision. Frieda had just taken Louis into the house to wash his grubby face and hands for tea, and Simone was busy getting the meal ready. Marie heard the click of the gate and looked up eagerly, expecting to see Jo. Inwardly she made a face when she saw who it was, but she came forward at once, saying, 'How do you do? I know you are Mrs Hart. I am the Countess von Wertheim. The others will be here presently. Won't you come and sit down?'

Mrs Hart stiffened. A *German* countess! What was she doing here? Meanwhile Marie was sending off the small fry to make themselves tidy, with Sybil and Wolfram in charge. Mrs Hart's attention was caught by Sybil, and she said, 'Oh, is that Sir James Russell's daughter? I heard he had been visiting you.'

Marie's violet eyes widened at this, but she only said, 'Yes, Sybil is the Russells' elder girl. She is Mrs Maynard's niece, and we brought her with us as Lady Russell has not been very well. Their youngest, little Josette, had a bad accident early in the year, and they nearly lost her. Lady Russell did a good deal of the nursing, of course, and it has pulled her down. So Sybil came with us, and her brother went off to a school-friend's for the holidays to give their mother a rest.'

'And you have two children, I hear. Which are they?'

'Wolfram and Josefa. They ran in just now with the others to get tidy for tea. They will come presently, and then I will show them to you.'

At this point, Simone appeared carrying a large tray, and Marie sprang to help her set it on the gipsy table in the centre of the ring of chairs.

'Simone, this is Mrs Hart,' she said. 'My friend, Mme de Bersac, Mrs Hart.'

'What a pack of foreigners!' thought Mrs Hart as she said 'How do you do?' to Simone, who set down her tray, and held out a slim hand.

But before anyone could go further, there came the sound of

light, swift steps, and Marie raced to the gate to welcome Jo, who was cross and tired, since Stephen had been fretful on the journey, and was not at all inclined for any visitors.

'Joey! Give me Steve! How is Phoebe?' cried Marie in one breath. Then added in an undertone, 'That's "The Sodger"—she's come to call!'

'I can see that with my own eyes,' retorted Jo. 'Oh, hang! Why must she choose today of all days to call? I don't call Saturday a proper afternoon for calling. Yes; take Steve, Marie. He's very cross and whimpery; I'm afraid there's another tooth coming, poor little man. I suppose I *must* be polite before I go and wash?'

'Of course you must,' returned Marie, lifting Stephen from the light folding pram. 'Leave this thing here, and come along. You need only stay to greet her, and then you can go and get tidy. Your girls are washing, with Sybs and Wolfram in charge. Come on, do!' And she led the way up the path to the house near which she had been sitting with her visitor. 'This is Mrs Maynard, Mrs Hart,' she said. 'Jo, Mrs Hart. And here is Stephen Maynard, our youngest but one,' and she held out the boy, who took one look at the grim-faced lady and then opened his mouth in a roar that showed him to be the possessor of excellent lungs.

Meanwhile Jo was saying 'How do you do?' with very little real greeting in her voice, as she laid a limp hand in Mrs Hart's.

'How do you do?' said Mrs Hart, giving her a searching look from a pair of light blue eyes which looked almost lashless.

'I am sorry I have not been able to call sooner,' she went on, 'but I have been away.'

'So we were told,' returned Jo, dropping into a chair, while Marie bore Stephen, who was still yelling loudly, off into the house. 'I hope you had a pleasant holiday?—Simone, I've more or less promised that you will go and see Phoebe when we get home. She's very much better, but not allowed to move under her own steam yet.'

'Oh, but it is good news to hear she is better,' said Simone. 'Of course I will go when we get home again. Here comes Frieda, so you had best run and make yourself fresh for tea while she entertains our guest.'

Jo got up. 'Please excuse me, Mrs Hart. We have just come off a journey and I would like to wash my hands and see to my boy.'

Frieda, with Louis clinging to her hand, came up to them at that moment, and under cover of her introduction to the Vicar's wife Jo slipped away, to return twenty minutes later very much refreshed by a wash and a change of frock. The hot weather had returned that morning, and she had found her tweed coat and skirt very warm wear. Stephen had been left in his cot, pacified and sleepy, thanks to a bottle which Marie had had ready for him. Mrs Hart was sitting in her chair, with Frieda offering her scones, and Marie was refilling her cup with Debby's excellent tea.

'Stephen all right now?' asked Simone with a smile, as she pulled up a chair beside her own for her friend.

'Quite. He's had his bottle, thanks to Marie, and he's drowsy now. We had a trying journey, though. It was so hot and dusty, and he whimpered most of the way.' Then Jo turned to the guest. 'What a pretty place this is, Mrs Hart. And the air is like wine. It has done our small folk so much good. Where are they, by the way—does anyone know?'

'Debby is giving them their tea in the orchard,' said Marie. 'We felt you would like yours in peace before the rush began. The girls are all right, Jo, and very fit. They have been quite good, too. But they're longing to see Mamma, of course. Josefa gave us a fright yesterday afternoon. She found a wasps' nest in the bank near that meadow where they play, and what must my lady do but try to stir them up with a stick? She came tearing down the road with a cloud of angry wasps after her, but luckily we got her into the house before much damage was done. She had two or three stings, but nothing much, and Frieda rushed to the rescue with an onion. The rest were safely away at the far side of the field, so escaped. Mr Allon, who owns the place, has put down cyanide and finished off the wasps early this morning. And Josefa has had a lesson which will make her leave such things alone for some time to come.'

Jo laughed. 'Well, at least they weren't *hornets*,' she said feelingly.

The rest joined in her laughter at this reminiscence, and Simone turned to Mrs Hart to explain. 'We had an adventure with a hornets' nest years ago when we were all at school,' she said. 'It was a Guide camp we had near a lake in Tyrol, and two people who had never seen such a nest before threw sticks at it to bring it down. They succeeded, and we had quite a thrilling time till the hornets departed. Do you remember their faces, Jo? Lonny was almost unrecognisable; and Margia Stevens looked as if she had suddenly developed mumps!'

'Is that the Margia Stevens who was making such a name for herself as a pianist?' asked Mrs Hart. 'She seems to have vanished now.'

'She's nursing in a hospital in Australia,' explained Marie. 'Yes; she was at school with us—one of the juniors, of course. She's a few years younger than we are.'

'It's to be hoped she is managing to keep up her music a little,' said Jo, as she handed her cup to Marie for more tea. 'It's so easy to lose way if you don't practise regularly. Margia has got to bring a few laurels to the school before she's done. Did you ever hear her, Mrs Hart? Her playing was always wonderful, even when she was a child. When last I heard her I thought she ought to get to the Myra Hess-Eileen Joyce class before she finished.'

'I heard her broadcast two or three times,' said the lady. 'I am afraid we have little chance of hearing much good music otherwise. We are too far from any large town, and even so, we are very busy people.'

'But you had *one* musical celebrity here for a short time,' said Jo thoughtlessly. 'I mean Nicholas Wychcote. Did you ever hear him?'

'Mr Wychcote scorned our poor little attempts at bringing good music into the lives of our village people,' said Mrs Hart icily. 'I did, indeed, try to get him to perform at one of our concerts, but he refused most rudely. I am afraid he thought more about his fees than sharing his music with others. And I am sorry to say that Miss Wychcote seems to have inherited his views on the subject.'

'But Phoebe doesn't play,' said Simone in puzzled tones.

'I am aware of that; also that it is impossible she ever should do so. That being the case, I think it is most selfish of her to refuse to sell her father's 'cello to one who could make real use of it. It shows a dog-in-the-manger spirit that I cannot approve.'

At this point, Rufus, who had been in the orchard with the children, and who had heard his mistress's voice a moment before, suddenly came tearing round the house and hurled himself on her, his great tail going like a flail. The cups and saucers on the table were in imminent danger, and Marie set up a shriek of dismay.

'Rufus! Jo! Make him lie down. Oh, my goodness! the milk!' And she made a vain effort to catch it before it went over. The jug fell on its side, and the milk streamed over the pretty cloth. Frieda jumped up to seek a cloth to mop it up, and Jo, whose own tea had been overturned in the excitement, ordered Rufus to lie down—with a hug for her treasured pet.

'You seem to be fond of animals, Mrs Maynard,' said Mrs Hart with a sour smile when peace had been restored again. 'Are you not afraid to have such a large dog with so many small children? I understand you have little girls as well.'

'Rufus has been my children's best safeguard,' returned Jo, looking down into the adoring eyes fixed on her. 'He is faithful, loving, and completely reliable. He would willingly die for any of our babies, I do believe. And none of us would know what to do without him.'

'Oh, indeed? Well, I should like to return to what I was saying just before he came on the scene. I have heard that, since you came here, you have made a great friend of Miss Wychcote. I trust you will try to make her see her conduct with regard to the 'cello in its true light, and show her how selfishly she is behaving—'

'I could never do that,' said Jo quickly. 'You see, I don't consider she *is* being selfish.'

'No!' Marie chimed in. 'The selfish one is the girl who is trying to make Phoebe give up her father's most prized possession, just to gratify a whim of her own. I am afraid, Mrs Hart, we all agree about that. In any case, the 'cello is no longer here. When Sir James Russell was here at the beginning of the week, he took it back with him. There had been an attempt to steal it, and to make our precious Rufus ill so that he could not interfere. We have no proof as yet as to who was behind the attempt; but we are in no doubt ourselves.'

'And then,' said Frieda's sweet voice, 'Phoebe is responding so well to this new treatment that the doctors hold out hopes of her being able to use it herself. Debby saw her at the beginning of the week, and brought that report home to us. In that case it would be unwise to sell what she values in any event. A musician's instrument is a great treasure to him, Mrs Hart. I play the harp, though I am no concert performer, and I know how I should grieve if, for any reason, I had to get rid of mine.'

'But that is silly,' replied Mrs Hart. 'One instrument is surely as good as another. And Miss Wychcote could never make the use of it that someone who is in normal health can. I maintain that it is selfish to keep the 'cello to herself. If she wants to play, a cheaper instrument would surely be good enough for her. I have heard Miss Burthill play, and I assure you she seemed to me to be quite out of the common. Her father tells me—we met in Llandudno a fortnight ago, at a hotel where they are staying—he tells me that she is making herself ill for want of this 'cello. She has set her heart on it, and Miss Wychcote would be wiser, as well as kinder, to give up this sentimental feeling, and let her have it. For one thing, this improvement you speak of may not be maintained. She may go back again; even become helpless. And then what use would it be to her? No doctor is infallible, you know,' she added with a slight sneer.

Kicking Jo to keep her silent—Marie knew that she was boiling inside—the young countess replied, 'We know that. But she has the best advice obtainable at the moment. Dr Peters has studied in America, and the treatment he is using is the latest there. We all hope that Miss Wychcote may be greatly benefited by him.'

'And now,' said Frieda, changing the subject firmly, 'we must show you our little people. Mrs Maynard has triplets, and we are all very proud of them. And I should like you to see my baby. I will bring them.' And she got up, and went to call the tinies, who came running at once. All of them were trained to be obedient, and it was rarely that even Margot the tempestuous did not do as she was told. On the other hand, as Jo once said despairingly, every one of them thought of things to do that no one would ever think of forbidding because no one would ever think of their even imagining such things! And then Marie told her that, so far as *hers* were concerned, it was a clear case of heredity!

The little ones trooped up cheerfully to say 'How do you do' to the stranger. Josefa came first, a miniature version of her lovely mother. Jo's daughters tripped after her, and Wolfram, holding 'Tante Frieda's' small Louis, followed. Shy Tessa clung to Sybil's hand, and only the babies in their prams were missing.

'This big fellow is my son,' said Marie with a smile at Wolfram. 'This is my daughter. Make your curtsy, Josefa, Liebling.'

Josefa curtsied as she was bidden, and Wolfram gravely raised the lady's hand to his lips. Marie had seen to it that they knew what she called 'proper' manners. Mrs Hart flushed, but she merely said, 'I should have known them for your children, Countess. They are both like you.'

Jo made a big effort and swallowed her wrath. 'These are my three, Len, Con, and Margot. Say "How do you do," my pets, to Mrs Hart.'

They said it, and, inspired by Josefa's example, gravely curtsied, much to their mother's amazement, for they had not done it before. Jo choked down the wild mirth that was secretly convulsing her, and drew Louis forward, since Frieda had gone to bring Stephen and Gerard.

'This is Louis, Mrs von Ahlen's elder boy,' she said, with a gentle touch on the primrose fair head. 'And this is our Sybil, my niece, and my sister's elder girl. She is a most useful person, and helps everyone.'

'I love being with you, Auntie,' replied Sybil with a smile at her adored aunt. 'And it's fun helping, too.'

Now Sybil was far and away the pick of the bunch for looks. Josefa was as lovely a small girl as you could find anywhere, with her mother's golden locks, violet eyes, and delicate features. Her skin was milk and roses, and she had enchanting dimples on both cheeks. But Sybil's chestnut curls, sapphire-blue eyes, and peachlike colouring, to which she united her mother's features and a little air of distinction all her own, would have made her outstanding anywhere. Her movements were a joy to watch, and her voice was low and musical. Her family were only too experienced in the effect she had on strangers, and were on the watch perpetually to try to check praise to her face, for there had been a time, and not so long ago either, when such things had been fast turning Miss Sybil into a most objectionable being. But Sybil had had some severe lessons this year, and was losing a good deal of her conceit. Everyone was doubly vigilant, for no one wanted her hard task of subduing her pride made any harder. Consequently Jo could cheerfully have shaken Mrs Hart till her teeth rattled in her head when that lady cried, 'But what a little beauty! I never saw such hair—or eyes. You look as if you had stepped out of a picture, my dear!'

Poor Sybil blushed furiously and looked imploringly at her aunt. She had learned to dread such comments. But Jo was quite equal to the occasion. 'Yes; Sybil has a great deal to thank God for,' she said gravely. 'But she knows that she has nothing to do with her looks except to keep herself clean and tidy, and to try to grow so that her expression can't spoil the beauty God has given her. And now, here comes Mrs von Ahlen with our babies. You have seen my Stephen, though I'm afraid you can't have had a very good impression of him. He is teething, poor little man, and he had a tiresome journey today. But what will you say to our newest comer? Frieda, show Gerard off this minute!'

Frieda laughed as she lifted the tiny fair baby from the pram, and held him for Mrs Hart to see. 'He is just ten weeks old,' she said. 'Would you like to take him? He is really very good with strangers.'

Mrs Hart drew back. 'I'm afraid I have no experience of babies,' she said with a little laugh. 'I like good children reasonably well; but I really know nothing about tiny babies. Has he been baptised yet?'

'Nine weeks ago,' said Frieda, surprise in her voice at the idea that anyone should ask that about a baby nearly three months old. 'Mrs Maynard,' she smiled across at Jo, 'is his godmother, and her husband is his godfather.' She sat down, and the children clustered round her to look at the baby. He blinked his blue eyes at them peacefully. What Frieda had said at the beginning of the holiday had come true, and her boys were as able to sleep through any ordinary din as even Jo's family.

Unable to think of anything to say, Mrs Hart rose. 'I must go,' she said abruptly. 'I shall, no doubt, see some of you at church tomorrow.'

'Only me,' said Sybil. 'I'm the only one. The rest all go to St Ignatius in Garnley when they can.'

'St Ignatius!' Mrs Hart exclaimed. 'I understand.'

'Yes, Mrs Hart,' said Jo wickedly. 'Sybil must represent the family for you tomorrow.'

'If she goes,' murmured Marie in an aside to Simone. 'Jo will be afraid to let her go in case the good lady says anything more about her looks to her.'

'Jo will send her with Debby,' returned Simone in the same low tones. 'Even Mrs Hart won't get a chance to spoil Sybs if Debby is there.'

Mrs Hart bowed to them, not offering her hand. 'Good afternoon,' she said coldly. 'Thank you for your kindness. Perhaps we shall meet again.'

'Oh, I expect you'll see lots of us for another week or so yet,' said Jo cheerfully. 'And we'll be coming again later on. We've bought this place, you know, to use as a holiday home. I don't suppose, among all of us—and we all have sisters, and some of us married brothers as well—it will go begging for any length of time.—Take Stephen, Marie. I'll escort Mrs Hart to the gate.' And she dumped Stephen into Marie's lap.

But when the lady had gone, Jo let fly with all the pent-up anger in her. 'The nasty, insinuating, narrow-minded old *hunk*!' she exploded, when Debby had gone off with Louis and Tessa to put them to bed, while the rest escaped to the orchard to make the most of the time left them.

'*Jo!*' protested Marie as well as she could for laughing. 'Where on earth do you pick up your language? As for Mrs Hart, we can only be sorry for her. But for goodness' sake, Jo, if you send Sybs to church tomorrow, get Debby to take her. Don't let's have a repeat of this afternoon's performance. It's not fair to any one, and to Sybs least of all.'

'Debby will take her if she goes. Oh, how I would have enjoyed wringing her neck when she talked that rot before Sybs!' said Jo, somewhat incoherently. 'I only wonder I was as restrained and ladylike as I was.'

'So do I,' agreed Simone. 'You show improvement, my Jo!'

'Well, I fully agree with Debby's estimate of her. She *is* a regular "sodger," and there's no other word for it. Now I'm going to get Steve off. I feel in my bones that we're in for a bad night, and he may as well get what sleep he can, poor laddie!' And Jo stalked off, followed by Frieda, bent on the same errand with her son.

Chapter XIV

Zephyr Tries Again

The knocker rapped sharply three times. Simone, alone in the house as she was cook for that day, gave a sigh and turned to find a towel to wipe the flour off her hands. Her pastry would never be done at this rate. First it had been the baker. Then the parcels post had brought a parcel for Jo, and she had to sign for it. The telephone had gone twice—wrong number each time, and she had banged down the receiver the second time with thoughts not lawful to be uttered. Finally, a lady had come, asking for a donation for charity, and that had meant a trip upstairs to seek her purse. Simone wiped her hands, slipped off the big useful apron she was wearing, and went to the front door prepared for anything, from a gipsy selling clothes-pegs to one of Jo's publishers. She threw the door open and got the shock of her life. Standing there was Zephyr Burthill—Simone recognised her from Jo's graphic description—and she was holding out her hand, saying, 'I am Miss Burthill. You, I think, must be another of the ladies who are living here and have befriended poor Miss Wychcote. So good of you! May I come in?'

Too stunned for speech, Simone silently led her to the little drawing-room which, mercifully, Marie had dusted only that morning. As they rarely used it, they were apt to forget it during their labours. She waved Miss Burthill to a chair, took one herself, and waited to hear what that young woman had to say for herself.

Perhaps Simone's continued silence alarmed Zephyr, for she said plaintively, 'I'm afraid you think this an intrusion.'

Simone found her voice. 'That will depend on why you have come,' she said gravely, her accent rather more French than usual.

'There is only one reason why I should trouble you,' said Zephyr. 'I do so want you—all of you—to use your influence with Miss Wychcote and get her to sell me that 'cello. I want it—I *want* it, and I must have it! I—I—I don't know your name, but oh, *won't* you do your best for me? Please, do! I shall *die* if I don't have it! I never wanted anything so much in my life before. I can't eat—I don't sleep. When I do I see that hateful girl standing flourishing the 'cello in my face and *laughing* at me! I *must* have it! We'll pay anything she likes—*anything*! You can tell her so. But oh, do help me! Please, do!' In her excitement she fell on her knees and clutched at Simone's hands, much to that young lady's discomfort. Even at her most emotional—and Simone had been an emotional child—she had never made such an exhibition of herself as this. She drew her fingers from those clutching at them, and sat back.

'Please get up, Miss Burthill,' she said. 'I must name myself. I am Madame de Bersac. I am sorry you came to me on such an errand. I cannot do anything for you.'

'I should think not!' said a voice from the open french window. 'Of all the babyish conduct! Do you *ever* think of anything but what *you* want?'

Jo pushed the window wider and stepped over the sill, and Simone turned to her thankfully. 'Oh, Joey! But I am so glad to see thee!' she cried in French, forgetting her English in her agitation.

'All right,' replied Jo in the same tongue. 'You go and get on with your cooking. *I'll* deal with this business.' Then she remembered her manners and turned to the unwanted guest. 'I beg your pardon, Miss Burthill. I am afraid we are so accustomed to speaking any one of three languages as they come handy, we tend to forget that it isn't the same with everyone. Simone, do go back to your work. I know you'd rather I saw to this. Sit down, Miss Burthill, please.'

Looking, despite her old cotton frock—all the girls were wearing out their most aged clothes here—every inch Mrs Maynard, she took Zephyr's hand, pulled her to her feet, and seated her in a big wicker chair. Then she sat down herself, and said gravely, 'You know, Miss Burthill, you are behaving like a very spoilt baby. And it won't get the 'cello for you, I can assure you of that. Miss Wychcote won't sell, and I think she is quite right. Why *should* she hand over to you a thing she values so highly? You say you can make the best use of it, but I doubt that.'

'I can play and she can't—not a note. I could use it, but *she* only wants it to stick it up in a corner. I call that silly sentimentalism.'

Jo could cheerfully have shaken this sulky girl with her insistent 'I want!' but that would get them nowhere. She tackled the most obvious remark in Zephyr's speech. 'How do you know that Miss Wychcote can't play?' she demanded. 'In point of fact, she learnt for four years, and was making real headway. The doctors at the Sanatorium all think that, although they cannot promise a complete cure, they can promise great improvement, so that she would be able to take it up again for her own and her friends' amusement. And, if you want to know, in that case I think she could make far better use of it than ever you could. She may not be able to get the technique—I grant you that—but the *soul* will be there. From your own account you have never really wanted for anything till now. You can only give real feeling to your music when you have learnt what it is to suffer. And so far I should think you haven't learnt that.'

'Then you're wrong. I'm suffering now!' cried Zephyr angrily. And she repeated the story of her dreams which she had told Simone. Jo nearly exploded in her face at the idea of Phoebe *flourishing* the 'cello; but she managed to control herself with an effort.

'That's not real suffering,' she said curtly. 'Oh, I don't say you are not enduring a disappointment. But there's more to it than that. You'll get over it in time. You've got plenty to console you.'

'But not what I want. Mrs Maynard, I *must* have that 'cello! I shall *die* if I don't.'

'Not you,' said Jo unfeelingly. 'People don't die for a reason of that kind—or even for a greater reason. I know that in books of the Victorian era the heroines seem to have been very easily killed off; but either our generation is tougher; or, what is more likely, the writers of the books were more concerned with making a "sad, sweet story" than with keeping to real life. So don't you worry about dying.'

'But I shall. I've always been delicate and easily made ill.'

Jo's thoughts went to her adopted sister, Robin Humphries. 'You've been easily made ill because everyone has given in to you,' she said bluntly. 'I know a girl, younger than you, and very much frailer. But I can't imagine her making herself ill just because she couldn't have all she wanted. And I certainly couldn't imagine her going on as you do when she was refused anything. She's had to put up with a lot of refusal in her life, just because she *was* so delicate. She's stronger now than we ever hoped she would be, but only because she learnt from babyhood to be obedient and accept what came without fretting, even if she didn't like it.' Then, by a sudden inspiration, she added, 'I wish you knew her. Upon my word, I'm very much inclined to send for her and make you stay here till you two have met. It would probably be the best thing in the world for you.'

'You couldn't *make* me stay. *You* couldn't make me do anything I didn't want. No one ever could!' Zephyr flung at her. 'And I *hate* "pi" people!'

Jo chuckled. 'Not much "pi" about Robin. No one in any of *our* houses could incline that way.' The mention of Robin had changed her mood. She suddenly turned to Zephyr, who was looking puzzled. 'Are you staying here—in Garnham, I mean?'

'No; I'm at the King's Arms in Garnley,' replied Zephyr.

'Staying for long? I mean, can you wait for a few days? I'd really like you to meet my Rob. She's staying with a school-friend at the moment; but she'd come if I sent for her. I think she'd make you understand things better than any of us. For one thing, she's much nearer you in age.' Jo spoke with an elderly air as if she were at least fifty.

Zephyr stared at her. 'I'm nineteen. How old is this Robin of yours?'

'Eighteen—and a half,' she added as an afterthought. 'We are all much older than that. Yes; Rob would be best. Will you stay, and I'll give her a ring? The Chesters are on the 'phone.'

'Did you say her name is Robin? I don't think I ever heard a girl called that before.' Zephyr was interested. 'What is it short for?'

'Nothing. Her real name is Cecilia Marya. But she was always called Robin from her baby days because she was round and chirpy and robin-like.'

'Is she musical? Does she play anything?'

'She has a violin; but her singing voice is lovely. Of course she's musical. No one could live with us and be anything else, I should think.'

'Do *you* play?'

Jo gave an involuntary grin. 'I can manage my own accompaniments on the piano if I have to. That's about all. But I sing. We all do, more or less. And little Primula, one of the nieces, is beginning to play the piano very prettily. Daisy, her elder sister, has a voice, and also a violin. They live with me, you know. But they're all away at the Chesters. Oh, music is a part of our lives. Rob will tell you. Well, will you do as I ask? If you will, I'll go and try to get the Chesters now.'

'Yes; I'll wait.' Zephyr was definitely intrigued by all this. For the moment, she had forgotten her wants. After all, she had had a lonely life with no real friends. Her own selfishness had prevented that.

Jo got up, tossed her an album of snapshots, saying, 'You'll find snaps of Rob in there. Dark, with curly hair. The fair, long-legged thing is Daisy. I'll go and see if I can get long-distance.'

She vanished, to come back twenty minutes later. 'It's all right. Rob will leave the Chesters tomorrow for a week, and I've rung up the King's Arms, and they've got a room for her. So that's all right. Will you know her when you see her, do you think?'

'I don't know.' Zephyr spoke doubtfully. 'Which is she? There seem to be two or three dark people with curly hair here.'

Jo took the book from her. 'So there are. I'd forgotten Elsie Carr and the rest. *This* is Rob.' And she pointed out a snap of a lovely girl of seventeen or so, with curly hair tied back from her face.

'That? But she's beautiful. I never saw anyone more lovely.'

'Oh yes; Rob's beautiful. That was taken last year. Here's our Daisy. She's younger by two years or so. Those are her two friends, Gwensi Howell and Beth Chester. Those three are great pals. Just as we four have always been. Well—what now?' For Zephyr was looking at her wistfully.

'It was just—do you know, Mrs Maynard, I've never been pals with anyone in my life. They look so happy. And *you* seem so happy.'

'Of course we are. But it isn't because we've all had everything we want all the time. We haven't. But we've learnt to live together, and to share, and to give in to each other. "I want" never got any of us anywhere. I don't think it ever does.'

Zephyr flushed. 'It's always got me what I wanted.'

'Only in the things that don't matter when it comes to the point. It hasn't brought you friends, and it never will as long as you make it your life's slogan. Now it's getting on for lunch-time. Will you stay and have it with us?' asked Jo, surprising herself almost as much as Zephyr by the invitation.

The visitor shook her head. 'I—I'd rather not today, thank you. I must get back to the hotel.'

'Well, will you meet Robin for me? She's coming by the train that arrives somewhere about midday. It would be difficult for me to get in for it. If you'd meet her, and have lunch together, then you could come out on the afternoon bus and have tea with us. You must see the others, and meet our families.' Jo glanced at her watch. 'If you go now, you'll just catch the bus comfortably.'

Accordingly, just as Simone and Marie were wondering what they should do about lunch, since Jo seemed to be still closeted with Zephyr, they heard the drawing-room door open, and then voices in the little hall. Two minutes later, Jo strolled into the kitchen to ask when the meal would be ready as she was hungry.

'Have you settled Zephyr?' asked Marie, lifting down the plates from the rack above the big closed range.

'I hope so,' said Jo, as she emptied the cabbage into the colander to drain. 'I've sent for Robin. She's coming tomorrow to the King's Arms.'

'Quoi?' cried Simone amazedly.

'Don't shriek at me like that! Why shouldn't she? She's eighteen, and responsible. Much more so than some people I could name were at her age,' retorted Jo, turning her cabbage into its dish. 'That's done. Come along, you people. We can't talk in front of the babes, but when they're fixed up for the afternoon I'll tell you all the news. But one thing I'll say now, if it hadn't been for that attempt on Rufus, I'd be ready to forgive her everything. As it is, I *am* very sorry for her in some ways.'

Her friends stared at her as she walked out of the kitchen carrying her dish. Then they turned and eyed each other doubtfully. Frieda shook her head. 'We shall get nothing out of her till she chooses,' she said. 'We had better have lunch and clear away. She'll tell us then.'

They had to wait till half-past two before Jo was ready, however. But then, over the teacups as they drank their after-lunch tea, she gave them a full account of what had happened, and explained her idea in calling Robin to the rescue.

'Rob is very sane. And also she's much the same age as this girl; I think she will probably get her to see a little straighter than any of us could. After all, we *are* six years older—at least, you three are, and I shall be in November. And then we're married, which is always ageing.' She heaved an elderly sigh.

Frieda and Marie laughed, but, to their surprise, Simone took it seriously. 'I think you are right there, my Jo. And it seems to me that our children make it seem even more so. I know that I always felt that for Gisela who was almost the same age as Gertrud Steinbrücke. Both were épousées, but Gisela had Natalie four years before Gertrud's little Gretel was born. I do wonder when we shall see Gertrud and Dr von Ronschlar again?' And she heaved a sigh, for it was now six years since any of them had seen Gertrud who had been one of the very early members of the Chalet School, and as they were all fond of her they mourned for the separation, though they had hopes that when they got back to Tyrol they would all meet again.

'I know I am,' said Jo, replying to the first part of Simone's speech. 'When one has babies of one's own to care for, it makes one older in some ways. And then all of us have had other experiences too. Beside us, Zephyr is a mere child. Robin herself is older in most ways. Oh, I know the young woman makes up *inches* deep—more idiot she!—and tries to be very sophisticated; but she really knows nothing about life. In my opinion, it is more than time that she grew up a little. I'd be sorry for any man who married her in her present state of mind. She'd lead him a dance! Of course I blame her people more than her. They must have been mad to let her grow up thinking that "I want" will get you whatever you want. However, it's not too late, even yet. We must do what we can for her. If only she takes to Rob, I think something can be done. I gave Rob a hint over the 'phone.'

'Then we must leave it to Rob,' said Marie. 'By the way, are we to see anything of her while she's at the King's Arms? And are you going in to meet her tomorrow? What time?'

'I am not,' replied Jo calmly. 'I told Zephyr to meet her, and showed her some snaps. They are both to come out to tea tomorrow afternoon. I felt it would be better that way. Whatever we do, we mustn't let Zephyr get an idea that we are trying to improve her. I don't know anything more maddening to the—er—improvee. Yes, Marie, I know you never heard *that* word before, but I've just coined it. Quite good, I think.'

'For calm conceit, Jo Maynard, I don't know your equal!' cried Marie. 'All right; we'll keep it dark. I only hope she likes Rob. But what a task to set our Vögelein! How will she meet it?'

'Easily! Rob has sense, and Zephyr is already very much impressed with her snaps. When she sees her in the flesh, I should think she'd be even more impressed. And Rob is a most lovable person, as you very well know. I hope that we shall find they've got together already when they arrive tomorrow. By the end of the week—Rob's week, I mean—they ought to be sufficiently friendly for Zephyr to want to keep in touch. I don't think her people will make any objections. Judging by what I've seen of her, I should think Miss Zephyr winds her family round her little finger.'

'What about Phoebe?' Simone wanted to know.

'Nothing, as yet. I'm not going to say a word till we see how it works out. But, knowing her as we do, does anyone doubt that Phoebe will meet Zephyr halfway? The young woman won't get her 'cello. I shan't allow it; I know what it means to Phoebe. But if she can only learn to feel for the girl who has had to bear so much in the way of pain and loss, I have an idea that young Zephyr will not only become a much nicer being, but will even make far more of her music than she could ever do otherwise.'

'Of course,' agreed Frieda. 'You are very wise, Joey.'

Jo flushed. 'I don't think so. If I have any wisdom, it has come to me through what life has brought me.' Then, with a sudden change of tone, she added, 'You must admit that in my school days I never showed very much wisdom; or common-sense, even.'

'You didn't!' said Simone emphatically. 'But you were always kind, Jo, and quick to see the needs of other people. It's the same thing, only in a more grown-up form. That is all.'

Jo laughed. 'I'm glad you look at it like that. Well, it's out of our hands now. Rob must stand by and do her best. We'll be there if she needs us, but, you know, somehow I don't feel that she will. What's the time, anyone? Half-past three? We promised the babes tea in the orchard. We'd better see about it. I'll go and put the kettle on if someone else will cut bread-and-butter and sandwiches. Then, after tea, let's play hide-and-seek all over the orchard and garden. They'll love it!'

'And so will Mrs Jack Maynard!' said Marie with a chuckle. 'Jo, you *are* a queer mixture. One moment, you're talking as wisely as the Abbess or Madame herself. The next, you might be about Sybil's age. How do you do it?'

'Simply by being Me, of course. That *is* Me. And don't pretend—you like hide-and-seek as much as anyone.' And Jo went off to the kitchen to fill the big iron kettle and put it on the oil-stove, since Debby, who usually saw to such things, was away at Howells Village for a couple of days so that she could visit her young mistress.

The improvement was maintained, and Phoebe, nearly a fortnight after her removal, was already feeling easier and in less pain than she had been for years. The doctors were growing less anxious about her heart too, for relief from continual pain was resting it. Jack had telephoned the night before, and had said that they hoped that after six months or so, Phoebe would be as nearly active as she could be, short of complete recovery.

Tea was a riotous affair, in which Sybil sent her mug flying, mercifully *after* she had emptied it; and Margot, not to be outdone, spilt all her milk down her frock as a result of rolling over with laughter. However, these were everyday accidents, and Margot would have a clean frock on the morrow in any case, so beyond telling her that she must be more careful, Jo said no more. After tea they duly played hide-and-seek, when Jo, having taken refuge up a huge old pear-tree, got caught in the branches, and had to be ignominiously rescued from her trap, with her frock torn under the arm and her hair coming down. The small fry watched Marie and Simone freeing her from the twigs and branches that had caught her, and shrieked joyously when at last she had reached the ground. Then it was bedtime, and for the next hour the elders were very busy while Sybil, having washed herself and brushed her chestnut curls, laid the table for the grown-ups' supper before betaking herself to a deck-chair on the lawn with 'Bevis,' which she was re-reading for about the sixth time.

No more was said about Zephyr, but all the girls were anxious for the coming of the next afternoon and the arrival of Robin and the queer case Jo had, as she herself said, 'wished on to her.'

Chapter XV

Robin

'Whyfor is you so singy, Mamma?' It was Margot, of course. Not much slipped that young lady's notice. So far as that went, none of Jo's three daughters was unobservant, but the other two talked less. Margot said everything that was in her mind, sometimes with disastrous results. On this occasion, Jo finished wiping the plate she had in her hand and put it away in the cupboard before she answered.

'Debby's coming back this evening, for one thing. For another. Auntie Rob is coming to tea this afternoon. And we haven't seen her for six whole weeks. Isn't that enough to make anyone singy?'

'Vewy nice,' said Margot. 'Is Auntie Daisy comin' too? An' Pwimula?' For some reason known only to themselves the little Maynards had taken to calling Daisy Venables 'Auntie,' and nothing would stop them. Daisy herself had been rather pleased by it; but her small sister Primula was very indignant, for the triplets showed no sign of giving her the title.

'Daisy isn't coming, nor is Primula,' said Jo, taking up the milk-jug. 'They are staying with Beth and Nancy Chester. It's only Auntie Rob.'

Con desisted from her attempts to ride Rufus to ask, 'Will she stay here? But where will she sleep? We're full up. Tante Mawie said so yesterday.'

'She will not sleep here. Tante Marie was quite right. Leave Rufus alone, Con, my lamb, and put this away for me, please. Auntie Rob is at the King's Arms in Garnley. But she's coming out for tea. So after lunch you can get into fresh frocks. I should like her to see you looking fairly decent for once. Thank you, Len. You can carry the forks and spoons into the dining-room and put them on the table. Sybs and Josefa will be down presently and they'll lay it all ready. We're going up to the moors as soon as the work is done.'

Jo and her little girls were washing up the breakfast things while Frieda dressed the two babies, and Marie and Simone were making the beds with the help of Sybil and Josefa. Tessa and small Louis were out in the garden in charge of Wolferl, and shrieks of joy were to be heard coming from them as he swung them gently in one of the hammocks.

Presently Jo finished, wrung out her scalded dish-cloth, hung up her towels to dry, and set to work to pack a slab of cake and some fruit in a big basket. They had all decided that they must do something to make the morning pass quickly, so they were taking the whole party up to the moors, which were about half a mile away. That meant taking 'elevenses,' for the fresh air made everyone hungry. Having finished her basket, Jo went out to the shed to fill a can with milk, while Len got the Bakelite mugs from the lower cupboard, and also took a biscuit for Rufus. Frieda came downstairs, a baby under each arm, and tucked them up in the big double pram Jem had brought, lashed to the top of his car, on his first visit. The girls used it continually. If Tessa and Louis tired, the two babies would be put side by side, and the tinies piled on at the bottom, so it was a very useful affair. From the dining-room came the sounds of Sybil and Josefa laying the table for lunch, and Simone vanished to the kitchen garden to pull lettuces for the salad she would make when they returned. Robin and Zephyr would not reach Garnham before half-past two or a quarter to three, so there would be plenty of time to put everything in order, and it was a lovely day, with bright sunshine and a fresh breeze; and, which was a consideration, a few hours spent on the moors made the children sleep soundly. So they all worked with a will, and by half-past ten they had closed the house, collected Reg on the way, and were headed for the narrow path that led from a white fence at the upper end of the village by a twisting track to where the moors unrolled, a purple glory for mile upon mile. Overhead came the strange, lone cry of a passing curlew; now and then they heard the bleat of the hill sheep. Looking down, they could see the village with the square tower of the church, and about it lonely farmhouses, embowered in trees. Jo and Frieda, pushing the big pram between them, stopped when they reached the edge of the moor, and looked round with sighs of delight. Reg heard them, and thinking they were tired, came to offer to push the pram.

'Not on this path, thank you, Reg,' said Jo. 'It's much too rough, and the pram is heavy. Tessa and Louis, I think you might walk a little now. Reg, take Sybil and Wolfram and Josefa, will you, and find us a nice place for elevenses. We'll follow with the others.—No, you three; you can't go. Stay with us, and help with the baskets.' For her trio had come to beg to go with the elder children. Reg gave them an understanding grin and set off, Sybil, Wolfram, and Josefa at his heels. Presently he set up a wild 'Pee-wit-t-t!' and the rest of the party made towards the place he had chosen. They had elevenses, and then Reg, armed with the basket and accompanied by all the children who could trot along, went to seek wimberries which grew about here.

'They'll make themselves filthy sights,' said Jo sleepily as she stretched out on the springy heather, her hat tilted over her eyes, her head cradled in her clasped hands, 'but "wots the hodds as long as you're 'appy," as it says somewhere. Simone, *must* you sew? Can't you just be lazy for a little? Put that mending away, and enjoy yourself for once.'

'But it's got to be done some time,' argued Simone. 'Oh, very well. What a tease you are, Jo!' And she laid aside Tessa's frock, which she was darning with the exquisite stitchery of her French fingers, and lay back too. The other three were frankly idle. They had brought no work, and Marie, curled up against the scented heather, actually fell asleep. When the others woke her, which they did with much jeering, she protested that the heather on a sunny day was the sleepiest thing she knew. Then Reg and the others returned with the big basket half-full, and fingers, clothes, and lips blue with wimberry-juice.

'It's been a jolly morning,' said Jo as she helped to pack the small fry into the pram. 'And this afternoon we shall have Rob with us!'

'Is that another doctor?' asked Reg eagerly. Then he turned scarlet at the shouts of laughter. 'Well, I couldn't know,' he said offendedly.

'I'm sorry, Reg.' Jo spoke in instant apology. Reg was a touchy young man, and she liked him, even if she had not wanted to befriend him, for Phoebe's sake. 'But it seemed so funny to think of Robin as a doctor. She is a girl, my adopted sister. I know it's a queer name for a girl, but it just fits her. Come to tea this afternoon and meet her. She's heard heaps about you. She'd like to meet you, I know.'

'I'll think about it.' Reg was still on his dignity. 'Mebbe I've got to go a message for Aunt. If she doesn't want me I'll come.'

'All right,' said Jo equably. 'We won't expect you till you turn up.'

'You'd better try, though,' said Marie. 'I'm going to make wimberry shortcake for tea. Ever tasted it? Well, you'll like it.'

'Another of your American dishes?' teased Jo as they set off down the path. 'What it is to be so far travelled!'

Marie, who had spent nearly three years in America—Josefa had been born there—smiled amiably, but said nothing; and by the time they had reached the village Reg was his usual sunny self. The church clock was chiming one, so he left them at his aunt's cottage, and they hurried on to get lunch and do all the things that seemed so many when they had less than two hours in which to do them. However, they were finished and changed by half-past two, and were sitting sewing, knitting, and chatting when there came up the village street the sound of light steps and merry laughter. Then a voice that was one of the loveliest voices in the world to Jo called, 'Jo—Joey! Here we are! Oh, *Joey*!' And the gate was flung open, and a small, dainty person came flying up the path to hurl herself on Jo, who had risen and was standing with open arms that closed tightly on the slender form which clung to her.

'Rob! My precious! How ever have I done without you for so long?'

'How have *I* done so long without *you*, you mean!' came the answer.

'You'll have to manage when you go to Oxford, Rob,' said Marie as she kissed the lovely face lifted to hers, for Robin was very small, shorter even than Simone who owned a bare five-foot-three, while the other three were all above five-foot-six, tall Jo boasting two inches more than that. Robin Humphries was only half an inch over five feet, and slender in proportion, so that she looked fairy-like, with her lovely face and curiously graceful movements. Zephyr, following her slowly up the path, was already fascinated by her new acquaintance, and, for the first time in her life, wanted to make a real friend.

Jo saw her, as Robin was greeting the others and answering the clamouring of the children who clustered round her with shouts, and went forward with a smile. 'Come along! You must forgive our ecstasies, but, as you see, we aren't accustomed to being parted for so long. Come and meet our children. I'll take you to see the babies while the rest are pulling Robin to pieces, shall I? This way. They're asleep in the orchard.'

She led the way to the orchard Zephyr remembered so vividly, and to a Li-lo on which the two babies were sleeping. 'This is

Mrs von Ahlen's new son, Gerard,' she said, bending over the tiny baby with his flaxen mop resting on the pillow. 'This big gentleman is *my* boy. When they're awake, you shall nurse them if you want to. Just at present I think we'll let sleeping babes lie. They're nice, but they can both *yell* if they're wakened at the wrong moment—which happens to be now. Now come and meet the rest.' And she tucked a hand in Zephyr's arm and steered her back to the noisy group on the front lawn.

'Can they sleep through that?' asked Zephyr in surprise.

'Oh, our babies have to learn to sleep through anything,' said Jo airily. 'I admit Frieda's house is quieter than ours; but six weeks with us has taught her boys the lesson all ours learn from the first.—Children! come and say "How do you do?"'

Her own three trotted up, very fresh and dainty in their blue frocks. Jo gravely presented them, and they held out their hands at once. 'How do you do?' said Len. 'It is nice to see you. Are you a friend of Auntie Rob's? She's stayin' with you, isn't she?'

Zephyr shook hands with her nervously. She had never had anything to do with small children, and this very self-possessed little person was a shock to her. When the other two followed, she touched their fingers quickly, and then turned and looked at Sybil, who was coming forward with that enchanting grace which had attracted even Mrs Hart.

'This is my niece, Sybil,' said Jo. 'And here are Countess von Wertheim's pair, Josefa and Wolfram. By the way, you haven't met their mother either, have you?—Marie! Stop eating Rob up, and come and be introduced.'

Marie von Wertheim joined the group with a laugh. 'How rude you are, Jo! I'm not eating Rob—no more than you did, anyhow.—How do you do, Miss Burthill? Do you think you'll be able to remember us all? We are a crowd, aren't we? Here is Mrs von Ahlen, and her elder boy, Louis. I think you did meet Mme de Bersac yesterday; but here is Tessa, her girl.'

'And now,' said Robin briskly, 'I want to go and see Stephen and Gerard while the rest of you entertain Miss Burthill. Do you know, Frieda, that this is my first view of him? Who is he like?'

'Me,' said Frieda mournfully. 'I did hope he would be like Papa, but he isn't. Jo consoles me by saying I must manage a daughter next time, and she is sure to be like Bruno, as girls usually take after their fathers. Come along and see him, and tell me what you think.'

The two took Robin between them, and led her off to the babies, while Marie, having given Zephyr a chair, sent the rest to play, with a reminder to keep themselves clean, and Simone slipped indoors to put the kettle on for tea, for they had all agreed that it would be best to have it early in case of any awkward pauses.

'Are you comfortable there?' asked Marie. Then she laughed. 'I'm afraid our crowd must be a little embarrassing at first. It's much worse when we're all together at home. You see, I have a sister, and she has three children. And Frieda's brother is one of the doctors at the San. His wife is an old school-friend. They have five little ones. When all our crowd get together with Keferl, Maria Ileana, and Baby Emmie, who are my two nieces and nephew; and Gisela's Natalie, Gisel, Louise, and Jo-jo, not to speak of three or four others, the children of more of our old school—it's like a monkey-house. So we're accustomed to it.'

'They all seem quite jolly,' said Zephyr shyly.

'Oh, they are!' Marie laughed again. 'It's such fun having the second generation all growing up together and being chums as we are.'

'How well you speak English,' said Zephyr. 'You aren't English, are you?'

'No: I'm Austrian—Viennese,' said Marie. 'But I was educated at the Chalet School, where we all spoke English every third day. Then I had a good three years in America—Josefa was born there. And we've lived in England since. So it would be queer if I didn't speak English well.'

'Why English every *third* day?' Zephyr's curiosity was roused by this mysterious remark. 'What did you speak on the others?'

'French one day and German the other. We were tri-lingual. You see, we had girls of all three races in the school—others, too; but those were the three chief ones. So it was necessary to talk all three languages well. I'm afraid we sometimes forget before strangers, which is very rude of us, of course. But we don't mean it. If we do it before you, please understand and forgive us. We don't mean it as rudeness.'

'I can't speak anything but English.' Zephyr sat revolving things in her own mind. 'You see, I didn't like lessons, and I only had to tell Daddy, and then he said I needn't.'

'Oh, but wasn't that a pity? I mean, it cuts you off from so much that is great and beautiful in the writings of other lands. Translations are never quite the same. You know,' went on Marie confidentially, 'Mrs Maynard speaks Italian quite well, and a little Russian too. She was always mad about languages. We always say that doing so much of it is what has helped her to write such jolly books.'

'Does she write *books*?' gasped Zephyr.

'Didn't you know? Oh, but I suppose you wouldn't. She's Josephine M. Bettany. Haven't you read *Cecily Holds the Fort*, or *Gipsy Jocelyn*? How proud we all were when "Cecily" came out! Quite a lot of our girls are doing interesting things; but Jo is our one and only authoress up to date.'

'How interesting,' said Zephyr, who had never read a child's book since she was thirteen, and had never even heard of 'Josephine M. Bettany.' 'And what do you do?' she asked as an afterthought.

Marie laughed. 'I'm just a plain wife and mother. Our family doesn't run to brains, I'm afraid. Jo and Simone led us there.

Frieda and I went with the ruck. Frieda is a harpist, though. Simone, now, is really brainy. She studied at the Sorbonne, and took her degree in maths.'

'What is the Sorbonne?' asked Zephyr helplessly. She had had no idea she was so ignorant, and only good breeding kept Marie from staring.

'It's the great Paris University,' she explained. 'Simone did very well there. When her course was ended, she came back to the school to teach. And if ever it is in trouble over maths, she goes back again.'

'And Miss Humphries is going to Oxford, she tells me. I—I—what a clever set you all are!'

'Not me!' said Marie emphatically. 'I married young, you see. And I really never was much good at school, though I did work hard. What about your music? Have you been to the Royal College or the Royal Academy?'

'No; I've only had private lessons. But they were good ones, of course. My 'cello was the only thing I ever really worked at. But I do love it. I—I feel so sure I should get on faster if only I could have Nicholas Wychcote's. I feel that somehow it would—would *inspire* me, and I should be able to—to *feel* the music better.'

Marie shook her head. 'Someone else's 'cello couldn't give you that. It comes from inside yourself, you know. You can only put into your music what you've got to give. If it isn't there, nothing will give it to you from outside. I'm explaining very badly; but perhaps you can see what I mean.' Then, as she saw Zephyr's bewildered look, she said, 'Oh, I never could explain things. You'd better ask Jo—or Robin. They can make you understand. But I'll tell you this much. Ask Jo to sing for you after tea, and you'll see what I mean. Her voice is really lovely, you know. It's not a concert-room voice; it isn't powerful enough for that. But she puts herself into her singing—and Jo has a lot to put.'

The talk ended there, for the others came back, and Jo went to help Simone to bring out the tea while Frieda and Robin chatted to Marie, doing their best to bring the stranger into the conversation. But Zephyr felt herself very much on the outer edge of their interests. They talked of books of which she had heard, but which she had not attempted to read. They discussed music, and she was amazed at the technical knowledge even Marie displayed. The talk turned to travel, and she heard descriptions of their beloved Tyrol, with its lakes and mountains and rushing streams. When the other two came out with the teapot, it was the same. They never left her out of the talk, but so much of what they said was so nearly Greek to her, that she felt as if they were using an unknown language. It was quite a relief when they had finished, and Frieda and Marie went to see to the children, and she could turn to Jo and ask her to sing.

'Oh yes, do, Joey!' cried Robin. 'It seems ages since I heard you.'

'It's six weeks or so,' said Jo. 'Oh, all right. What do you want?'

'"Rosebud in the Heather." I love that, and it sounds almost as well without an accompaniment as with it. Go on, Joey!'

Jo lay back in her chair, dropping her hands in her lap, and opening her mouth, sang with a voice like gold, every note as round and true as a choir-boy's, Schubert's lovely little lyric. Zephyr was a really musical girl, and she appreciated the purity of the singing and its easy, effortless production to the full. When the song was ended, and the children, their tea finished, came flying to demand more, she joined her voice eagerly with theirs, and Jo laughed and gave way. She chose the old Northumbrian folk-song, 'Bonny at Morn.' As the last perfect note died on the air, Zephyr suddenly felt that Marie was right. Mrs Maynard must have a great deal in her to sing like that. She tried to say something about it.

'I should be sorry if I couldn't sing lullabies,' said Jo briskly. 'I've had four babies to sing to sleep. That teaches you a good deal, you know.'

'Yes; but—but you singed to *us* togever, Mamma,' cried Margot.

'Together?' Zephyr turned a puzzled look on Jo, who shouted with laughter.

'Miss Burthill! Has no one told you yet? My girls are triplets—the only triplets in our crowd. Rob! Did you really never say anything about it?'

Robin laughed and coloured. 'I'm afraid I forgot. We take them so for granted nowadays. It really is true, Miss Burthill. Jo was as proud as a peacock with two tails when she found what she'd done. And so were we.'

'Oh!' burst out Zephyr suddenly, 'can't you stop calling me "Miss Burthill" all the time? Mayn't I be "Zephyr" to you? And can't I call you "Robin" as everyone else does?'

'Why, of course,' said Robin quickly. 'It would be silly of us to spend a week together as we propose, and "Miss" each other.'

Zephyr glanced at the others; but what Robin, so near Zephyr in age, could do easily, was not quite the same for them. There was still too much to consider for them to come to such terms yet. So no more was said, and presently Robin discovered that they must leave if they did not want to wait for the last bus, which would mean that they could not reach the hotel before nine.

'Oh, we mustn't do that!' cried Zephyr. 'They don't serve dinner after half-past eight unless you make a real fuss. Will some of you come to Garnley tomorrow and have tea with us?'

'Tomorrow is Sunday, and the buses are awful,' said Jo. 'You come out to us, if you like. But with all the small fry, I think we'll stay put.'

'We'd better all stay put,' said Robin. 'All right, you people.

You can come on Monday and spend the afternoon. We can take the babes to Garnley woods, and have tea at the hotel later. They have a small room they let to private parties. I saw it when I came down for lunch. We'll speak to the manageress and book it. You don't want to bring all the families to the lounge, I know.'

'No; and I shouldn't think the other visitors would want us to, either,' said Marie. 'What a sensation we should create, though!'

'One I'd rather be excused,' said Frieda decidedly. 'There are moments, Marie, when you are quite as mad as Jo herself. I believe you would rather *enjoy* the episode. But in that case, you'll go without me.'

'And me,' chimed in Simone. '*I* am not going with a small kindergarten anywhere. If you and Jo like to do it, Marie—'

'No one is going to do it,' said Robin firmly. 'Zephyr and I will see to booking the room, and we'll have tea there. Now we really must go, or we shall miss that bus. Come along. Zephyr.' And she led the way down the path, the triplets clinging to her, and the rest of the children running about them. Zephyr contrived to get Jo alone for a moment. 'I like her,' she said quickly in an undertone. 'I—I do hope she'll be friendly. I never saw anyone like her before. Thank you, Mrs Maynard.'

Jo glanced at her. 'Rob will be able to help you better than anyone else,' she said gently. 'I hope she *will* be friendly with you. Rob's a dear.'

That was all; but that night, as the four stood on the bedroom landing for a few last words before bed, she told them what Zephyr had said, and they all agreed that Robin would help Zephyr better than anyone else.

Chapter XVI

Jack Arrives

Rob stayed her week, and then went back to her friends, having given Zephyr Burthill a thing she had never known before—a quiet, disinterested friendship. The spoilt child of a rich man had had acquaintances, but she was quite clever enough to realise that most of them showed her friendship for what they could get out of her. At one time she had rather enjoyed the feeling of power this gave her. But lately she had been thinking more deeply than she had ever done before, and she was slowly beginning to know that such things would not easily satisfy her. Robin Humphries wanted nothing that she could give unless it were friendship. And from her talk Zephyr had gathered that she was already rich in friends. Suppose, after thinking it over, Robin decided that they should not go any further! When she got this far, Zephyr suddenly realised something else—that the 'cello had taken second place in her desires. If it came to a choice between that and Robin's friendship, then the 'cello must go.

If Jo had known of this, she would have known how successful her hastily conceived plan had been. But Zephyr was too shy to tell her, and they said goodbye without the older girl learning the truth of the matter.

The next excitement was the arrival of Jack Maynard for his week's holiday. He brought more good news about Phoebe. It was too soon yet for them to say anything certain about this improvement. But they all hoped that it meant the beginning of better things for her. She was having massage now, and was doing a few easy exercises to tone up long disused muscles which were flabby. The exercises were very carefully supervised, and so far had done good and not harm.

'We have to go slow because of her heart,' explained Jack, as he lay on his back in the heather in an attitude frankly suggestive of having overeaten—it was after lunch, which had been a picnic affair, and the girls were boiling the picnic kettle on a little Etna set in a biscuit-tin to make coffee. 'It's stronger than it was, but any strain would send it right back to where it was. No one wants that. But,' and he sat up, clasping his hands round his knees, 'I rather think things are going to happen.'

'How do you mean?' asked his wife as she put the coffee into the pot.

'Aha! That's just it!' he said wickedly.

Jo finished her task, set the pot down carefully at a safe distance, and came to sit beside him. 'Elucidate that statement,' she said, laying her hand gently on his head. But he knew what it meant, and gave a quick wriggle to get away from her. Not quite quick enough, though. She was prepared, and as he squirmed away from her, her fingers closed firmly in his hair, and she said threateningly, 'Tell; or I'll thin your locks!'

'You do, and just see what you get!' he retorted, sitting still perforce. 'Pull my hair, and your own will be down in half a moment.'

'Oh, don't bother with him, Jo,' urged Marie. 'He's only talking nonsense to tease us. There isn't any special news.'

'Oh yes, there is. So that's all you know about it!' he declared.

'Madge is all right, isn't she?' demanded Jo, her mind suddenly flying to the beloved sister, who had been mother to her as well, since they had been orphaned when Jo herself was a baby of ten months old.

'Perfectly all right, so you needn't worry,' he said quickly. 'Get the coffee made, like good girls, for I'm dying of thirst, and

I'll tell you all about it. It's news all right, and I think you'll be pleased.'

'The kettle is just boiling,' said Frieda. 'Bring the pot here, Jo, and Jack can have his drink. Then he can tell us what he means—if anything.'

'Oh, I do mean something!' And Jack chuckled to himself.

When they were all settled with their coffee, he held out his cup for a second supply, and then told them. 'Peters had a long talk with me yesterday about Phoebe. He says that he thinks a good deal can be done for her so that, in time, she will be able to lead an almost normal life. But, of course, she will need care all her life. He has seen a great deal of her in the past few weeks, since she is mainly in his charge, and what he wanted to ask me about was if I thought there was any chance for him with her.'

'Jack! Oh, what a lovely thing to happen!' And Jo clapped her hands.

'Do you really mean that, Jack? But if only Phoebe feels the same about him, surely it would be the very best of all for her?' said Marie, leaning forward, her lovely face flushed with earnestness.

'I mean it, of course. And I agree with you, Marie. Peters is a fine fellow. He isn't any film star for looks, I know. But he is honest and upright and faithful, and, I should say, thinks any amount of Phoebe. He'd watch over her like a hen over a duckling, so *that* would be all right. And he knows what to look for as well. The thing is, he's afraid to do anything about it in case she doesn't feel that way about him. Then, he says, just having to refuse him would probably have a bad effect on her, and he's afraid to risk it. So I thought I'd get you girls to try to find out what she feels about it. If it's all right, he can go ahead. In that case, it would almost certainly be an additional spur to her to get well. If it's all wrong, he'll say nothing, but—well, just go on hoping and try later when she'd be more able to stand it, I suppose.'

'So that's why you've told us? I was rather surprised after the first shock, for it isn't like you to betray a confidence,' said Simone.

'Oh, it's no betrayal. He asked me if my wife would try to get some idea from Phoebe about it, so that he could know what to do. It's an awkward position, you see, girls,' went on Jack, rumpling up his thick hair with an impatient hand. 'He seems to be falling more and more in love each day, and if he goes on seeing her—well, there's a limit to every man's endurance, and he may break some day, and say something. If she likes the idea, well and good. If she doesn't, it would mean worry and upset for her; and he would have to hand her over to someone else as a patient. Now do you get me? Frieda, what do you think? You've said nothing so far.'

'I think it would be the very best thing of all for Phoebe, and I hope—oh, I do *hope* she loves him!' replied Frieda, her soft voice full of happiness. 'What a wonderful thing to happen! Whoever could have thought when you took her away that Sunday, so ill, that this would come of it!'

'It hasn't—yet,' he said hurriedly. 'No one knows what Phoebe thinks. She's certainly very friendly with him; but no more so than with Jem, or me, or Gottfried, or any of the rest. At least, I've seen no signs of it.'

'You are all men,' said Jo. 'I don't suppose you *would* see. Does Madge know? Can't she give you some idea?'

'Madge hasn't been to the San. yet. Jem wouldn't let her risk it. And it isn't a thing we could ask of anyone else. You four are all fond of Phoebe, and I thought you might be able to help us out.'

'It isn't as easy as all that,' said Jo gravely. 'Phoebe might confide in us, but it would be another thing to tell you. I mean, I could let you know, perhaps; but it would be for your ears only, and for no one else. In that case, I don't see how you would be any better off.'

'I don't want you to ask her outright if she loves him, dear. I thought you might be able to find out if she liked him more than the rest of us. That would give Peters something to go on.'

'Well, that *might* be just possible. You'd have to leave it to my judgment how much I told you; or if I told you anything at all,' said Jo.

'I thought that. If you will do that, Joey, I know I can trust you.'

'I'd have to get rid of Reg. We couldn't talk with that young man there.'

'I can manage that for you. I've got to go over on Wednesday for a consultation that can't be put off any longer. I thought I'd take you and Reg with me. He could see Phoebe first, and then I'd turn him off on to Oliver's hands in the X-ray room. He'd be happy enough there, and Oliver could answer all his questions. Then I'd leave you—and one of you other girls too—with Phoebe. I propose to take two of you. Jo has an imagination, and she might see things that weren't there, so to speak.' He gave his wife a teasing look as he spoke, but to his surprise Jo did not rise to the bait. Instead she sat silent, gazing gravely toward the distant blue hills on the horizon.

It was Marie who replied. 'I see what you mean. It would be such a wonderful thing for Phoebe if it were true, just *one* of us might be ready to see what really wasn't there. But *two* of us would check on each other. Isn't that what you mean?'

'That's the idea. What do you say, Joey?'

'Yes; I think you are right, both of you. But, I do hope it's true. It would mean that Phoebe would know the happiness we all have—or most of it, anyway. You are sure it can't be a complete cure, Jack?' Jo looked wistfully at him as she spoke.

'So far as human knowledge goes—no, Joey. Only God can

cure like that. But it may be His Will that way. We can't say. With Him, all things are possible. We can only do our best and leave the end in His hands.' Jack spoke as gravely as she had done, and felt repaid by the look she gave him. These two were united in every way, and in their religion as well as in other things. To them, God was a close Friend indeed. The other girls felt the same, and there was no jarring element among them.

'We'll all pray harder than ever for her now,' said Marie. 'But even if it is not God's will that she should be completely cured, if she really loves Dr Peters, she will know far more happiness than if she had lived on alone in Many Bushes, with just Debby to care for her.'

'And Debby is getting old,' said Frieda. 'A day would have come when she couldn't have gone on as she has been doing. She was talking to me one day when I stayed at home, and she told me how often she had felt tired, and how much better she was for just these few weeks of rest with us. She was terrified the day would come when she had to give up.'

'And now it need not happen!' Marie's voice was full of joy. 'How very happy Debby will be if it comes to pass!'

'When—oh, but you said Wednesday,' said Jo. 'That's a long time to wait. Jack, this really is wonderful news, and I'm sorry I threatened to pull your hair. But you really are aggravating,' she added.

'I'll forgive you. And it won't hurt you to wait. You'll be getting accustomed to the idea. There'll be less chance then of your flying in to Phoebe crying, "Oh, Phoebe, are you in love with Dr Peters?" That *would* be a shock for her,' chuckled Jack. 'Well, how is my friend Reg? Is he still anxious to be a doctor? You know, girls, we must give that kid a hand. He's really keen, and he asks sensible questions. Why didn't he get a scholarship to the nearest secondary school? He's a bright lad.'

'Measles at the time of the exam. And the next year he was

over-age. At least, I think that's what it was. Something of the kind, I know. Yes, Reg has a good brain. We see quite a lot of him. But he's a huffy young man, and we have to be careful what we say, or he goes off, and won't come back for a day or two.'

'He'll have to get over that if he means to do anything in the world.' Jack spoke sternly. 'Heaven defend me from a sulky man! There's no doing anything with him. Master Reg will have to learn to take teasing and snubs and so on without losing his temper over them.'

'I think,' said Simone, 'it is because he has had no one to understand that he is like this. His aunt is good to him, but she doesn't understand him in the least. I should think she never has done. She sees that he is well-fed and has good clothes. But I don't think she bothers more.'

'That may be. And if the boy resembles his father as Phoebe seems to think, then he wants more than just creature comforts. But she won't understand that.'

'Tonsils and adenoids!' said Jo suddenly.

They all turned and eyed her as though she had taken leave of her senses.

'What are you talking about?' asked Jack. '*Who* has tonsils and adenoids?'

'Reg did—when the exams for the Garnley Grammar took place. I said measles, but it was tonsils. Phoebe says that old Mrs Thirtle could quite well afford to pay for him there, but she doesn't approve of "all this here eddication," so she won't. She'd have let him go if he'd got a free place, I believe. As it is, she expects him to leave school when he's fourteen and get a job of some sort. Reg once told me she'd spoken to Mr Jaycott about him to go and learn farmwork. He said he'd run away sooner. I asked him where he'd run, and he said, "I dunno; but I'm not going to be a farmer for anyone. I hate the work—always mucky." Poor kid!'

'If he wants to be ... gracious! who's being killed?' as a terrific uproar arose from where the children had been playing happily a little way away among some trees.

'No one.' Jo got to her feet. 'That's Margot in a rage. What's happened now, I wonder?'

'You sit down. This isn't going to be allowed. Margot must learn to control herself. Sit down, Jo. I'll see to it.'

So imperative were Jack's tones that Jo meekly sat down again, and he strode away over the heather to where his youngest daughter was standing in the middle of a circle, stamping with both feet, and screaming at the top of her voice. Her eyes were tightly shut, and tears were streaming down her cheeks. Her father came up in time to hear Len say, 'Margot, Con didn't mean it. Don't scream like that, Margot! Mamma will put you to bed when we get home if you do. Don't scream so. Con, say you're sorry!'

'But I'm not sowwy,' said Con. 'Margot *was* bein' g'eedy an' takin' the best of evewything. *Vat*'s like a little pig, Mamma says.'

'Yes; but *you* needn't say it,' said the anxious eldest sister. Then their father was among them, demanding, 'What is the meaning of this? Margot, are you hurt? Got a pain somewhere? No?' as Margot shook her head. 'Then stop that noise at once!'

Slightly subdued by the sudden appearance of her father, Margot gulped noisily once or twice, and then stopped screaming. The rest turned rather scared looks on him. Jo had generally contrived to keep Margot's sudden fits of rage from him, and he was very little at home during the daytime. This was the first time for more than a year that he had met one of them, and he was determined to put a stop to them as soon as possible. He turned to Len who was standing looking worried.

'Len, what is all this about?'

'Margot was angry with Con because Con said something she didn't like.'

'What was it, Con?'

'I said she was like a little pig,' confessed Con, lifting truthful brown eyes to her father's face.

'Oh? What had she been doing to make you say that? You girls are not to call each other names like that. You've been told that before.'

'*Not* a pig!' sobbed Margot, who had dissolved into tears. 'Con is howwid to say it! I *aren't* a pig, Papa!'

'I don't know about that. You look more like a fury than anything else at the moment. No; I don't want to pick you up. I don't like little girls who fly into the kind of tempers you flew into a few minutes ago.'

Margot sobbed loudly, and he turned and looked at the other children. 'You people run away and have a game. I must settle this.—Len, you don't seem to have anything to do with it. You go with the rest. Run along.'

'But please, Papa, can't I 'splain a bit first?'

'No, my pet. Con and Margot can do the explaining. You go and play.' He bent and kissed the dear little troubled face. 'Don't worry, Len. I'm not cross with anyone—yet. But I must know why Con said Margot was like a pig; and Margot must learn to take such things without showing temper.'

Jo had trained her children to obedience, so Len had no more to say. She went off after the others, and Jack was left with Con and Margot. He sat down on a fallen log, and called them to him. 'Now, I want to know the meaning of all this. Con, what exactly did you say?'

'I said Margot was actin' like a pig, and I wasn't goin' to play if she went on,' said Con, her head drooped, and her cheeks red as she spoke.

'What were you doing, Margot, to make Con say that?'

'Nuffin'. At least it wasn't much, anyway,' said Margot. Her cheeks were red too, but not with shame. Her eyes were sparkling with anger, and her lips were set in a straight line.

'But it was something?' Jack waited for an answer, but none came. Con was trying not to cry, and Margot was not anxious to tell her father what she had been doing. He tried again. 'Margot, I want to know what it was.'

'Please, Papa, I'll say I'm sowwy to Margot, and she'll say she's sowwy she was cwoss. Won't that do?' pleaded Con, trying to shield her sister. 'You'll tell Papa you're sowwy, won't you, Margot, if I do?'

'Shan't!' Margot was still rebellious, and very far from any sorrow. Jack looked at her. Then he turned to Con. 'Kiss me, pet, and go to the others. No; not another word. Off you go, now—run!'

Con turned and went with lagging steps. The triplets loved each other dearly, though they sometimes squabbled. It was bad enough when Mamma was cross with them. But that Papa should be angry was nothing short of a calamity. He had been so much away from home during their short lives that they had had it impressed on them that they must always be good when he was with them. He was such a delightful playfellow, too. Con couldn't remember ever seeing him so grave as this. Oh dear! Why hadn't she just let Margot have her way and say nothing? Mamma would be so sorry.

Meanwhile, Jack turned back to his small rebel. 'Now, Margot, we stay here until you tell me what you were doing to make Con call you a pig. Come here and sit down beside me.' She came, and he lifted her on to the log. 'Now then; as soon as you are ready to tell me, I will listen. But I must know why you were so naughty. I am ashamed to think you are one of my little girls!'

That nearly settled the matter. Like the others, Margot adored her father, and to be spoken to by him in this strain was almost the worst punishment he could have given her. She sat very erect, struggling with tears. But she was a very proud little person, and she wasn't ready yet to say that she was sorry for her temper. Jack glanced at her as she sat there, her lips set, her brows knit in a baby scowl. She looked so tiny, and so pathetic in her naughtiness, that he nearly relented. But he had very high ideals of his duties as a father. He knew that she must learn to control her temper, and the sooner the better for everyone. They had had sad scenes with Sybil Russell when she was younger; and Sybil was still paying the price for selfwill earlier in the year. So he took a paper from his pocket, and began reading it, taking no more notice of the poor little sinner by his side.

In their hollow, the girls looked across at the trees. The pair were hidden from view, and they had no idea what was going on. Jo looked worried, but Stephen roused from his nap just then, so she had to go and take him out of the pram, for Gerard was still fast asleep.

'Don't look so anxious, Jo,' said Marie. 'Margot's temper really is dreadful when it's roused, and Jack was bound to meet it sooner or later.'

'I have tried to make her control it,' said Jo, 'but it seems to flare out so suddenly. Poor little soul! It's a hard row for her to hoe.'

'It will be worse later on,' said Frieda. 'You don't want to have the trouble with her that there's been with Sybil. What Jack says may impress her more than your scoldings. You're with them so much, and they see so little of him. Besides, it's right that he should help to train them. I only wish Bruno were at home again to help me with my little boys.'

'I suppose you're right,' said Jo with a sigh. 'I certainly *don't* want Margot to have the struggle poor Sybs is having. And they *are* Jack's children as much as mine, so he certainly has a right to control them. But I have tried to get them always to be at their best with him just because he sees too little of them. I can't think where Margot gets her temper. I don't remember ever flaring up as she does, even at my worst. And I know, for Bob told me, that Jack was always sweet-tempered as a child, and he hasn't changed in that respect. And Madge and Dick are the same. It isn't in our family—unless—I believe my father was by way of being irritable. I don't know. I don't remember him at all, you know. Perhaps that's where both Margot and Sybil get it. I must ask Madge when I see her again.'

'Let's be getting tea ready,' suggested Simone. 'Everyone will want it by the time the kettle has boiled. Give me the meth bottle, Marie, and begin to unpack the baskets, will you?—Frieda, I believe I heard Gerard.'

In the meantime Jack was reading, to all outward appearance quite placidly, and Margot, perched up beside him on the log, was as unhappy as ever she had been. Why did she fly into rages? The others didn't. It was most unfair. Len always gave in to other people, and Con was very rarely angry. It was only she who did it. And it was so horrid to have to say she was sorry. But somehow she knew that Papa would no more let her off it than Mamma did. Oh, if only she didn't do and say such awful things when things happened that she didn't like!

At this point she could hold it in no longer. A sob burst from her, and then Papa had tossed his paper down, and was lifting her on to his knee, and holding her so closely. Margot felt the comfort of that tender hold, and she turned her face to him and cried out all the naughtiness.

'Are you sorry, my pet?' asked Jack presently, when the heavy sobs had ceased a little, and she was lying in his arms, still heaving with the violence of the storm.

'Yes, Papa. I'm vewy sowwy. But oh, *why* can't I be good like Len and Con? Vey never say fings or stamp. I don't mean to, and ven someone says somefing to make me cwoss, and I forget, and it's *dweadful*!' And Margot gulped again.

'I know, my darling. But God gave you your temper, and He

gave you the power to keep hold of it. Only you don't always try, do you? Now tell me what you had been doing to make Con call you a pig?'

In muffled tones Margot made her confession. 'We was playing at house, and Len had such a pwetty house under a may-bush. And I wanted it, and I said so. And ven Sybil said I'd chosen the one I had when Josefa wanted it, and wouldn't give up, and *she* had, and I must keep it. And I said I wouldn't, 'cos I wanted Len's, and Josefa could have mine if she liked. Ven Wolferl said I was always selfish and twying to get ve best for myself, and Con said Mamma would be cwoss if she knew how like a little pig I was being—and so she would!—and I was *vewy* cwoss. Vat's all.' And Margot heaved a sigh of relief as she ended.

Jack nearly smiled; but he pulled himself together. 'It was very, very naughty,' he said gravely. 'I don't wonder Con said Mamma would be cross. We want our little girls to learn to give in to others when it is right, and not try to get all the best things for themselves. You have made everyone unhappy this afternoon; yourself as well, because I don't think you were really happy, were you? Now you must tell them you are sorry. And you must tell Mamma, too, for she was very worried when she heard you screaming like that. And you *must* try to keep hold of your temper, or we shall have to punish you for it, and we don't want to do that.'

'Mamma sends me to bed,' mumbled Margot, scarlet-faced.

'Yes; well, *I* shall spank you if I see it again. We don't have spankings in our family as a rule, so don't be the one to bring them there. Try to be good, my pet. Now kiss me, and then go and tell the rest how sorry you are to have spoilt their fun, and we'll say no more this time.'

Margot held up her face for his kiss. Then he put her off his knee and saw her start off on her unpleasant task. He sighed. Then he laughed softly, and getting up and rescuing his paper, returned to the girls, where he found tea nearly ready. He told them the story while they waited for the kettle to boil, and Jo both laughed and sighed.

'My poor little pet! It *is* a hard struggle for her. I haven't ever let it pass, Jack; but it is so hard for her to remember to control herself.'

'I know, Joey. Don't worry. Once she *has* learnt to govern it, she will make all the finer woman. Is that kettle boiling at last, Marie? Then make the tea, and I'll give the kids a yell.'

And so the matter ended, though Jo had to listen to a sad confession at bedtime. She was so grave over it, that Margot cried again; but she had had a lesson which helped her to make greater efforts to control herself, while Con, who was equally penitent at having made the remark which had set a match to the fire, made resolutions to be more careful about what she said to her sister in the future.

Chapter XVII

'I Can Never Repay Him!'

'Now, Reg, I'm going to send you in to see Miss Phoebe while Mrs Maynard and Mme de Bersac go to visit one or two other patients they know. When they come to Miss Phoebe, you run out, and go along to the X-ray room. Mr Oliver, the head of our X-ray staff, will be there, and he will explain everything to you far better than I ever could. I believe he's got some very interesting plates to show you as well.'

There was sheer worship in the eyes Reg turned on Dr Maynard as he heard this. 'D'you mean that, sir?' he asked breathlessly. 'Truly? Oh, that's ripping! I'm going to be a doctor some time, you know, though it will be years and years before I can get enough saved up to go to college. But I—I'll even go to Farmer Jaycott's if I can save enough from my wages to pay for it. And I guess I can be reading books an' things till the time comes so's I know a bit to start off with.'

Jack swerved his car slightly to one side to avoid a rabbit that seemed bent on committing suicide under his wheels before he said, 'I'm going to have a talk with you some day soon, Reg. Until then, I want you to get it into your head that being a doctor means a long, hard training. It's no use your thinking of it if you aren't prepared for that. But if you are, and if you're prepared to work, and really want to make it your life-work, then be sure that some day the chance will come to you. A man can generally do what he makes up his mind to do if he sets about it the right way. *Think* about it, *want* it, *do* what you can to bring it nearer, and, last and most important, *pray* about it. You can't hope to make a real success of anything if you don't take God as your partner. Remember that!'

Reg nodded.

'Yes, sir.' Reg would take from Jack Maynard what he would never have taken from anyone else. The two had already had a talk in which Jack had expressed himself very forcefully on Reg's tendency to sulk if anything offended him, and the young man had made up his mind to conquer this tendency. His adored doctor had told him that he would get nowhere if he went round with a chip on his shoulder all the time, and had ordered him to get rid of it as fast as he could, especially if he meant to be a doctor.

In the back of the car, Jo and Simone smiled at each other. Jo was very proud of the influence her husband had already gained over a difficult boy, and the other three all sympathised with her. Reg never sulked with Jack Maynard. He had only tried it on once, and the ticking off he had got on that occasion had taught him a lesson.

'Poor Reg!' murmured Simone in French. 'He has so much to do battle with that one feels very sorry for him. I do hope he will get his wish!'

'He'll get it,' said Jo in the same tongue. 'Jack means to see that he does. He thinks that it's a hereditary thing with the boy. His father's father was a doctor, you know, and it's quite likely that Reg's own father would have been one too. But there was no money for his training, so he took up teaching instead. Don't you worry over Reg, Simone. Jack means to see him through. He's going to pay a call on Mrs Thirtle one day before he goes back. He's going to offer to pay for Reg's education at Garnley Grammar. It's a very good school, you know, and Reg must get through his School Certificate before he can do anything else. If she won't agree, then we must just wait till Reg is twenty-one. But I hope she will, because it would be so much more difficult for him to begin the work then. He would have lost nearly eight years.'

This brought them up to the door of the Sanatorium, and Jack, after seeing the two girls to the door of the room where an acquaintance of theirs was undergoing treatment for a diseased ankle-bone, ushered Reg into Phoebe's room, and then went off to his consultation.

Jo and Simone stayed for half an hour chatting, then said goodbye, and went to Phoebe, feeling inwardly excited, but looking outwardly as cool as a couple of cucumbers. Simone had been chosen to come because, as Jack said, 'she hasn't an ounce of imagination, and she *is* logical and clear-headed, which—if you'll forgive me for saying so, you two—can't be said of either Marie or Frieda.' Thereby he offended all three. One mayn't have very much imagination; but to be told that one hasn't an ounce of it is, as Simone declared, an insult. And no one likes to be told that she is neither logical nor clear-headed. He had to apologise all round before anyone would agree to make him after-supper coffee, and explained that he only meant his words to apply to such a case as the present.

Simone felt at the present moment that she was anything but clear-headed. They were all so fond of Phoebe, so eager to do anything they could to make life easier and happy for her, that it was hard to sit down firmly on the flights of imagination that, Jack to the contrary, were stirring in her.

'Now for it!' whispered Jo as they reached the door. 'Pull up your socks, Simone. I'm going to tap *now*!' And in her agitation she performed a positive rataplan on the door.

Phoebe was delighted to see them, and Reg made his farewells and ran off for a paradisial hour or so in the X-ray room, by which time the pair had seated themselves and brought all their wits to bear on their task.

'How much better you are looking, Phoebe!' said Jo, when

the first greetings were over. 'Upon my word, I believe you're beginning to get fat! Don't you think so, Simone? Or is it my imagination?'

'If so, then it is mine as well,' declared Simone. 'Your face is getting round, Phoebe, ma chère. It is very becoming to you.'

Phoebe laughed. 'Oh, I know I'm putting on weight. They weigh me every week, you know, and Nurse told me the last time that I had put on exactly three and a half pounds since I came here. And look at this!' And she slowly but proudly lifted both arms till they were above her head. 'There! When I first met you, I couldn't have done that if you had paid me for it.'

'Oh, Phoebe! How splendid!' cried Jo. 'Why, you'll be able to go on with the 'cello before we know where we are! Do they let you walk yet?'

'Yes; but not very much. They are so careful, you know, and my heart has been so tiresome, they are afraid if I try to do too much at first it may go back a little. But even *it* is better. I haven't had any of those horrid flutterings that used to bother me so—not for nearly ten days now. Oh, girls! You can't think how wonderful it is to feel so much better! And to think that if you had never come to The Witchens none of it would ever have happened.'

'You don't know that,' said Simone quickly. 'Very likely someone else would have come along and done quite as much for you, if not more.'

Phoebe shook her head. 'Who would there be? Dr Thompson doesn't pretend to be more than a G.P. He told me so. He could carry out the treatment prescribed for me, but he wouldn't have done anything else. The Harts—well, you know what happened there. I'm sure he would do what he could, but, as Debby says, Mrs Hart rules the roost there. After Father refused to play at her concerts, she hadn't anything bad enough to say for us. And there wasn't anyone else very much. No; it had to be you four.'

'Well, it's very nice to look at it like that, and we're grateful, but I still think you're making far too much of it,' said Simone. 'What do you do to pass the time? Give us an account of your days, won't you?'

Phoebe laughed again. 'Oh, it isn't a very interesting tale. Nurse brings my breakfast at eight o'clock. She comes back at nine to wash me, and brush my hair, and put me tidy for the doctor's visit, which is about ten o'clock. When that is over, I have a hot drink and then it is time for my exercises and massage. After that, I rest for half an hour, and then, if I'm not too tired—or if *they* think I'm not too tired—I get up for lunch. After that, I have to lie down till three, and as a rule I go to sleep. I get up again, and have tea. At six Nurse puts me to bed. During the intervals I sew, or read, or write letters. Sometimes I do jigsaw puzzles, but they rather worry me, so I get on slowly with them. But Dr Peters taught me demon patience when he was in the other day, and do you know, I find it quite thrilling. I got it out yesterday for the first time, and I felt almost as pleased as when I lifted my arms above my head for the first time. He said when I did, he would teach me another as soon as he could get time. But he's very busy today. They have an important consultation this afternoon.'

'We know. Jack had to come back for it, and that's why we are here,' said Jo. 'He said he'd bring two of us and Reg to see you. We're going back tonight for once. But this is really his holiday, so he doesn't want to miss more of it than can be helped. Well, had Reg anything to say to you? What news did he tell you?'

'He's more set than ever on being a doctor. I don't see how it's to happen. I don't believe Mrs Thirtle will ever agree, and he has no one else. Oh dear! How I do wish I were rich!' And Phoebe sighed.

'Don't worry over Reg, my child. Jack and I are going to see him through,' said Jo. 'Jack says it's hereditary, coming from his doctor grandfather, and it would be a sin to let it go. He's very keen on it. So set your heart at rest about Reg. He shall be a doctor by hook or by crook, even if we have to wait for him to matriculate when he is twenty-one, supposing his aunt won't agree.'

Phoebe considered for a moment. 'I wonder what she will do. Mr Hart on the one occasion he visited me told me that Mrs Thirtle could quite well afford to send the boy to the Grammar. Only she disapproves of education for boys in Reg's position. *He* knew, of course, for he always had to help her with her business. If Dr Maynard offers to pay for Reg, she may accept. Or she may say she'll do it herself. Or, which I am afraid of, she may insist that he's got to stay in the class to which she considers he belongs—his mother's class. She was in a shop, you know. That was how his father met her. She never thinks that Reg also belongs to his father's class. In one way, it's understandable. She has had him since he was seven, and done everything for him.'

'That's true, but it doesn't give her the right to spoil his life,' said Jo. 'And spoilt it may be if she refuses to let him go to the Grammar. If she were poor and needed his wages, one wouldn't say anything. But from what you say, she doesn't. It's just an idea she's got into her head, and she hasn't any right to sacrifice him to an idea.'

'Reg won't let her,' said Simone. 'He has ideas of his own, and he is very obstinate. She may be able to stop his going to the school, but he will work by himself. And as soon as he is twenty-one he will insist on doing as he chooses. That will be very hard for her, so I hope she will be wise, and give in. And now, Phoebe, haven't you any work to show us?'

'Yes; I've finished your other little frock, Jo. I'll get it—and the bill,' she added, with a laughing glance at Jo.

'Mercy! I hope you won't insist on immediate payment, for I

haven't got my cheque-book with me, and I've only a few shillings in my bag!' cried Jo.

'Oh, I can wait. But I want you to have the frock in case you need it suddenly. You never know!'

'No,' agreed Jo, her mind going back to a spring day years ago in Tyrol when Jem had come to bring her and some of her friends from the Chalet School to Die Rosen, the beautiful house in which the Russells had lived on the Sonnalpe, for the half-term, and had sprung on her the startling news that she had a new niece. 'Sybil, for instance, came along a good month before anyone expected her. She arrived at half-term, which we—some of us, anyhow—were spending with Madge and Jem; and Jem celebrated the event by having a naming party for the young lady. *My* choice was "Malvina." And the heroine of the first book I ever wrote was "Malvina" too. That book never came to anything—except the incinerator.'

'I was going to say this was news to me,' said Simone, laughing.

'Oh, no one knew anything about it but Matey. I was down at school because the twins—my nephew and niece, Peggy and Rix Bettany, Phoebe—were indulging in measles, and I wrote about seven or eight chapters of it. Then Matey came and found out about it. She insisted on reading what I had written; and *was* she scathing! No reviewer could ever make me turn a hair after Matey's comments on that work of literature. Hence, I put it in the incinerator. And I've always had a hate at the name since.'

Phoebe came back with the frock, laughing gaily. 'What adventures you seem to have had! Here you are, Jo.'

Jo unfolded it carefully. 'Phoebe! You really have a genius for this work! I thought the other was lovely, but this beats it into a cocked hat!—Look at this, Simone. Did you ever see lovelier work in your life?'

The little frock was of finest merino, and round the neck, sleeves, and hem Phoebe had embroidered daisies with pink tips and golden hearts so beautifully that it almost looked as though real flowers had been woven into chains to make the wreaths.

'Winter is coming. I thought one warm frock might be useful,' explained Phoebe, sitting down. 'I'm glad you like it, Jo.'

'Oh, I do! And Madge will be thrilled. I sent her the other two days ago. I'll give this to Jem to take back, perhaps. He's here, too, for the consultation, though we haven't seen him yet. The new baby is a lucky boy to have two such marvellous frocks waiting for him.'

'It may be a girl,' Simone warned her. 'Don't be too sure, Joey.'

'If it's a girl, she can just pack up and depart. They have two girls in that house. It's time David had a brother, as I've said before.'

'You've three girls of your own to one boy.'

'I know. The next is going to be a boy—to be called John James.'

The other two shrieked in protest at this, and Simone pointed out that Stephen's second name was John. 'You can't have two Johns in one family,' she said.

'My dear, we've done that already. Have you forgotten Jackie Bettany?' asked Jo crushingly. 'However, perhaps you are right there. I'll think it over again.' Then she turned to Phoebe. 'Enough of this! Phoebe, I want to say how amazed I am at your improvement. I knew Dr Peters was very clever, but I didn't think even he could do so much. You aren't the same girl. You're getting plump. You have a colour in your face—just a faint one so far, but it's a real pink for all that. And you're walking without crutches.' For Phoebe had used only a stick to lean on when she went to the drawers to get the little frock. 'It—it's a miracle!'

'Oh, it is,' agreed Phoebe, dimpling—yes; the dimples were really there now. 'Of course, I couldn't do more than just those few steps without crutches as yet. But to feel that I can do so much is a real joy.'

'It must be,' said Simone. 'I think Dr Peters is a wonderful man.'

'I take off my hat to him,' said Jo airily. 'He's no beauty to look at. In fact, I don't think I ever saw a plainer man in my life—'

'*Plain?* You call Dr Peters *plain*?' exclaimed Phoebe.

The two girls looked at her. 'Well, don't you?' asked Jo. 'He hasn't a really good feature in his face.'

'He has beautiful eyes,' said Phoebe. 'They are so kind and gentle.'

Jo nodded. 'Yes; I'll grant you he has kind eyes. But have you ever looked at his mouth? It's a real gash.'

'It has a smile I should like to have with me if I were in danger.' Phoebe spoke emphatically. 'And his hands are so strong and gentle. And he is so unselfish. When I was so bad just at first, he used to come along at all hours, night *and* day, just to see if he could move me into an easier position, or give me something to relieve the pain, or just to sit and say a word now and then to help me through.' Then she added quietly, 'I think he must know himself just how dreadful the night can be when you are in pain, and it's dark, and it seems as if the darkness would *never* end. I know that Sir Jem came and sat with me that night I was so ill at Many Bushes, and did everything he could to help me. And I've not forgotten how your husband did the same thing. But there's something more than that in the way Dr Peters does things. He's been through it himself.'

'No,' said Jo, who had been talking of all this to Jack. 'But his mother died of heart trouble caused by rheumatoid arthritis, and he helped to nurse her through the last months. She was never out of terrible pain, and he learned then just how long the nights can be to those in pain. That's why he went to America after she had died and made a special study of rheumatism. He wanted to help other people with her trouble. When I see you as you are now, Phoebe, and remember what you were when we first knew you—only seven weeks ago—when I think of that awful night when Jack was with you, and of the other when Jem sat with you, it makes me feel that Mrs Peters did not suffer all that agony for nothing.'

'I didn't know about his mother,' said Phoebe quickly. 'But of course, seeing her suffer so, and knowing he could do little to help her, is what made him understand so well how I felt. I can never repay him!'

'I think you will find a way some day,' said Simone gently. 'One never knows just when one may be able to help people. Even if you can't, no doctor expects any special payment for what he does.'

'You can repay him by going on improving,' said Jo. 'I know what it means to a doctor to know that he is being able to help, even a little, to relieve pain. As Jack once said to me, it's a life of hard work, and often of disappointment. But you get your reward when you see a patient recovering. Don't worry, Phoebe. As Simone says, you'll probably find a way one day. It will come, so don't fret about it.'

Phoebe nodded. 'I won't. But Jo, I want to say one more thing as we are on the subject. I shall never forget I owe this in the beginning to you—all you people; but Simone won't mind if I say that *you* began it.'

'Of course she did,' said Simone promptly. 'I've known Jo since we were little girls at school, and she's always been like that. All of us like to help where we can; but we often have to have it pointed out to us. Jo sees where it's wanted and just plunges to the rescue.'

'With exciting results sometimes,' said Jo, with a grimace at her. 'I hear footsteps which tell me that my husband is coming to remove us, so I'll say goodbye … Yes; I thought so!' as the door opened, and her husband and brother-in-law came in with Dr Peters. 'Well, you three, how did the consultation go?'

'Well on the whole,' Jem replied. 'But, Joey, Jack must come back on Friday instead of staying till Monday as we'd arranged. I'm sorry, but we need him.'

'Friday? But that's the day after tomorrow!'

'I know, dear. It can't be helped. You and he are to have ten days later on at Pretty Maids. The girlies will have to come to us, for Jack can't be spared till the end of October. But you shall have a second honeymoon then.'

'It won't be much of a honeymoon with Lydia round! Oh, well, a doctor's wife gets accustomed to such things. Where's Reg, anyone?'

'Gottfried went to bring him. Say goodbye, girls, and come along. We have a good drive before us, and I'd like to do as much as possible of it by daylight.—Goodbye, Phoebe. The girls will be back at the end of next week, you know, and one or other of them will be up every day once they've settled down again. By the way, Debby is coming to live with Frieda for the present. So you'll be seeing her fairly often too. She is up to the eyes in cleaning Many Bushes before closing it for a while. Is there anything you'd specially like to have brought? Make out a list, and send it, because we aren't going to let her go back there to be alone. And Jo insists on having Reg for a few days before his holiday ends, so that's settled too.'

'Oh, how good you all are!' Phoebe's eyes shone like stars, and her cheeks were flushed. Jo, glancing at her, thought that she was almost beautiful at that moment. Then she realised that someone else thought the girl quite beautiful, though Dr Peters only said quietly, 'I think Miss Wychcote has had enough excitement for one afternoon. I'll see you people off, and then I'm coming back to help Nurse settle her for a rest.'

They went after that; but when she had got the latest news of Madge from Jem, Jo fell behind the rest, touching the young doctor on the arm to hold him back. He looked at her as she faced him, her soft black eyes glowing with feeling.

'Dr Peters, go in and win! You *can*! That's all!' Then she was off, leaving him looking after her with incredulous delight in his face. But it was with an even lighter step than usual that he returned to his patient, and there was something in the way in which he helped Nurse to make her comfortable that gave Phoebe a sudden strange idea. When she was alone, she pondered on it. Then she gave a little gasp.

'Oh, was *that* what Jo and Simone meant? Oh, but it couldn't be! And yet—' And she fell asleep with a smile.

Chapter XVIII

ALINE ELIZABETH

'HEIGH-HO! This time next week we shall be at home!' Marie heaved a sigh and went on with her work of dusting the dining-room mantelpiece.

'What's that?' asked Jo in muffled tones, for she was on her knees, her head under the sofa, while she polished the floor industriously.

'I said that by this time next week we should be at home. We shall have to forget that we are Jo and Simone and Frieda and Marie, and remember that we are married women with families. Doesn't it sound *aged*?'

'It certainly does the way you say it,' agreed Jo, emerging from under the sofa and sitting back on her heels. 'But I shouldn't say we've had much chance of forgetting the families,' she said with some grimness. Stephen had given her another bad night, and only fallen asleep as dawn broke. She yawned widely, and then shuffled further along to continue her polishing while she talked. 'Well, I've finished two frocks here, anyway. My old blue cotton is only fit for dusters; and the green isn't much better. Might get a couple of overalls out of it for the babes. It has a good wide hem, luckily. I'll get Anna to dye it for me.'

'You'd better!' Marie dropped into a near-by chair and shrieked with laughter. 'After your exploits just before Stephen arrived, I'd advise you to leave dyeing strictly to other folk. Oh, Jo! You *were* mean to keep it dark as you did! You might have let us three in on the fun, at any rate!'

'No, thank you! Even Rob and the babes saw nothing of it.

Nurse and Jack were the only ones; and quite enough, too. There! this side is done. Have you finished the dusting?'

'Very nearly. But we must leave it as beautiful as possible. How long will it be before Madame comes? Have you any idea?'

'None at all. It all depends on the new baby. He's not due for another fortnight or so. I suppose it'll be about six weeks after that. Let's see. That'll be just after Jack and I get back from Pretty Maids.'

'That'll bring it into November. Well, luckily, November is often a very pleasant month. Jo, you all talk of this new baby as *he*. What will you do if it's *she*? It may quite well be, you know.'

'Put up with it, I suppose. I hope it isn't, though. Both Madge and Jem want another boy, and so do I. We've our fair share of girls.'

'To hear you talk, anyone would think David and Stephen were the only boys in the family instead of there being three others. You've five boys.'

'And eight girls! It's out of all proportion. Hello! There's the 'phone. I wonder what it is now?'

'It's all right. Simone's going. There! that's the last of that, and you can get on with your polishing. I'll go and dust the drawing-room.'

'Joey!' called Simone from the little hall, 'you're wanted on the 'phone. It's Jack.'

'All right; I'm coming!' Jo pulled off her gloves, tossing them down on a chair, and went out to take the receiver and ask, 'Hello, Jack! What do you want *now*?'

The other two were about to vanish when they were pulled up short by her wail of: 'Oh, Jack! *No!* What on earth did she go and do that for?'

'What's wrong?' demanded Simone. 'Is anything up with Phoebe?'

'No—idiot!—It's all right, Jack. That was to Simone. She

wanted to know if anything was wrong with Phoebe. Hang on, you two, and I'll tell you in a minute.—Jack! It's all right otherwise? You're *sure*? Oh, good! Well, you can tell her I'm bitterly disappointed. When can I come and see them? Oh, well, perhaps I'd better wait. As you say, it's only three days now. But I shall say exactly what I think.'

The pips ended her remarks, and she hung up with a final 'Goodbye,' and faced on the anxious pair. 'Where's Frieda? Call her, and I'll tell you all at the same time.'

Frieda was summoned from the garden, where she was picking runner beans, and the three waited for Jo's news, though they guessed pretty shrewdly what was wrong.

'That's what comes of *my* being away,' she began. 'If I'd been at home I'd have kept Madge up to her duty. As it is, the baby arrived this morning, and it's another girl! An eight-pounder, Jack says. And both are splendid. But I do think Madge might have managed a boy!'

'I told you you were talking far too much of *he*,' said Marie. 'It's a judgment on you. You're sure they're all right? Oh, well, that's good news, anyhow. I don't suppose Madame really minds how little—what is her name to be, by the way?'

'No idea.' Jo began to laugh. 'Perhaps they'll call her "Malvina."'

'And perhaps they won't. Why should they? It's a silly sort of name, and I shouldn't think they'd hark back to that old name party of Dr Jem's. If they did, what about "Esmeralda"? Didn't someone go for that?'

'They did, though I forget who. I know David wanted Sybs to be called "Tibby" after the cat. Jack will ring me up tomorrow unless anything goes wrong, which no one expects. I'll ask him then. And now I'd better find Sybil and tell her she has a new little sister. There's one thing. We shan't have all the trouble with her we had when Josette was born. Oh, how badly she behaved!

I don't know how Madge had patience with her.'

'She's in the orchard with the others. I must go and get the beans done, so I'll send her to you as I go past, shall I?' offered Frieda.

'Yes, do. Is that bad son of mine still asleep, by the way?'

'Sleeping like a little angel. I expect the tooth's through, and you'll have no more bother with him for a while now. You must lie down this afternoon, Jo, and try to get a nap,' said Frieda consolingly.

'It's an idea. I can scarcely keep my eyes open as it is.'

'We'll take all the children up to the moors and leave you alone in the house,' said Simone. 'You get undressed and go properly to bed. Stephen has given you two or three broken nights lately, and you need it.'

'I think I will. I don't want to go home looking like something left out overnight. I can't imagine why Stephen should be giving me so much trouble. The girls got their teeth easily enough.'

'Oh, they vary. Wolferl was as good as gold. We only knew the teeth had come when we saw them. But Josefa had a bad time with two or three of hers, poor lamb. And Wanda was nearly distracted over Keferl's first four. It was funny, for there was no trouble with any of the others. Perhaps Stephen's will be that way too.'

'I hope so, I'm sure. Here comes Sybs! I wonder what she'll say?—Sybs, Uncle Jack has just rung me up to say that a new little sister arrived for you three early this morning. What do you think of that?'

'A sister? Are you sure, Auntie Jo? Oh, goody, goody!' And Sybil began to perform a *pas seul* which ended in her tripping over Marie.

'Well, I'm glad you're so pleased, but I thought you all wanted a brother this time.'

'Oh, *I* didn't. And David won't care one way or the other.

When can I see her and Mummy? Did Uncle Jack say what she looked like?'

'You won't see her till we go home on Saturday. As for what she's like, she's a big baby, anyhow. Your uncle didn't tell me any more. You can't say much in three minutes, you know. Now you'd better run out and tell the rest, but get far away from the pram before you do. I don't want Stephen wakened if it can be helped.'

'I'll take them to the other end of the orchard,' Sybil promised as she darted out of the front door.

Jo looked after her. 'Thank goodness! Though, as I said, I didn't think we'd have any trouble there now. But I shan't forget how jealous she was of Josette, poor baby. But Sybs is much older, and she's a very much nicer girl. Well, I'd better get back to my polishing, or it won't be done.'

Simone took her arm firmly. 'You can leave the rest of the polishing to me. I've washed up, and done the potatoes, and put the sausages ready for frying. The rice puddings are in, and the stewed apples are cooling in the shed. There's nothing more to do till Frieda brings in her beans. She can cut them up while I make elevenses. In the meantime, you go and tidy yourself, and then you can take a book out on the lawn. It's a beautiful morning, and it will do you good to sit out in the sun. This afternoon you can have a sleep, and then you'll look like yourself again. At the moment you are a real scarecrow. Jack would be horrified if he saw you. I never saw such a creature for going all eyes when she is tired as you are! Off you go and wash and change!' And she walked Jo to the foot of the stairs.

'Do you think I ought? It seems so mean to leave all the work to the rest of you. A nap this afternoon is really all I need, you know,' said Jo, yawning fearfully as she spoke.

'There isn't very much to do now,' agreed Marie. 'Simone is right, Jo; you go and rest, and leave it to us.' Then, as Jo went up the stairs, she turned to the others. 'We'd better be very firm about this afternoon. Jo really looks ill for want of sleep. I'll go and dust up the drawing-room and then we'll let everything else go for the rest of today. If she rests, and has a good night tonight, she'll be all right tomorrow. But I shouldn't like Jack to see her looking like this. Let's hope she falls asleep over her book. If she does, we'll leave her till dinner-time.'

Frieda, who had come back to get her basket, which she had forgotten, and so heard this, nodded. 'I agree. Let's hope no one comes this afternoon and wakes her up.'

'Debby has nearly finished at Many Bushes. She said this morning that she was going to pack the things Phoebe wanted, and then there'd be very little left to do. We'll ask her to come over here for the afternoon, and she can answer the door if anyone comes.'

'Very well. I'll finish the floor, and we'll have elevenses when you bring the beans in, Frieda. Oh, and Frieda! Send the children to get their milk and bread-and-butter, will you? They can take it to the orchard. It's all ready for them. I saw to it before I did the potatoes.'

The friends parted, and set to work, and by the time Jo came downstairs, looking better for a wash and a change of frock, coffee was waiting for her, and she was ordered out to the lawn with it and her book, where she speedily fell asleep. Marie laid a shawl lightly over her, for though the sun was hot, there was a fresh breeze, and, as Simone wisely remarked, there was no sense in *asking* for a cold. Jo slept till the dinner-bell brought the children tearing back from the orchard, still very excited about the new arrival at the Round House, the home of the Russells. Then she woke up, looking much better, but, as she acknowledged, quite ready for an afternoon in bed. The others packed tea-baskets, and saw to the little ones getting into hats and taking blazers with them—even little Tessa had a tiny one made for her by her mother's clever fingers—and Marie popped in to make sure that

Jo was safely in bed. Then, with Debby sitting comfortably in the kitchen to answer the door and the telephone, they set off for the moors, taking every child, even Stephen, with them. He was sleeping again, and looked rosy and well, and they had a bottle and some rusks for him, so Jo, relieved of all worries, snuggled down on her pillow, and fell asleep again.

She was roused a couple of hours later by the tread of a light step at her bedside, and opened her eyes to gaze straight up into her husband's face. 'Jack!' she exclaimed, sitting up. 'What on earth are you doing here?' Then, with a sudden memory, 'Madge is all right, isn't she?'

'Perfectly. But our ambulance had to come within a couple of miles of here, and I could be spared, so I thought I'd run over and see how you were. Simone rang me up about noon and said Stephen was giving you trouble with his teeth again. Where is he, by the way?'

'I'll wring Simone's neck when I see her again! Stephen? Oh, they've all gone up to the moors. We love them, you know, and we haven't much longer to go to them. He's all right now. I think the tooth must have come through just before he dropped off this morning. I haven't looked yet. Simone gave him his bottle at dinner-time. They made me go and sit on the lawn with a book, and I fell asleep, and they'd fed him and got him off again before I woke up. I must have had a good two hours then. And I've slept all the afternoon, so I've about made up what I lost. How long can you stay? I'll get up and we'll have tea together.'

'I've to meet the ambulance at half-past five at the foot of the bank, so we've got an hour or so. I met young Reg in the village, and he's coming down with me on his bicycle and wheeling it up again. Let me look at you. Yes; well, I've seen you look better. However, a good night will probably bring you back to your bonny self, so I'm not worrying.'

'"Bonny self," indeed!' jeered Jo. 'You go and ask Debby for tea on the lawn while I dress, and I'll be with you in a few minutes.'

'Right you are. By the way, I delivered your message to Jem. He says I'm to tell you that you can't talk. You've got three daughters to one son yourself, so the less you say, the more you'll shine. Now don't rag! There isn't time for it. Get dressed, like a good girl, and join me on the lawn, and I'll tell you what I can about your new niece.'

Jo gave up her attempt at ragging, and began to hunt round for her stockings as he went out laughing. Ten minutes later she was out on the lawn, where Debby was getting tea ready, and Jack was stretched out in a deck-chair, smoking peacefully.

'Well, now about Madge,' she said, when she was pouring out the tea. 'It was like her to do things in a hurry. You're sure she's all right?'

'Fit as a fiddle. As a matter of fact, she rather expected it this week, but she and Jem decided not to say so to you. They knew you would insist on coming racing back a fortnight ago, and you needed a holiday, Jo. This has been a pretty trying year for you, what with Stephen coming, and all the worry about Josette, and the business at school, and so on. The baby arrived at six this morning, and Madge was fast asleep an hour later. I saw her at eleven, and she was feeling very fit then, and looked it too. The babe is a bonny little soul—turned the scales at eight pounds—with long black lashes, and a mop of dark curls.'

'What are they going to call her? Do you know? Have another scone and some of that blackberry jelly, by the way. Reg found them last Saturday, so we went berrying on Monday, and made the jelly on Tuesday. We divvied up, and there are four pots each to bring home.'

'It's nectar!' Jack spoke with his mouth full. 'The babe's name? Well, I regret to tell you that I don't know. I did suggest that "Malvina" of yours to Jem, and he made hooting noises, so I don't think it'll be that.'

'We've about used up all the family names. They'll have to branch out. I wonder what it'll be? By the way, Sybs is thrilled to have another sister. What does Josette say about it?'

'She's thrilled too. We haven't let her see the baby. Jem thought it best to wait till all the children can see her together. Wanda von Glück heard of the baby's arrival and came at nine o'clock and carried her ladyship off for the next week or so, and David won't be home till Friday at ten at night. So he can quite well wait till Sybil arrives. When are you coming? Anna keeps me mended up, and feeds me well, but her menus are rather lacking in imagination. Rob is coming back tomorrow, and Daisy and Primula will come with her, so I think you'd better get off early if you can.'

'We're leaving here at ten, and catching the eleven-twenty-five train. If we can make our connections, we ought to reach Plas Gwyn about three-thirty or so. But it's all rather iffy.'

'And what about Phoebe? Have you forgotten her?' asked Jack teasingly.

'Of course I haven't! Jack! Do you mean that it's all right?'

'That depends on what you are referring to, my dear. She is certainly making headway. She walked to the end of the corridor and back yesterday with only her stick. But if you mean anything else—' Jack stopped.

'Of course, I mean Dr Peters and her! Jack, don't tease! Are they engaged? Oh, they are—they *are*! How marvellous! Oh, I *am* so glad!'

'Here! where are you off to?' demanded Jack, for she had sprung to her feet and was making for the house, regardless of the cup she still held.

'To tell Debby, of course! She'll be delighted!'

'Let Phoebe tell her own news herself. I've got a letter here for her. One for you, as well. I told her this morning that I was coming here, so she begged me to bring them with me, as then you would know sooner. Here's yours; and here's Debby's. You can take it to her, but for goodness' sake put that cup down first or you'll spill it all over yourself or her in your excitement.'

Jo laughed and put her cup back on its saucer. 'I never noticed. Thank you, Jack. Here's a reward for you!' And she dropped a kiss on the top of his head before she fled with the precious letters to the kitchen, where Debby was placidly toasting her fourth round of toast, with the pot stewing on the hob. 'Debby!' cried Jo, bursting into the kitchen, 'here's a letter for you. Dr Maynard brought it—and one for me. Open it! It's great news!' And she dropped the letter on to Debby's aproned lap and turned round and was off before the old woman could do more than gasp her amazement.

'Now for mine!' she cried gaily as she reached her chair. 'Give me your penknife, please, Jack. Oh, I *am* so excited! This is the best news I've had for many a long day. *Now*!' as she slit open the envelope and pulled out the letter. 'Let's see what Phoebe has to say for herself!'

She opened it, and scanned it eagerly. Then she looked up. 'I'm going to read it to you, Jack. There's nothing really private in it—just a sentence or two. I'll miss them. Here's the rest!' And she read aloud:

'"MY DEAR JOEY,—I scarcely know how to write to tell you my great news. And yet I must, for if it had not been for you, I should never have had it to tell. Oh, Joey, I wonder what you will say when you learn that I am lonely no longer? I am engaged to Dr Peters—he says I must call him Frank now—and as soon as I can walk down the stairs with only my stick, we are to be married. I wanted to wait till we were surer of my being so much better; but he won't. He says that if we are married he can look after me properly. So I have had to give in. And what do you think? He wants me to be married in white with a veil! I am going to embroider it myself—the dress, I mean. In the big, cedar-lined chest in the box-room at Many Bushes there is a length of chiffon. I have had it for years. I meant to make evening scarves with it, but I never did somehow. Now it's there, just waiting. There are nine yards of it, and as I am so small, I think it will be enough. I shall have to buy a veil, but perhaps I can get some lengths of lace and darn them together." She won't,' put in Jo, looking up, 'I'll lend her my own veil. They say that the veil of a happy bride brings luck to other brides. I was the happiest bride that ever went to her wedding, and I'm the happiest wife in the world.'

'Thank you, Joey. That's worth hearing,' he said quietly, laying his hand on hers for a moment.

Jo smiled at him, her eyes suddenly moist. 'I've always pitied every other girl who wasn't married to you—even Madge, though Jem is such a dear. But there's only one YOU in the world, and I've got you!'

'Well, there never was any other girl in the world for me but you, even when you were just a kid at school. How old were you when we first met each other? Fifteen, wasn't it? I made up my mind then to wait for you, even though it would be a long wait.'

Jo laughed. 'You *were* sure! But it wasn't so very long after all. I was only twenty-one when we were married. Well, I must go on with the letter. Where was I?' She found her place, and read on: '"Thank goodness I have plenty of undies—" Oh, this won't interest you.' She skipped the next two paragraphs which were for her eyes only, and then went on: '"And now, Joey, I am going to ask a big favour. May I be married from your home? And will Dr Maynard give me away? The Vicar of Howells has been up to see me, and I do so like him, and his wife too. We should like to be married by him, for Frank likes him as much as I do. You have been so good to me, Jo, that I think you will say 'Yes,' or I should never have the courage to ask you such a big thing. I want to be married from your home with your little girls as my bridesmaids, and Dr Maynard to take my father's place, and you to be to me the mother I never knew. Will you? And make me the happiest girl in all this world.—My very dearest love to all of you.

'"PHOEBE."'

'What about it?' asked Jack. 'Do you feel prepared to play mother to a girl nearly your own age?'

'It's a funny thing,' said Jo slowly, 'but when I first met Phoebe I told the rest that I wanted to mother her. Yes, Jack. If you will, I certainly will. Oh I here's a postscript!' The next moment she was crying, 'Jack Maynard! Did you ever! *Where* have they got that, I should like to know?'

'Where have *who* got *what*?' demanded her husband.

'Just listen to this! "Sir Jem has just been in to see me, and tell me about Aline Elizabeth's arrival, and they've asked me to be one of her godmothers! It seems too good to be true!" Where in the world,' asked Jo dramatically, 'did they get hold of such a name? "Aline Elizabeth"! But, on the whole, you know, I like it … What are you doing?' with a sudden change of tone.

'Time's up. I've got to go. So that's what they've chosen, is it? Well—well! It might have been worse, I suppose. And now I *must* go. Can't keep the ambulance waiting, never to speak of young Reg. Goodbye, my Joey girl. Take care of yourself. Thank God, I shall have you back in three days' time!' His arm went round her as he drew her close.

Jo lifted her face for his kiss. 'Goodbye, Jack darling. I don't know how ever I've managed to stay away from you so long. Two months! It seems impossible, doesn't it?'

'Kiss my babies for me, and tell them Papa is longing to have you all back. Tell the girls they've got to help you with the wedding when it comes off. But I don't think I'd advise Phoebe to have our three for bridesmaids. There's no knowing what they might do.'

'Oh, they'll be good. Must you really go? Well, good-bye, Jack! Only three days now!'

Jo hung over the gate, waving to him until he turned the corner, and then went back to clear away the tea-things, and carry them to the kitchen, where she found Debby in such a state of tearful joy that the rest had got back before she had succeeded in calming the old woman. Among them they managed it, however, and Debby was cheered by what Phoebe had said in her letter. Many Bushes was to be let, and Dr Peters had found a little house at Howells Village where he and Phoebe and Debby would live. Jo was able to tell her that Ty-Gwyn was nearly next door to Mrs von Ahlen's house, and only ten minutes' walk away from her own home. So Debby went to bed that night a happy woman; and, as Stephen was over his trouble, Jo had a good, long night. Next morning she examined his gums, and shrieked wildly. Stephen had cut not *one* tooth, but *two* at once. No wonder he had cried so!

'But what a lot of changes in just one little holiday!' she said to the others. 'Aline Elizabeth has arrived. Stephen has three teeth. A girl we never knew before has become a firm friend; and, best of all, she is going to get well and to be married! I *am* glad we came to The Witchens!'

Chapter XIX

A Nice Rounding-Off

'Margaret Daphne Russell! I wonder you dare to face me!'

Lady Russell, lying comfortably against her pillows, chuckled. 'Josephine Mary Maynard, you can't talk! Who created the sensation of the year by presenting us with triplet daughters? I haven't been so wholesale as that. Come and see her, and stop being so scathing.'

Joey closed the door, and advanced to the bed. 'Bless you, my child! It's a treat to see you looking so well. Here's a small gift for her—another of Phoebe's frocks. It's even prettier than the other.'

'Impossible! That was the daintiest thing I've ever seen.' Madge was opening the parcel as she spoke. Then she gave a cry of delight. 'Oh, Jo! what a lovely thing! Such embroidery! And such material! Where in the world did she get that? It's pure wool, and as smooth and fine as silk.'

'Says she had it a long time. She chose that because of winter coming.'

'Aline will love it. And I'm more than glad to have it. Three babies have made my first supply shabby. And, of course, a good many of them are worn out. She sent me three for herself—two first frocks, and another about the size of this, but much plainer, though very lovely. And your woollies are most acceptable. Where is Sybs? What did she say about it?'

There was a little anxiety in Madge's voice, and Jo hastened to end it. 'Sybs is thrilled to have another sister. She's dying to see her, but Jem said not till tomorrow. He's bringing Josette up for an hour or two, and calling for Sybs on the way. So the three can see Aline all together.'

'Yes; it's much the best plan. I saw David for a few minutes last night, as I was awake when he came. But Baby was asleep in Jem's dressing-room. She's lovely, Jo—quite the prettiest of all my babies, I think.'

'Ho! You said that about each one,' quoth Jo. 'As a matter of fact, the pick of your family so far as looks go is Sybs herself. She's very well, Madge, and has been a real help. I don't know how we'd have managed without her. She helped to look after the tinies, and gave a hand in the house, and was everybody's errand-boy. Thank you for letting me have her.'

'Are you sure, Jo? You've often been so scathing about her that I was nearly afraid to let her go with you. There's a lot of good in Sybs, only it got overlaid by all the silly nonsense people talked to her and about her. But I knew it was there all the time.'

'Sybs is a changed being. I've always been very fond of her, you know, Madge. And I was desperately sorry for her in the spring when there was all that trouble with Josette. I thought Sybs would break her heart. By the way, how is Josette? Jem said she was all right—he was in a hurry, as usual—but what do *you* think about it?'

'Oh, she is very well now. The scars are still very bright, and she hasn't got her flesh back yet. But she's coming on now, and every day sees her better. The heart trouble has cleared up, and the doctors all say in another six months she'll be herself again. But they advise us to let her run wild for another year or so, so she won't be starting school till next September. And what about your family? I hear Stephen has been having a bad time with his teeth.'

'That's over for the moment, at any rate. He's cut three, and as he is only seven months old, I think he's well forward with them. As for the girls, they are as usual—very fit and full of beans. You shall see them next week. They are growing, of course. They're going to be tall, I think.'

'Well, both you and Jack are tall. It's two months since I saw any of them, so I expect I'll see quite a change in them. Tinies alter so fast at that age. Now, don't you want to see your new niece?'

'Of course I do. Where is she? Can I get her?'

'Nurse has her in the dressing-room. Go and bring her here. I must show her to you myself. You'll love her!' And Madge smiled happily.

Jo got up from her chair and crossed the room to the dressing-room door, where she was met by Nurse, who had helped to bring all Madge's babies into the world as well as Jo's own four. She looked up with a smile into the clever, sensitive face above hers, and laid a bundle in a big white shawl into the arms opened to receive it.

'There you are, my dear,' she said. 'Take her to Lady Russell and let her show you the latest addition to the family herself. How is Stephen?'

'Splendid! He really is a show specimen; fat as butter, and placid as a cow mostly,' said Jo. 'Three teeth, Nurse, so he's beaten his sisters.'

'He certainly has. I must see him soon. I suppose you didn't bring him with you, by any chance?'

'Not this time. He doesn't need me so much now. And he looks a duck with his cup and spoon. We had one or two bad nights with the teeth, but nothing to speak of really. I'll bring him next time I come; but I can't stay long. I must get back and see what my family are doing. I left Robin in charge, and Daisy and Prim are there to help her. But I've got to go up to the San. this afternoon, so I mustn't be too long away from Plas Gwyn now. If only we'd been able to make our connections I'd have been here last night. But it was an awful journey, and the babes were all so tired when we finally got home that I had to get them to bed as soon as possible; and by that time it was after seven, and Jack wouldn't hear of my prancing off then. So I had to leave it till this morning.'

'Oh, well, you're here now,' said Nurse comfortably. 'Now I must go and see about some malted milk for your sister, so I'll leave you.'

She turned on her heel, and Jo carefully carried her precious burden back to the bed and laid it in Madge's arms. 'There you are! Undo all that flummery and let me see her.'

Madge laughed and unwrapped the shawl to show a small pink face with a frame of black curls. Long black lashes lay on the chubby cheeks, and the little mouth was closed firmly. Jo gave her a critical look.

'She's a pretty baby all right, even if she *has* only a smudge for a nose. What enormous lashes! They beat even Sybil's. What colour are her eyes?'

'Blue-grey, so far as we can see. She sleeps a good deal as yet. And what do you mean about her nose?' demanded the baby's mother indignantly. 'It's just what a baby's nose should be. If she had a perfectly formed one at her age, she'd probably produce a Wellington beak when she was grown up. You know that as well as I do.'

Jo chuckled. 'Thought you'd rise! Yes; she's nice. When is the baptism to be? Phoebe wrote to me that she was to be godmother.'

'In about a month's time, I expect. Yes; I wanted to do that for her, and Jem agreed. Elizabeth Ozanne is to be the other godmother, and we've asked Frank Peters to be godfather. I suppose those two will be thinking about their wedding shortly after that, by the way?'

'Not till the end of November, if then, I believe. Phoebe wants to wait till the New Year. She's so terrified of not being well enough to look after Dr Peters. But he won't agree. So they'll wait till we get back from Pretty Maids, and then Phoebe ought to be well enough to come to us. The idea is to have it about the twenty-ninth. They'll have a ten days' honeymoon somewhere near at hand, and then come back and settle into their new house before Christmas. I was on the 'phone to Phoebe last night after I'd got my family to bed, and heard all about it.'

'I'm very glad for her,' said Madge quietly as she lay smiling at Jo, who was cuddling her tiny niece. 'She's been so lonely since her father died. I wasn't able to go to San. to see her, you know; but we've been writing regularly twice a week, and we've struck up a real friendship.'

'You'll like her even better when you know her in the flesh,' prophesied Jo. 'Here's Nurse with your milk, and I must go. I'm going up to the San. after lunch for an hour or two, so I'd better get back to my family now. Can't leave everything to Robin, can I?'

'She's quite capable,' smiled Madge as she took the baby from Jo.

'Oh, very. But I don't like asking her to do too much. She's always ready to do far more than one asks. Oh, by the way, why "Aline"? Is it a fancy name? It isn't in our family, and I never knew Jem's had it.'

'No; it's his choice. He had a fancy for it, and as I chose Sybil's and Josette got your name by unanimous vote, I thought it was his turn.'

'And the rest comes from Elizabeth Ozanne, I suppose?'

'Quite right. How do you like it?'

'I've heard worse in my time.' And Jo departed on this note with a chuckle for her sister's righteous indignation.

She reached home just as the bell sounded to call the small folk in to wash for lunch, and when it was over, and Stephen had

had his dinner and was put down for his afternoon nap, she declared herself ready, and got into her husband's car with a final, 'Be good girls, you three, and do what Auntie Robin says. Daisy, if you and Prim want a walk, see that she takes her mac. It's fine at present, but I'm not sure it's going to last. The hills look too clear-cut. If it *does* rain while you're out, mind you both change when you get back. School begins next week, and I don't want either of you held up by colds. Goodbye, everyone. I'll be back shortly after tea, I expect.'

Then Jack, growing impatiently bored, let in his clutch and they whirled off down the drive. 'What a chatterpie you are, Jo!' he said as they turned into the road. 'Well, what do you think of Baby Aline? Fine specimen, isn't she? Jem's as proud as a peacock over her.'

'Oh, she's splendid. Madge thinks her the prettiest of them all, but I think she's wrong there. She's no prettier than Josette and David were, and not nearly so pretty as Sybil.' Then she added complacently, 'I left Madge hopping mad. She asked how I liked the name, and I said I'd heard worse in my time. I ran after that! But it is pretty, and, thank goodness, *not* likely to be badly duplicated when she goes to school. Hilary Burn told me last term that she had five Margarets in one gym class, and seven Joans in another. I do think it's so unfair to date girls like that by their names. Do you know, Jack, I read the other day that when the present Princess Royal was born, Queen Victoria wanted her to be called "Diamond" because she was born in the Diamond Jubilee year.'

Jack chuckled. 'That would have been a give away of age if you like! Not that I think it can matter much about Royalties. Most people have a very good idea of that and every other detail about them. But "Mary" is a much better name than "Diamond," I quite agree.'

'Well, we want another boy next time, of course. But if it

should be a girl, then she'll have a name that doesn't date. I'll see to that.'

'Quite so. Now we're getting to the sticky bit, so don't talk for a few minutes, there's a good girl.' And Jack gave his full attention to guiding the car past several bad potholes in the road. As it was nowhere much wider than ten feet, it was a tricky business, and Jo was obligingly silent until they had got past the worst and were running along the broad highway that led past the gates of the Sanatorium. Then she asked him about Reg's future.

'Have you heard from Mrs Thirtle? I wish she had given you a direct answer at once when you went to see her.'

'Yes; there was a letter for me at San. when I got there this morning. She thanks us for our interest in Reg, and accepts our offer. But only on the understanding that until he goes to college he spends most of his holidays with her. After that, he must please himself.'

'Well, that's what we want. He certainly ought to be with her part of the time. She's been very good to him in her own way, and he owes her that. When does he go to the Grammar?'

'He doesn't go there at all. I made inquiries, and there were no vacancies left. So I've entered him for Polgarth, where Peters's young cousin was. It's fairly near at hand, though it will mean being a boarder, and it's a good school of the same kind. I just got him in, so he goes next week. Mrs Thirtle is providing all his clothes and books, and so on. She says she always reckoned to do that. But pay good money out for more school learning, she will not. She's got funny ideas.'

'Oh, well, what does it matter so long as Reg gets his chance. Here we are, and I'm longing to see Phoebe and wish her happiness.' Jo uncoiled her long legs, and sprang out as the car stopped. Jack grinned.

'It's as well we have the all-weather one,' he said. 'You'd

have hit your head a nice blow if you'd tried bouncing out of the Morris like that. I'll leave you till five. Then we must get back. Phoebe is to give you tea. Off you go, and don't give the poor girl headache by headlong gabble! I'll bring Peters along for tea about four, so you've an hour.'

In too much haste to answer this, Jo waved her hand to him and raced up the steps and into the great cool hall, where she was met by the porter, who gave her a hearty welcome—everyone in San. knew and liked Mrs Maynard. Jo paused a moment or two to ask after his wife and daughter, and then sped off up the stairs and along the corridor to Phoebe's room.

As she opened the door, she heard the tap of the stick, and there stood Phoebe with welcoming arms open for her.

'Jo! Oh, how glad I am to see you! It was nice to talk to you over the 'phone; but it's far better to talk face to face! How well you look!'

'The same to you and many of them! Phoebe, if you go on at this rate you'll be getting fat! What a colour! Is this what being engaged has done for you?' teased Jo gently. 'Come and sit down, and let's *talk*! I have heaps to say to you. There you are. I'll perch on this window-sill. But first, my dear, I do want to say how glad I am about your engagement. It's the best news I've heard for a very long time. What fun it will be to have a wedding from our house. The girls will be thrilled to be your bridesmaids, but are you sure you care to risk it? You know what they can be like when they are excited. And what about the other girls?'

'Do you mean Sybil, and Josefa, and Tessa? Joey, I can't have six bridesmaids! It would make such a show of it, and I don't want that.'

'No; I suppose not. Well, they must all come, anyhow. Oh, we won't make a big affair of it—nothing swagger. Just our little crowd, and Madge and Jem and their family. And Debby, of course. You couldn't be married properly if Debby wasn't there. She's to stay with Frieda till you two get back from your honeymoon, and the day you come she'll go in to Ty-Gwyn and have it all ready for you to come to. She can amuse herself with getting it into order while you are away. By the way, I'm afraid the whole of Garnham knows where you are and that you are going to be married. I gave it away myself. The day after Jack told me I met Mrs Thirtle and she asked how you were, and I told her—never noticing that the world's two worst gossips were within earshot. Of course, that did it. It was all over the place in under an hour, I believe. By the way, I must tell you about Reg. He's going to get his heart's desire, we hope. He's going to Polgarth School next week. Garnley Grammar was full, but Jack got him into Polgarth. He's to spend most of his holidays with his auntie, but I expect she'll spare him to you for odd weeks. He must get School Certif. with matric, and then he's to go to Edinburgh and work for his medical degree. I haven't seen him yet, but he's coming next Thursday for a day and you'll hear all about it then, I know. He goes to Polgarth on Friday. Now I've talked enough—too much Jack would say if he were here. It's your turn. Tell me your plans, if any.'

Phoebe laughed a little. She was very pink, and her eyes were shining, and the happiness in the face she lifted to Jo was clear. 'It's rather early to make plans. We're just engaged, you know. But here is my ring.' And she held out her hand to show Jo the ring with its diamond cluster. 'It was Frank's mother's ring. He asked me if he should get me a new one, or if I would rather have that. Of course I chose that. I know how he adored his mother. Her ring means a lot to him—and to me, too.'

'It's a lovely ring. How thickly the diamonds are clustered! You could not have had anything prettier. A big, modern stone wouldn't have been like you.'

A tap at the door broke in on Jo's speech, and Phoebe called:

'Come in!' It opened, and to their amazement no less a person than Zephyr stood hesitating on the threshold.

'I—I'm afraid I'm intruding,' she faltered.

'Miss Burthill!' cried Jo. 'Whatever brought you here?'

'Not to make trouble! Please don't think that!' said Zephyr breathlessly. 'Miss Wychcote, I am Zephyr Burthill. Mrs Hart wrote to me to tell me where you were so that I could come and see you myself and ask for the 'cello. I was glad to know, but not for that.'

'Will you come in and sit down?' said Phoebe flatly. Her glance went to the corner where the 'cello stood, and Zephyr's followed it.

'I'd like to. I'm not going to stay, but I did want you to know that I won't worry you about it any more. I'm—sorry—I was selfish—please forgive me.' Zephyr's voice quavered and faded away.

Phoebe looked at her. 'Of course I forgive you. I—I can't let you have my 'cello. You see, it was Father's. It means—him—to me. And they all think that in time I may be able to use it myself. I shall never play really well. It's too late for that now. But I can play it in time, they say. And that is such a joy to me.'

Jo thought it time to take a hand. 'Oh, but even if you couldn't. Zephyr wouldn't take it,' she said cheerfully. 'I'm glad to see you, Zephyr. You must wish Miss Wychcote happiness. She's engaged, you know.'

'Mrs Hart told me when she wrote. I *do* wish you every happiness,' said Zephyr. 'You must tell me when it is to be so that I can send you a present. Tell me some of the things you'd like so that I can get one.'

'Phoebe refuses. She'll be delighted with anything,' said Jo airily, seeing that Phoebe was too much overcome to say anything. 'The wedding will take place about the end of November, we expect, so you've plenty of time to choose. How did you come here, by the way? I mean, if you're staying anywhere near, Rob's at home, and I'm sure she'd like to see you. What about coming to tea tomorrow?'

Zephyr stared at her. 'Do—do you mean that?'

'Shouldn't waste my breath if I didn't. Well, shall I tell Rob to expect you? Where are you? You haven't said.'

'I'm staying in a private hotel in Armiford. I'm there for a week. If you think Robin would really like to see me, I'd love to come to tea tomorrow.'

'I'm sure she would.' Jo looked at the girl with keen eyes. Then she said gently, 'Zephyr, did you think Rob's friendliness was only for the week you were at Garnley? That was a mistake. Rob is either friendly for keeps or not at all. So long as you play straight, she'll be your friend.'

'Do you mean that, Mrs Maynard?' Zephyr suddenly looked down. 'Do you know, I've never had a real friend in my life.'

'Why, you poor kid!' cried warm-hearted Jo.

'No; but then I never valued friendship,' said Zephyr steadily. 'I can begin to see what I must look like to you people. I—I'm sorry about your dog and the burglary, Mrs Maynard. I—I'm afraid we can't do anything about that now. But I'm never going to want anything so badly that that sort of thing can happen again. Or if I do, I'll keep it to myself.'

'It's all right,' said Jo shortly, for Phoebe's eyes looked ready to fall out of her head. 'We'll wash it out. And Rufus was always all right. Now, suppose you go and find the 'phone and ring up Rob and tell her you are coming to tea tomorrow. We'll talk then, shall we?'

Zephyr agreed. She said goodbye, and, escorted by Jo, went to the call-box at the end of the corridor where Mrs Maynard left her, while she herself went back and gave Phoebe an extremely watered-down version of the night's alarms. She rocked with laughter as she described how she had showered the bacon over the would-be burglars, and Phoebe laughed too.

'But if I had known, Jo, I should have been dreadfully upset,' she said when they were grave again. 'I'd no idea such a thing would happen.'

'Oh, but I always run into adventures one way or another,' said Jo calmly. 'I'm noted for it. You ask the others. And now, here come Jack and your young man—why blush like that? He *is* your young man—very much so, I should say. Not that it isn't exceedingly becoming,' she added.

By the time the two men were in the room, followed by the ward-maid with an inviting tray, Phoebe was as red as a rose, but luckily for her Jo dropped the subject, and they had tea with gay chatter about the future, the new Miss Russell, and Reg's career.

Finally, Jo rose to go. She bent over Phoebe, and took her into her arms. 'Phoebe, dear, I talk a lot of rot at times. But I want you to know how glad I am about everything.'

'Everything?' queried Phoebe.

'Yes—your getting so much better—your engagement—Reg—even Zephyr. I think—I really do think that there's a chance now she may turn out better than one would have thought. Rob will do her all the good in the world. Yes; in spite of all our alarms and excursions, the holiday at Garnham was a good thing. Now I must go. Goodbye, Phoebe, dear. Let me know if there's anything I can do for you at any time, won't you?'

Half laughing, half crying, Phoebe clung to her. 'Honest injun, Jo, I believe you'd go to the rescue of anything!'

'Don't you believe it. The only thing I ever really rescued was Rufus from a watery grave when he was only a few days old.'

But Phoebe shook her head. When Jo had gone, she sat in her chair looking out at the hills. 'Jo may say what she likes,' she said aloud. 'But I know I'm right, from beginning to end—even if she lives to be a hundred Jo will be a rescuer. She couldn't help it—that is just Jo.'

APPENDIX: ERRORS IN THE FIRST EDITION

The few errors in the 1945 hardback of *Jo to the Rescue* were largely typographical ones, and we explain below how we have dealt with them. We have not attempted to correct either EBD's French and German or her occasionally idiosyncratic use of commas.

PUNCTUATION We have corrected obvious misplaced apostrophes (eg 'wasp's nest); on pages 98 (last line) and 145 (line 21) it is possible that there should be a possessive apostrophe after 'The Witchens', but as the usage is consistent we have not changed it. We have inserted missing opening and/or closing quotation marks, and have changed commas which were obviously meant to be full stops as they were followed by new sentences.

MISSPELLED WORDS We have changed the occasional use of 'Joe' instead of 'Jo', and have corrected mistakes such as 'he' for 'be'. We have inserted any missing letters—both 'he' and 'sh' appear where it is obvious that 'she' is meant—and on page 161, in the last paragraph, we have corrected 'Jo shook his head' to 'her head'.

INCONSISTENCIES On page 208 both 'His Will' and 'God's will' appear, so we do not know which is correct; on page 192, in line 16, we have corrected 'the moors, which was' to 'which were', to match the usage in the rest of the book.

POSSIBLE MISTAKES There are a few places where it seems as if there are errors, but as we do not know what the originals were intended to be we have not changed them:

page 41, para 2: 'She was to have come and have tea'—possibly 'to come and have tea' or 'to have come and had tea'
page 44, line 12: 'five-months-old baby boy'—possibly 'five-month-old'
page 79, line 12: '*He* said; *I* didn't.'—possibly '*He* said it;'
page 120, para 2: 'I shouldn't like to think I'd never known another'—possibly 'I'd never know'
page 193, line 27: 'wots the hodds'—possibly 'wot's'
page 213, line 2: 'her brows knit'—possibly 'knitted'

There are also places where the definite or the indefinite article seems to have been omitted—'at sight of him' rather than 'at the sight of him'; 'it's waste of time' rather than 'it's a waste of time'—but this was often EBD's style.

Laura Hicks
2006

Girls Gone By Publishers

Girls Gone By Publishers republish some of the most popular children's fiction from the 20th century, concentrating on those titles which are most sought after and difficult to find on the secondhand market. Our aim is to make these books available at affordable prices, and to make ownership possible not only for existing collectors but also for new ones so that the survival of the books is continued. We also publish some new titles which fit into this genre. Authors whose books have already appeared, or will be published in 2006, include Margaret Biggs, Angela Brazil, Elinor M Brent-Dyer, Dorita Fairlie Bruce, Gwendoline Courtney, Monica Edwards, Antonia Forest, Lorna Hill, Clare Mallory, Violet Needham, Elsie Jeanette Oxenham, Malcolm Saville and Geoffrey Trease.

We also have a growing range of non-fiction titles. Those already available, or to be published in 2006, include a new edition of the seminal work *You're a Brick, Angela!* by Mary Cadogan and Patricia Craig, and books about Elsie Oxenham (*The World of Elsie Jeanette Oxenham and her Books* by Monica Godfrey, and *Island to Abbey* by Stella Waring and Sheila Ray), Antonia Forest (*The Marlows and Their Maker* by Anne Heazlewood) and Monica Edwards (*The Monica Edwards Romney Marsh Companion* by Brian Parks).

For details of available and forthcoming titles, and when to order the latter (please do not order any book until it is actually listed), please either visit our website, www.ggbp.co.uk, or write for a catalogue to Clarissa Cridland or Ann Mackie-Hunter, GGBP, 4 Rock Terrace, Coleford, Bath BA3 5NF, UK.

Founded 1989